"One of the brightest young stars in the
tion, Daniel Braum is among the best sho.
If you haven't read Daniel's brilliant, poignant, and often heartrending
short fiction, we can recommend him and his exceedingly beautiful collection, *The Night Marchers*, highly enough.

—This is Horror

"Daniel Braum is a true storyteller. By that I mean he spins tales of wonder
that grasp at ideas and themes that human beings have been pondering
since our brains become up to the task. These stories will also make you
laugh, cringe, and damn near weep. This is such a big-hearted and wide
ranging book and Daniel Braum is the real deal, a writer to treasure."

—Victor LaValle, author of *The Ballad of Black Tom*

"Daniel Braum is a master at capturing the feel of a place and a time. From
the jungles of South America to the mean streets of New York's suburbs his
stories wind through territories that feel at once familiar and strange, exotic
and dangerous or maybe just dangerously personal."

—David Wellington, Author of *Monster Island*

"Tales of music, magic, tortured spirits, desperation, and even hope await
you in *The Night Marchers*. Braum presents our world through a lens that
reveals the wonderful and the horrifying with masterful, elegant prose. *The
Night Marchers* is a stunning debut from a writer who's been adding to the
field of darkly weird literature for years, but who's name is only now beginning to emerge, and it's about time!"

—Lee Thomas, Author of *Torn*

"Faithless women and adventuring lone wolves populate these trippy, fantastical stories of music, magic, and the search for connection. Take some
Neil Gaiman, a dash of Kevin Brockmeier, and a whole lot of Long Island
garage band, and stir."

—Sarah Langan, author of *Good Neighbors*

"Braum has a knack for describing the indescribable in extraordinarily acces-
sible language. No mean feat. The plight of the underrepresented features
prominently in a number of stories, like the title story (set in Hawaii.)"

—Tor.com

"I give very few quotes. I only make exceptions when a novel or collection knocks me out. So...short and sweet: buy Dan Braum's *The Night Marchers*. It's good, damn good. This man has one hell of a career ahead of him, and *you* get to be at the party before everyone else."

—Jack Dann author of *Concentration* and editor of *Wandering Stars*

"The strength of Daniel Braum's writing is the strength that comes from patience, from a writer trusting his audience with a steady, slow pace that allows details to accumulate in the mind so that the story becomes consistently more vivid until it reaches a conclusion that is profound in its subtlety and restraint."

—Matthew Cheney, The Mumpsimus /
Author of the *Last Vanishing Man and Other Stories*

"*The Night Marchers and Other Strange Tales* is a story treasure map for those who want a bit more from their spec-lit and horror--the weird, the strange, the unsettling from not just a Western perspective. Within these pages you'll tread across and in-between the lines of speculative literature and into Weirder terrain. Braum pares away layers not immediately visible with the human eye with an effortless fluidity that builds to unexpected climaxes, rather than easy twists. Indeed the sacred and the supernatural may seem like something one could slip a hand through, but in Braum's fiction, they have sharp edges that can cut you."

—Anya Martin, The Outer Dark / Author of *Sleeping With the Monster*

Vivid and haunting, Daniel Braum weaves stories rich in old school strange and rife with creeping dread. Jellyfish Moon in particular is a subtly constructed tale where beauty is overshadowed by quiet menace. It reminds me of nothing so much as one of the tributary side stories in Neil Gaiman's *American Gods*, alive with cultural texture and otherness."

—John C. Foster, author of *Leech*

"Braum's stories feature music and musicians as a means of exploring human attempts to "capture" transcendent experience. He is a genre-crossing acrobat, and he couches his ideas within the well-executed spinning of yarn. These stories are genuinely surprising, strange, and unpredictable. Working with a geographically diverse set of plots, he's adept at portraying the sense of being lost and out of touch in unknown environments. Sometimes the book itself feels this way—like a new and unknown space, tantalizing but full of quietly and slowly emerging creepiness."

—Mike Thorn Thorn's Thoughts / Author of *Shelter of the Damned*

"Braum's collection flirts with horror and weird fiction for sure, but there is something else going on here that almost makes the stories defy categorization. The stories themselves often have a very dream-like quality to them and one aspect of the writing that I particularly enjoyed was the choice of location Braum successfully weaves a web of mysticism and magic through his stories, making them addictive and often unpredictable. It's this unusualness and unpredictability that I really enjoyed and made this collection really shine for me. Highly recommended reading for those looking to take a journey to a far away place where anything is possible."

—The Grim Reader

Braum is a masterful wordsmith. His talent lies in his ability to create what one might call "literary" fiction absent even a scintilla of pretentiousness. His prose is poetic without being self-consciously elevated, gorgeous without contrivance, effortlessly musical. Like no other author writing short fiction today, with the possible exception of Jack Ketchum, Braum communicates a sub-text in his stories that is deeply, deeply emotionally affecting. There is often an ache here, hiding behind the words, revealing itself just enough to resonate with the reader before ducking out of sight once again.

—Hal Bodner, Goodreads Review

Carefully crafted tales written in concise, meaningful prose, taking his reader on flights not just of fancy but of the strange, the mysterious, and the out of the ordinary.

Braum's stories are atypical in that there is hardly any traditional horror trope utilized: no gore, blood or spilled guts; violence and sexuality is generally described in subtle tones. His is "quiet" horror which is not to imply that Braum's stories aren't unsettling. It is the fantastical and highly original images Braum carefully crafts in his stories which seizes and holds the reader's attention and imagination. What also makes Braum's stories engaging is the restrained but ever-present throb beneath his various enigmatic fantasies of a pulsing tenderness and care for humanity. Readers are bound to enjoy all the tales in *The Night Marchers and Other Strange Tales* as there isn't a weak story among them.

—Dan Studer / Tales of An Eclectic Reader

The stories in this collection do not fit conveniently into a neat box. *The Night Marchers* is full of sadness, beauty, and unprecedented wonder. Two cups of literary dark fiction, a heaping scoop of magical realism and urban fantasy, a tablespoon of horror.

If you're looking for something thought-provoking and elegant, yet still dark and somewhat mad, you'd be a fool to pass this book up.

—Chad Stroup / *Subvertia*

There is something in each of these stories that makes it impossible to stop reading them.

But what something is that?

Maybe it's the way the reader finds themselves so immediately immersed in each new story. The entry is sharp and complete and vivid, a spell only the best short stories are able to snare us with.

Maybe it is the voice of each character, crystal clear in the reader's mind, so clear that no matter what they are telling the reader, it is immediately real, no matter how strange or unfamiliar. This is because no matter how fantastical the details, the human element at the heart of the story is so strong it pervades everything within.

Maybe it is the velocity of each story, a living current that sweeps the reader along—you are caught, you are part of that moment in that world, you are led into the jungle, the ratty apartment building, the ocean, the burning building.

Whatever these dark and magical ingredients are that he's been playing with to achieve this wondrous collection of tales, Daniel Braum has succeeded in mixing them in new and different combinations that surprise and captivate, startle and thrill.

—Michele Souliere / The Green Hand Bookstore

These tales are unlike anything thing else I'm reading today. Bold, adventurous, strange, and totally enjoyable.

I can pretty much guarantee the stories in *The Night Marchers and Other Strange Tales* will be unlike any you've read before and will leave you wanting more. 5 out of 5 Stars

—Frank Errington Michaels / Horrible Book Reviews

THE NIGHT MARCHERS

AND OTHER STRANGE TALES

THE NIGHT MARCHERS

AND OTHER STRANGE TALES

BY DANIEL BRAUM

CEMETERY DANCE PUBLICATIONS

Baltimore

2023

The Night Marchers and Other Strange Tales

Copyright © 2023 by Daniel Braum
All rights reserved.

Cemetery Dance Publications
132B Industry Lane, Unit #7
Forest Hill, MD 21050
www.cemeterydance.com

Trade Paperback Edition

ISBN:
978-1-58767-869-1

Cover Artwork and Design © 2023 by Dan Sauer
Interior Design © 2023 by Desert Isle Design, LLC

TABLE OF CONTENTS

To my family. For everything.
I would be one of the lost without you.

—Dan

INTRODUCTION

What is a strange tale?

Take a journey through these pages with me and we shall find out together, as I did while writing this eclectic set of stories.

You might call this a book of "Quiet Horror." There isn't blood and gore. The human-centric stories evoke Ray Bradbury and are full of the mystery and wonder of the old Twilight Zone show.

Flip around and you might find…

A song that heralds the end of the world. * A girl possessed by a hurricane. * A singer who could be the reincarnation of Crazy Horse. * A small time arcane practitioner chased by demons through the jungles of Central America. * A has-been rock star haunted by exotic tropical fish * An alabaster Sphinx lumbering not towards Bethlehem but the Belt Parkway in Brooklyn… and more!

Welcome to the Cemetery Dance reissue of this, my first collection of short stories. If you are new to my work I'm fortunate to have wonderful colleagues to help me with the task of making an introduction. Victor LaValle author of The Ballad of Black Tom says:

"These stories will make you laugh, cringe, and damn near weep. This is such a big-hearted and wide ranging book and Daniel Braum is the real deal, a writer to treasure."

THE NIGHT MARCHERS   DANIEL BRAUM

And Lee Thomas author of Torn will tell you:

"Tales of music, magic, tortured spirits, desperation, and even hope await you in *The Night Marchers*. Braum presents our world through a lens that reveals the wonderful and the horrifying with masterful, elegant prose. *The Night Marchers* is a stunning debut from a writer who's been adding to the field of darkly weird literature for years!"

It has been a privilege and a pleasure to work with the talented editors Norman Prentiss and Kevin Lucia. What you hold in your hands is the definitive edition of this book brought to you the way I always wanted it to be. It collects a trio of my hard to find stories from Cemetery Dance Magazine, along with other out of print material, and a trio stories original to the collection. Critics such as Chad Stroup, of Subvertia, have said things like:

"The stories in this collection do not fit conveniently into a neat box. The Night Marchers is full of sadness, beauty, and unprecedented wonder. Two cups of literary dark fiction, a heaping scoop of magical realism and urban fantasy, a tablespoon of horror."

And (the late) Frank Michaels Errington said:

"It's true. These tales are unlike anything else I'm reading today. Bold. Adventurous. Strange. And totally enjoyable."

I wish you welcome whether you are a long time reader or experiencing my strange tales for the first time. Welcome, welcome, welcome! Before we begin I would like you to know one thing by means of introduction; while these stories are full of mystery, hope, a sense of wonder, and the unexplained they all take a winding journey through the strange and dark side of this thing called life. Are you ready? Thank you for coming along into the night with me. Let's go.

—Daniel Braum, New York
  November 7, 2022

MUSIC OF
THE SPHERES

The song was a year long and had been playing for months when I stumbled into the room. Sometimes I imagine I'm still there, my hands chasing the Shepherd's up and down the keys. On late August afternoons, especially when the cicadas are singing, I think I'll never drive the spiraling refrains of his song from my mind...

———

A couple of weeks ago, one afternoon before rehearsal I sat at my piano waiting for Jack. The top was open and the mikes were set up, the back room where we recorded was full of gear—but no Jack. Ancient oaks shaded the yard and my old house from the late afternoon heat. Hidden among the summer green leaves, cicadas buzzed symphonies.

A Long Island Railroad train was rumbling into the station down the block. Hopefully Jack was on that train. We had a CD to complete, and after that, a show to put on. We weren't getting any younger, and life, rock and roll especially, waits for no one. The problem was that an hour here, an hour there didn't seem like much, especially to easygoing Jack.

After months of rehearsing and recording after work and on weekends I had recently admitted to myself, and to Jack, that something was missing, even on the tracks we both liked. I could hear that elusive "something" in my mind but we could never translate it, never hit it when the tapes were rolling. Jack knew it too. He was born ready to be a rock star but the hard work of laying down tracks and writing focused songs didn't come easily to him. Session by session, as he realized all the sweat that went into making an album, a sadness grew in him.

We loved to play and sing. When we clicked, which more often than not we did, it worked pretty well. The dream was alive. Another candle lit against the darkness. Each song more fuel to keep us going another day.

The gate opened. Jack and a slender African American guy with thick, long neatly tied dreads walked past my window. Their instrument cases were slung over their backs. There was always an element of chance to every session with Jack. He might show up one day high as a kite, the next on no sleep with a trio of exchange students he had met the night before at the Knitting Factory. Other times he was bristling with energy, brilliantly nailing his parts after only a few takes.

I let them in through the back door into the kitchen and offered them the iced ginger tea with lemon and honey I had ready for my vocals.

"Dave, this is Roger," Jack said. "I was practicing my parts, singing them on the F train and we got to talking, talking about the project. He plays with Noah Sol."

"Nice to meet you, brother," Roger said in a rich, deep baritone with a humble smile. "Thank you for having me today."

MUSIC OF THE SPHERES

"Thank *you*," I said.

Noah Sol was a serious old-school big-band leader, from the fifties and shit, which meant this guy probably had serious chops.

"Noah Sol?" I said. "You look a little young to be playing with that crowd. He's still alive?"

"And kicking!"

I wasn't sure why Roger was here but I trusted Jack. I also trusted him to make colossal, yet heartfelt mistakes.

"Shall we?" I said. Some of my hesitation must have showed, though.

"I'd be honored," Roger said. "Noah encourages all his players to expand their horizons and experience what other music is being brought into the world by our brothers and sisters."

He spoke like some hippie-Rasta; hopefully he didn't play like one.

"Cool," was all I said.

Jack plugged in. Roger opened his case, and took out his slender soprano sax.

"Cue up the rhythm tracks to 'Sacred Spiral'," Jack said. "We can jam over it."

"Sacred Spiral" was our most ambitious song. It started out slow and built up into a long instrumental meant to symbolize the desert waking up and the creative awakening we had felt when we'd gone on a road trip last March into the Utah desert near Moab.

I cued the tracks and let them roll. I knew from the first harmony that Jack was on. Roger came in with whispery, breathy notes acting as a third harmony. I liked it. By the time we came to the crescendo, we were locked in. Roger was making runs and trading trills with Jack as if they had been playing together for ages.

"Run it again, run it again," Jack said. "This time roll the tapes."

"Already on it," I said.

We recorded our next take and it was good. Real good. Not what I originally had in mind for Sacred Spiral, but I thought it might be even better. We put down our instruments and went into the kitchen for more tea.

"Nice playing, man," I said. "Where you'd learn to play like that?"

"Jupiter," he said, matter-of-factly.

After an uncomfortable pause I smiled, realizing he wasn't going to say anything else.

"Jupiter as in Jupiter?" I asked.

"Yeah, brother, as in I travel the space-ways, learning music as I go," he said.

A cicada careened from the trees, buzzing and clicking against the window.

"Come on, man," Jack said, smiling. "What kind shit is that? You're from Jupiter and I'm Mork from Ork. Nanu, nanu."

If I had said the same thing, it would have sounded all wrong and hostile, but Jack could speak his mind like that and get away with it.

Roger laughed. "Of course I'm not *from* Jupiter," he said. "Though sometimes I can feel its eye upon me, its great storms alive with energy. I say I'm from Jupiter in recognition that we all come from the same place. The stars. Not in spaceships, no, no, no. But you and me and everyone and *everything* around us were all born in the stars. Right?"

I nodded and listened, letting him go on.

"Our bodies are organic machines made of carbon and water and heavy elements all born in the hearts of stars. The stars burn hydrogen into helium and then it gets older and older and hotter and hotter forming every element ever known. When it dies, it blows up, spouting them into the universe. That's how we are born. Everything. So when I say we are brothers, I do not say it lightly. We may have once been molecules side by side waiting to be born in the womb of a star or traveling the space-ways together."

"Whoa, dude," Jack said. "Sacred Spiral. He gets it."

Roger laughed. "Yes, you could call it a sacred spiral. I feel an echo of it in your song."

"I hear you, brother," I said. For some reason I was uneasy with his praise. "Sacred Spiral is just about feeling free in the desert. All this peace and star-love is cool, but I just don't buy it. Look at the world today. I don't want to talk negativity under this roof, but look around at what a mess is out there."

Jack was listening intently.

"It doesn't care whether you buy it or not," Roger said. "The universe is one whole. Fractured at the beginning of time. All this fussing and fighting, it is just the universe trying to find its way back together again. You may not know it is so, but it is so. You touch this truth in every pure moment you have ever experienced. In everything true, like our playing just before."

I didn't have anything to say to that but Jack look really awe-struck. Roger packed up his case and thanked us for the jam. "Our ensemble meets at fifty five Saint Robinson, at the corner of Tenth," he said. "We're always there." He shook my hand, hugged Jack, and left whistling the melody to Sacred Spiral.

"Man, he can really shred," Jack said. "And he's heavy. Makes sense."

But he didn't make sense and I didn't like to think Jack had been buying into all of it. I sensed a heartfelt disaster coming on.

———————

Jack was late for the next rehearsal and flat out didn't show for the one after that. He didn't even call.

Instead of working on the tracks, or returning long overdue calls or going to see my new niece, I spent time in the basement. I had been building Jack a guitar. He'd picked out the body and the paint job a few months ago and probably thought I'd forgotten about it. I'd bought two sets of pick-ups and a new solid one-piece neck. I shaved the frets down so the action was real nice, so even I could play the high notes easily. When it was done it would sound like an old Gibson, real warm and resonant, but without the two grand price tag.

I was worried about Jack and I kept working on the guitar. Though all the elements were there, I just couldn't get it together. Couldn't get the wiring right. Finally I put it away after a few days and kept calling Jack until I got him on the phone.

He hemmed and hawed about being busy and told me everything was fine. I could tell it wasn't, so I told him to please just talk to me and to cut the shit.

"Alright, alright," he said. "I've been jamming with Roger and Noah Sol."

"How's it been going?" I asked. I'm sure it came out a bit angry, but I was genuinely curious too.

"Going pretty good," he said. "All things considered."

"Like what?"

"Demanding precision from imperfect machines. Using flawed formulas, you know, but we're trying."

"What kind of shit is that?"

"Yours," he said. "It's one of my favorite lyrics of yours from the Dawnstar sessions, five years ago."

I was flattered to be quoted, but embarrassed I had forgotten my own lyrics. The song was about unrequited desire and imaginary relationships. But, I still didn't know what the hell he was talking about.

"Thanks man, but what's the deal? You don't show up. You don't call. Is it the record? You think we can't pull it together?"

"All right, sorry, man. I mean, I'm sorry. I don't want to bum you out. You know that? Right? Tell me you know that."

I did. And I told him.

"It's like this." He paused and sighed. "It's kind of hard to explain. He's got a band. Anyone can join. Dude, you could, if you wanted. There are lots of members, they rotate in and out. But it's one song. One massive, super-long song. I'm going to be rotating in soon."

"What about the record?"

"Yeah. Well, this song man, if he's right, the record isn't going to matter anymore."

"What the fuck is that supposed to mean?"

"Sorry, I gotta go."

"Hold on. You can't say shit like that and just go—"

But he'd already hung up.

I went online and looked up Noah Sol. The first hits were newspaper articles with pictures of him in a robe on the streets of New York. He was really odd looking. Tall as hell. Long, spindly arms and legs and a really big head. It almost looked elongated, like one of those odd-ball pharaohs I'd seen on the Discovery Channel.

The caption read, "Spaced-out jazzman on NYC walkabout arrested by New York's finest."

The next article was his obituary. Noah Sol had died nine years ago. So who the fuck was Jack jamming with?

———

I called around to the record shops, the ones that still sold LPs and had big jazz collections down in the Village. Some kid told me his boss did a weekly jazz show on public broadcast and probably knew a boat-load about Noah Sol.

I jumped on the LIRR and an hour later I was in the city and on the subway to Bleeker Street. The record shop was bustling and I asked a portly man with a bad comb-over if he had any Noah Sol.

"So, you're the cat that called about the Shepherd? You look a little young, but right on."

"The Shepherd?" I asked.

"Noah Sol. The Cosmic Shepherd. His nickname. And one of his signature songs, from Sixty-two, sorry, sorry Nineteen Sixty One. 'We tra-vel…the space-ways…'" he crooned in a croaky falsetto. "Sol used to be a straight up be-bop guy, if you can believe it, until he started getting into that fucked up mysticism shit. He was new age before there even was any new age. Music of the Spheres, is what they call it. Pretty far out philosophy. Complicated stuff."

"Try me."

"Okay, for starters, it was the dominant worldview before the renaissance. As in what everyone believed in as to the nature of everything. The big thing was sacred intervals. Had to do with the space between the planets, and some sort of correlation to the space between everything. You ever see those books where they show telescope pictures of far out galaxies side by side with pictures of cells under microscopes and they look the same?"

"Nope."

"Of course not, you're some punk-ass kid and this is Nineteen Ninety-nine. Don't feel bad, I only know 'cause I'm so into the Shepherd. You know I do the jazz show Sundays, midnight to four on WNGO?"

"The kid told me."

"Right on. All right then, check this out."

He fumbled through a box of video cassettes under the counter, then went over to the VCR beneath the wall-mounted TV and took out the Sarah McLachlan video and put another in. The screen filled with a full brass orchestra assembled in the Hollywood Bowl.

Noah Sol stood before them in long, colorful robes and what looked like a cheap foil crown. He conducted, danced, babbled, and played his piano. The players were out of their chairs, some dancing solo, trance-like, and others marching off the stage, and into the crowd. It was wild.

"You dig it?"

"Yeah," I said. "Not what I expected," I admitted. "But it's cool."

"You into jazz, taking a class, or what?" he asked.

"Research, honestly. Helping out a friend."

"Right on. Okay, okay, here's one more fucked up thing about him, then. Sol claimed to be working on a song based on the sacred intervals that would bring about the end of the world. The rumor among Music of the Spheres purists is that such an end-all song is possible, but the debate is whether it would lead to the end of the world or a gateway to a new reality."

"Is it real?"

"Stupid question—we're still here. But he did die before he could complete it, so who knows? Supposedly his old players have resurrected the ensemble and are still working on it. But that's all bullshit."

I wandered out of the store and into the street feeling dazed. It was all bullshit like the guy had said, but I still had a bad feeling.

I phoned Jack's place. One of his roommates told me he had left hours earlier with his guitar. Of course. I knew where he was going. I headed towards Tenth.

———

Saint Robinson was a tiny side street right at the base of the Meat Packing district where renovated warehouses, now chic and trendy lounges and eateries, mingled with meat and fish distribution centers. 55 was an old walk-up plastered with faded paper flyers advertising shows and parties with dates long past. I went up the steps and found the front door unlocked and ajar. Then I heard the music.

A soprano sax played a whispering refrain, like a bird waking up in the dark of night. You could hear the darkness, and the bird singing despite it. Roger. Congas moved the beat beneath, and then I realized dozens of other instruments had joined in, their simple parts together forming a complicated whole. I walked inside.

The front room was packed with black music stands and folding tables. Notebooks covered the tables. Musical scores. Star charts. All annotated in a wild, flowing scrawl in a language I did not recognize. The music was louder, more layered, but I couldn't figure out where it was coming from.

I cut through the room and into the kitchen. Two construction workers, who looked like they had just come off work sat at the table, strumming guitars. Their playing was sloppy, but they were intensely focused and didn't bother to look up at me. As I realized their amateur chops somehow fit into the song, the bad feeling I'd been carrying around began to vibrate like noise through my body. I can't explain it, these two amateurs playing sloppy chords was the scariest thing I'd ever heard.

I backed out of the kitchen and into a hallway off the main room. They never looked up. A trio of girls, NYU students or wanna-bes were high-stepping down the hall banging pots and pans with wooden sticks. An old lady in a cocktail dress grabbed me by the wrists, forcing me to dance with her.

"Which way do you see it?" she implored. "Infinitely expanding, or someday collapsing back from a lack of force, to just become another super black hole to explode and start again?"

"What?"

MUSIC OF THE SPHERES

"The universe! The universe! We're all tracing the steps of this dance, we just don't know which one."

"Infinitely expanding," one of the girls said, with tears in her eyes. "I just know it."

I saw an open door and stairs leading down at the end of the hall. I broke the old woman's grasp and dashed down the stairs.

Batik tapestries covered crumbling brick walls. Brown water stains blended into the crude diagrams of the solar system drawn in black magic marker over the batik's yellow and orange designs. Light filtered in through dirty cellar windows onto the forty-plus musicians sitting on folding chairs playing their hearts out.

Jack was there, crammed in between Roger and a trumpet player, strumming his old Ovation with the absent look in his eye I knew so well. The look that told me he'd been struggling to catch the groove and had finally locked in. His shaggy hair was a bit longer and his boyish face covered in stubble, but it was him all right. I loved him like a brother, and musical moments, like the one I knew he was having now, (fleeting glimpses of gentle true spirit, he had once said), were what we lived for. And yet I had come to bring him away.

A heavy reek of sweat and old guitar strings, spit and valve lubricant oil hung in the air like ozone. I could feel in my bones, as sure as the ringing when Jack and I locked pitch while harmonizing, that something was brewing here, something was being birthed in the music. I wanted to join in, get behind a piano and add the fat syncopated chords that the song was just crying out for. They belonged with Jack's guitar part which, along with the drum and bass, was weaving a basket, tightly wrapping around the snaking cadences blaring from the mad cacophony of horns.

Then the player next to Jack trembled and dropped his horn. I saw the whites of his rolled up eyes as he slumped forward. In the seat behind him sat a sax player, dead and rotting, his horn still hanging around his neck. Whatever it was that I had heard in the music was gone. I dashed across the room. Song or no song, I was getting Jack out of here, now.

I pictured my hand closing around Jack's wrist. I pictured myself yanking him out of that chair, pulling him across the room, up the stairs and out of this mad place, but I didn't actually do any of these things. I couldn't move.

The music went on. Dust circled like planetary rings. Jack was locked in the groove. The cadences and circling phrases deepened, widened. In my mind's eye I pictured two serpents entwined in the double helix shape of infinity. The song was calling out for a piano part to bridge all these parts together.

"Noah Sol, join us," Roger said, his voice pitched to carry over the music. "Your spirit is in this place."

There was an old piano against the wall. I could sit there for a moment. Play a few chords just to see what they sounded like and then I could do whatever it was I had come to do.

I sat at the bench and stretched my hands across the keys, let them hover there waiting to catch the downbeat, to come in. My hands tingled, like they had been asleep and were now waking up. I thought of Noah Sol, asleep at this very piano, groggily waking up to the jamming refrains of his beloved band.

My hands were on the keys. A big fat chord, my thumbs grabbing the black keys, augmenting the seconds, filled out the tones with a slight dissonance that rang over the drums. The band had cut to just the percussion, the bass, and me. Then Roger and Jack came back in, trading a soft, fast trill that reminded me of Sacred Spiral. It was powerful. Thrilling. It felt right. It felt like home. Jack smiled. Not at me. To himself, but I knew what he was feeling. I felt the same way.

MUSIC OF THE SPHERES

My hands moved up and down the keyboard; in my head I was still watching Noah Sol, his hands moving with mine until I was unsure if he were following me or I following him. They were right about the song. There was power here, something real, something alive, and they were very, very close.

To what, I didn't know. But I knew in my bones that there was still something missing. Noah Sol knew it too. My playing had brought them closer—I could feel it. I knew it as sure as I knew that rain would fall from the sky, as sure as the cicadas' summer symphonies would cease come fall. I was far too familiar with the maddening feeling of being so close. Was that why he brought me here? To search with them? Was that what I brought to the equation?

They were ready for the next movement. I didn't know where it would lead us. But I wanted to know, so I played on.

The band came back in hard. Roger and the other sax players stood in their seats, swaying and bopping like in the video. The construction workers had come in from the kitchen. They were pounding on their guitars like drums. The girls from the hallways danced with the conga players. The old woman had some weird three-stringed instrument in her grasp.

After a few more measures half of the band was on its feet, marching around the room in interweaving orbits. I stayed at the piano. I couldn't see Jack anymore. I craned my neck and saw a trail of musicians marching up the stairs. The dead guy was on the floor in front of his chair.

We flung the song outward with all of our intent, and in that instant, I knew what the crying girl had meant. The universe was either going to infinitely expand into the blackness of the void, in an eternal wave of creation, or when we stopped it would finally collapse back onto itself. Which one it would be, I didn't know. No one knew, but the song, the song was hot on the trail.

THE NIGHT MARCHERS   Daniel Braum

I kept playing. I closed my eyes, and when I opened them, the last of the musicians were disappearing up the stairs. My cadences slowed. I rang out fat chords, and with each of them I thought of something true. My first love. My parents. My brother. My newborn niece. Jack. The girl from the music store I wanted to make it with so badly. These things were true. These things were expanding, racing into the future. I kept playing, letting each chord ring out until it was no more, then replaced it with another. Noah Sol watched, then too he was gone and I was left with the fading sustain of my last chord and the settling dust in the last of the sunlight.

When I stopped I was alone with a dead guy in an abandoned building. I felt I had done something, but wasn't sure what. Some decision had been made but I wasn't sure what, or even what all the choices had been.

The next night I received a call from Jack.

"I'm going to Jupiter," he said. "I want you to come."

I just listened, didn't say a thing. He knew my answer was no.

"I'm going to be okay," he said. "Maybe after Jupiter it will be a new galaxy."

"Why don't you stop by before you go?" I asked.

"I can't, dude. That's why I'm calling. Got to go."

And that was the last I ever heard from him. The world didn't end. Obviously. I wouldn't be writing this. Part of me hoped Jack would turn up a few months later, living with his sister in North Carolina, or with some fling of the month in Jersey City or Amsterdam, all of which had happened before.

It's been six years. I don't think I'll ever see him again.

MUSIC OF THE SPHERES

I finished the CD. It's cool. Not what I envisioned. So be it. I think of Noah Sol's song all the time. I hear it in everything. Everywhere. In the dark of night when Jupiter is shining and especially on late August afternoons, when the cicadas are singing and I go in the basement to continue my endless tinkering with that old guitar I never got to give to Jack.

HURRICANE SANDRINE

L ike a spirit given substance, the gentle humidity of the Caribbean air touched everything, creating an unseen bond, as certain as breath, between the creeping growth crowding the runway, the locals hustling a living, and the mockingbirds scavenging near the taxi stand.

Steven tramped down the metal stairs pressed against the side of the plane. Walking to the terminal with the other passengers, he opened the top button of his short-sleeved white shirt. The sun's heat on his exposed neck made him more aware of his body and the elemental nature of the Caribbean, even in the airport in the heart of Belize City.

Vacationers filed by as he entered the terminal, their forgettable faces bronzed by the touch of the sun. Relaxed and courteous, they waited in line to return to the States, where more likely than not their newly found Caribbean goodwill would fade with their tan. Seeing these people so full of this spirit emphasized the emptiness in his bones. He yearned to be filled, to feel the completeness, the optimism, he knew when Elise was still alive. Here, in Belize, it seemed the elements were trying to find their way in to fill that void. The sun sought to burn his skin, the air to fill his lungs.

In his mind's eye he pictured Elise on the beach, her dark hair streaming in the wind. Six months ago they were together, sharing a carefree day on the Malibu coast. He couldn't shake the image of her hair spread out almost the same way as when they pulled her, lifeless, out of the water.

Outside customs, a dozen Belizean men hungry for work greeted him at the taxi stand. Steven pointed to a quiet man in the back of the group who smiled, took his pack, and led him to a dark blue sedan. They drove out of the small airport, leaving its manicured lawns, flourishing palm trees, and well-tended flower gardens behind. He started to outline the picture in his mind, but since Elise died, he could no longer bring himself to paint.

As the image of the painting faded, he read the taxi license on the back of the seat. Fredrico Reyes.

"Thanks for the job, man, it's been slow," Fredrico said. "Where you going?"

"The Water Taxi station. I'm heading to Caye Caulker."

"You a diver?"

Steven almost said, "My wife was," but a harsh, "No," left his lips.

"Too bad. It's good place to dive," Fredrico said.

Steven knew. He and Elise honeymooned at a resort on Ambergris Caye twenty miles away. She dove the reef. He painted. They shared lazy afternoons. Matt even showed up once for dinner.

"I'm going to find my wife's brother. He's a diver," Steven blurted out. "She's no longer here."

Matt wasn't at the funeral. Elise had always wanted to seek out and reunite with her rebellious brother, who had spurned America for the Caribbean life, but now she never would. They hadn't heard from him in over a year and all Steven had was this address. In the rear view mirror, Fredrico looked at him sympathetically.

"Such a nice place for so sad a task," Fredrico said. "Go slow. That is the first thing they tell you."

Steven noticed dead flowers, a chicken bone and an incense holder at the base of a trinkety Mayan statue on his dash. Fredrico watched him look.

"I tell you, use common sense and mind your own business," Fredrico said. "Caye Caulker is a strange place, like an island of lost souls. Pirates used to hide in the coves and the Maya once had shrines out in the jungle. If your girlfriend's brother doesn't want to be found, he picked the right place to disappear to."

"Why's that?"

"There is nobody to answer to. No church, no police, and no governor, though I guess the island is somebody's responsibility somewhere in Belize City. When a problem gets bad enough, they take it in their own hands. Someone will go to the mainland, to the jungle, to find a medico de selva."

Steven shifted uncomfortably in the back seat.

"Don't worry. Most of the bad people are either in jail or kicked off. Now it's just a five mile strip of mostly fisherman, dive boat captains, and few drug dealers," Fredrico said. "Just don't buy any smoke and you'll be fine."

The taxi drove past foundations and rubble. A haggard man with short frizzy dreadlocks stumbled across the road, uncaring of the speeding car. He spat as they drove past.

"What happened here?" Steven asked.

"Iris. Last year. Hurricane Iris."

They passed two kids playing kick the can outside a broken-down house with no windows.

"Does the city get hit often?"

"Sometimes near the shore. Some places get hit hard, some places not at all. Caye Caulker, where you are going, lost many houses, restaurants, and most of its palm trees to Iris."

Steven noticed the broken tops of the big palms lining the road. "Did Iris do this?"

"No, Keith. Two years ago. Remember the one where twenty-two divers drowned? From Virginia, I think."

Steven felt water filling his throat. Since Elise died, he'd been dreaming of choking. When he decided to come to Belize to find Matt, the dreams had stopped.

"Looks bad," he said, viewing the devastated city block.

"It is bad for us when a hurricane comes."

Steven didn't know what to say.

"I hope the weather stays good," Fredrico said. "The weather says tropical storm Sandrine is moving towards the coast. I hope she blows away. Business can't handle another hurricane."

"Isn't it late in the season for a hurricane?" Steven asked.

Fredrico didn't answer. He maneuvered the cab through the narrow streets. Steven remembered when he was a child a hurricane had hit New York. He had stuffed his and his brother's pockets with pennies to avoid being blown away, till his father told him not to worry. That was the only hurricane he could remember other than the quickly forgotten names on the news that alternated, girl-boy, alphabetically. Here, the threat was real and came not once in a lifetime, but dozens of times a season.

"Just before Iris came, I went to see the beach," Fredrico said, his concerned look disappearing for an instant. "The tide was so low. I never saw it so low. I walked out on the sand. Far, far out, man. My boy asked 'where is all the water?' We didn't stay around to see it come back."

HURRICANE SANDRINE

They drove over a drab green swing bridge. Steven glimpsed the ocean at the end of a channel lined with boats.

"Station is there," Fredrico said. His smile retreated inside him like a frightened ghost. He stopped just out front of the low stone building housing the Water Taxi station. Six rough men sat on the uneven curb. Weathered brown skin absorbed the sun beneath faded t-shirts, their faces a mix of broken teeth and cold watching eyes. Steven handed Fredrico an American twenty and two singles.

"Thanks, man," Fredrico said, handing Steven his pack.

Steven walked past wood benches filled with sweaty people, and purchased a ticket at a small ticket booth that looked as if it belonged to an old movie theatre. The girl inside gave him change in colorful, animal-adorned Belizean bills.

As he scanned for a seat, he noticed a woman in an orange tank top and jeans sitting on the second bench. Her skin glistened with perspiration. Slender legs crossed, she fanned herself with a delicate paper fan adorned with a heron. A hint of strong calves showed beneath her raised jeans and a clog balanced lazily on her foot. Like everyone else, she looked as if she had been waiting for a long time. Her impatience reminded him of Elise. Elise was never good at waiting, especially waiting to go diving. The woman watched Steven look at her.

"1:30 to Caye Caulker here," the man standing at the door called before Steven could find a seat.

Still looking at Steven with her summer green eyes, the woman picked up her bag and smiled with her thin pink lips, the almost red of a lotus blossom ready to open. He got the feeling she smiled at everyone that way.

She grabbed the wrist of a skinny young girl who couldn't have been more than ten. The girl followed her, like a walking rag doll, into the line of people gathering to board the boat.

The sweaty people filed out of the station, handed their blue paper tickets to the man at the door, and carefully stepped over the gap between the dock and the boat. Steven sat down on the narrow bench lining the inside of the deck, his shoulders pressed up against his neighbors. The woman in the orange tank top, wearing sunglasses now, carefully boarded. Her silver thumb rings and copper bracelets caught the sun as she stepped over the gap between the dock and the boat, creating a brief blinding flash. She sat down. The girl followed, quietly sitting next to her. Before the woman even settled into her seat, a young unshaven American wearing a UCLA cap a few seats down from Steven introduced himself to her.

"Nice to meet you, Forrest," she replied, with a thick Spanish accent. She didn't give her name.

Forrest took out a tube of sunscreen and began rubbing it onto his arms.

"Want any?" he asked.

"I don't need any. I'm a gypsy," she said with a smile.

Steven thought her big gold-rimmed glasses were more suited to Beverly Hills. She did not offer the lotion to the young girl who stared, glassy-eyed, out to the water.

The boys running the boat started the engine and slowly navigated the boat through the channel.

"Can I have some?" Steven asked over the sound of the engine. "Mine's in my pack."

"Sure," Forrest said, handing the tube to Gypsy Woman who handed Steven the tube.

Faded green and blue tattoo lines wrapped around her wrist, forming strange spirals and symbols. Glyphs and animals decorated her silver rings. A single charm, a Mayan character, hung around her neck. Steven wanted to ask what it meant but Forrest spoke.

"You here on vacation?" he asked, apparently unaware the quiet little girl was with her.

"Me? Vacation?" She laughed and looked at the girl. "No. I used to live here. Today I'm working."

Steven wondered what she did. The boat cleared the channel and picked up speed.

"Your daughter?" Steven asked, nodding to the girl.

"No. No," Gypsy Woman said, shaking her head. "I'm...taking care of her."

The girl continued to stare, seemingly unaware of the conversation about her. As the boat sped them further across the water, rushing air made it hard to hear. Forrest stopped talking and Gypsy Woman turned to the sea. Wind pressed her tank top against her, outlining the shape of her breasts, revealing her belly and slender waist. Steven closed his eyes partially, softened his gaze, and imagined the blurry form before him was Elise.

In the shallows, just outside the channel markers which kept them in the safety of navigable depths, a blue heron seemingly walked on water.

———

A half hour later the boat's engines slowed as it pulled next to the long wooden dock. Boys with bicycle carts waited to take luggage.

"Welcome to paradise," they said in unison with the boat crew just after the engines were cut.

A group of old fishermen greeted Gypsy Woman and the girl and led them away down the sandy street

"Where you going?" a kid asked Steven. "Let me take your luggage."

"I'm O.K."

"Come on, man. Just give me a job. If the hurricane comes there'll be no money for a long time."

"O.K." Steven threw his pack in the basket. "But I'm walking, I can't have you pedaling me around in that thing."

"No problem, man. Go slow. That's the only rule around here."

Steven didn't want to go slow. The first time he dove, he remembered Elise had told him to breathe slow. Life moved fast, not like a snapshot image of a painting, but like animation— thousands of paintings in the blink of an eye. The day at Malibu he felt like he had blinked and all his happiness escaped with Elise's last breath.

"No worries," the kid said. "I know a good place. The Caribbean Paradise, right on Front Street."

"Let's go," Steven said.

The kid pedaled and Steven walked. They moved past lush red hibiscus, thriving bougainvillea and small orange flowers on a vine whose name he didn't know. They passed rickety homes, many that doubled as restaurants or businesses. "Martine's Grill", "Anita's Laundry", "Fresh bait here", the handmade signs read. A small jail stood next to the bank. A man with a rifle stood outside, apparently guarding both. The kid waved and the man smiled.

"Do you happen to know someone named Matt Kensington?" Steven asked the kid, "Last I heard he was a dive captain around here."

"My boss might know."

"Who's your boss?"

"Ricardo, he used to be a dive boat captain too. I sometimes help him with errands."

"Where can I find him?"

"Today's Bob Marley's birthday," he said with a look that suggested Steven should know. "Big party at the Lazy Iguana, tonight."

"Where?"

HURRICANE SANDRINE

"It's the tallest building on the island. You can't miss it," he said, pointing proudly to a big thatched roof poking up above the tattered palm trees.

The three-story, rickety-framed building had no walls. Catwalks and uneven stairs branched off from it haphazardly, like a tree house.

"You think Matt will be there?"

The boy shrugged. "My boss will."

Outside the Caribbean Paradise, Steven handed the boy a rumpled American five and took his pack. A dozen cabanas jutted up from the beach fifty feet from the gentle reef-protected shore. A white stone wall separated the property from a small graveyard. Most of the stones were old and flat on the ground or leaning over. New white paint and bunches of fresh flowers adorned a few of the crosses.

A young child swung from a tire in a tree just outside a small white picket fence enclosing the graveyard. She twirled her short dreadlocks and watched a European couple enthusiastically hit a ball back and forth with round wooden paddles.

"Hello," said a voice from inside the office's screen door. Steven walked in, signed a piece of paper, and paid for the room.

"Welcome to paradise," the clean-cut young man said.

In his room Steven threw his pack on the floor and flopped onto the bed. Within minutes the sound of wind and the lapping of waves on sand coaxed his tired body to sleep.

———

Steven awoke with a jump from a choking dream. For a second he didn't know where he was. Elise's face and wind-swept hair filled his mind. As he caught his breath, he heard a mournful song underneath the rustle of the late afternoon breeze in the palms. He looked out the window and saw the gypsy woman standing in the graveyard.

He ran his hand through his hair, and went outside. She stopped singing as he approached.

"Hello, man from the boat," she said.

"Hello," he said. Now that he was talking to her he didn't know what to say or why he even came outside, other than to be near her.

"What were you singing?" he asked.

"I'm praying."

Steven looked at the small gravestone at her feet. "1997-2000," it read.

"What a place to be buried, huh?" he said.

She looked at him as if he had just said the stupidest thing. "These people loved the island, loved the sea. It is as fitting a place as any if one must be buried at all."

A quick glance around revealed other stones with the years 2000 and 2001. Iris and Keith, he thought.

"My daughter is here. Next to my grandfather," she said, pointing to the white stone cross. "The rest of my family is buried on the other side of the island."

"I'm sorry," Steven said.

"You remind me of him."

"I do? I'll take that as a compliment."

"Don't. He was stubborn and had his nose in everything. You Americans have your noses in everything."

"We mean well, at least I do."

"The road to hell is paved with good intentions, isn't that how the old saying goes?"

"What is that supposed to mean?"

"It means that there are things you are not supposed to interfere with." She turned from him and arranged flowers around the tall glass candle holder at the base of the cross. Steven watched as she placed chicken bones next to the flowers.

He thought of asking who the candle was for and telling her why he was here. He wanted to kiss her and to forget Elise and Matt and everything. The desire felt potent and strange.

"I don't want to hear your story," she said. "I don't care if you are ignorant or disconnected or whatever you are or think you want from this island."

Steven watched her as she spoke. She smelled like sand and sweat and incense.

"You've talked to the pretty girl from the boat, now be on your way. There's work to be done."

She lit the candle beneath the cross. Its dim light flickered on the stone. Steven opened his mouth to ask her anyway, but decided to go.

Storm clouds gathered on the horizon above the dive boats return-ing to shore. A group of pelicans sped by in a line just above the reflection of the red setting sun rippling on the waves. Sandrine was coming. Steven could almost hear her voice in the rustling fronds.

He walked the short distance to the Lazy Iguana. Reggae ema-nated from its three-story haphazard frame. People were already celebrating. He pushed his way past lanky, dreadlocked teens crowding the rickety stairs. Barefooted vacationers surrounded the second floor's bar. Divers well on their way to being drunk sat on swings and tires hanging from the rafters.

Steven bought a rum punch, then saw the kid who'd helped with his pack. The kid saw Steven and ran to a man, not much taller than the kid himself, and pulled on his sleeve. The short man looked Steven's way and whispered something back. The kid disappeared into the crowd. The short man and the American-looking blonde girl he was chatting with turned and smiled as Steven approached. The man's ears were pierced with dozens of hoops. A six-inch shark tooth hung from a leather band around his neck. He looked like a little pirate.

"Nice necklace, I didn't think they made them that big," Steven said.

"Not anymore, this is a fossil. The shark that once owned this has been extinct for a hundred thousand years."

"It ate whales," the girl said.

The short man shrugged. "This is my girl Angie," he said. "I'm Ricardo. Do a shot with us."

"Steven," he said, shaking Ricardo's small strong hand. "I have a rum punch."

Ricardo pointed over his shoulder to a sign nailed to a beam that read "body shot table."

"Rum punch is for girls. That's what the little girls from the States who say they want to run away to Belize to live with me drink."

Angie smiled and clicked her tongue piercing on her teeth.

The kid re-appeared, squeezing his way through the crowd. He precariously held a bottle of tequila, a stack of glasses, a saltshaker, and a cup of cut limes.

"I'm looking for Matt Kensington, you know him?"

"Go slow man, we got tequila here."

"Why don't you just do me a favor and point him out to me?"

Steven didn't want to be drinking. He wanted to find Matt and say, "Why the hell did you miss her funeral? What are you running away from down here?" Maybe he'd punch him.

"He don't come out and party no more," Ricardo said. "Why you want to see him so bad? He fuck your girlfriend or something?"

Angie giggled and rubbed salt on her neck.

"You're at the body shot table. Do a shot." He laughed.

Angie laughed again and put the lime in her mouth.

Ricardo moved closer to Steven and stood on tip-toe to whisper in his ear. "My girl thinks you're cute. Win me some points. Do a shot with her and then we'll go find your friend. Don't be so stiff."

Steven shook his head.

"No takers then."

Ricardo salted his lips on Angie's neck and then downed a shot of tequila. He placed his hands on her shoulders, pulling her down to take the lime from her mouth. The men around Ricardo let out a cheer followed by "Bob" in unison as another Marley song came on.

A diver passed Ricardo a joint.

"Happy Bob's Birthday," he said.

"A happy day indeed. The storm has gone away," Ricardo replied. He took a hit and passed it to Angie.

Steven noticed the sky had cleared and the wind died.

"You're next," Ricardo said to Steven.

Steven shook his head.

"I don't trust no one who don't smoke with me when Bob is playing," Ricardo said.

Angie inhaled deeply off the joint. She grabbed Steven's face and planted a kiss on his lips, blowing the smoke into him.

Steven struggled but Ricardo put a reassuring hand on his back.

"Hold it now," he said.

Steven held it, then extended his lower jaw, releasing the smoke. He sucked it back though his nose.

"Take another hit. Blow it into me." Angie said.

Steven took a drag and blew the smoke into her as instructed.

"I feel so much closer to you," Angie said, tendrils of smoke wafting from her mouth. "What's been inside me has been inside you."

"Satisfied?" Steven asked Ricardo.

Ricardo leaned in to whisper in Steven's ear again. "Do one shot with us, I'm tryin' to liquor her up, take her to the jungle—know what I mean?"

The kid poured another round of shots. Steven noticed the drinks looked a bit milky.

Ricardo toasted, and they downed their shots. Steven drank a sip and purposefully spilled most of his all over his face. He wiped his mouth with the back of his hand.

"O.K. Let's go," Ricardo said and slid his arm around Angie's waist.

They weaved through the crowd to the stairs and stumbled down.

As they walked through the yard, Ricardo lit another joint. Steven checked his pocket for his wallet.

As they walked away from the Lazy Iguana, the sounds of the night replaced the fading reggae bass lines. Ricardo frowned and looked at the trees.

"What?" Steven asked.

"Something's wrong. Geckos are chirping," Ricardo replied. "Means it's gonna storm."

Ricardo walked along the moonlit road with Angie slumped against him.

Steven followed, noticing the rag-tag houses giving way to trees and dense undergrowth. At the end of the road, near some abandoned remnants of a house, a cluster of headstones and crosses jutted from the light, almost white sand.

"Where you taking me?" Steven asked.

"To your friend, may the bastard rest in peace."

Angie murmured something, but her speech was too slurred for Steven to understand.

HURRICANE SANDRINE

Steven ran the few steps to the small graveyard. He could smell the ocean and hear the waves on the beach, stronger now than the afternoon. He looked at some of the newer, less weathered stones and found Matt's name chiseled into a simple unadorned stone.

Ricardo had moved up behind him. Angie was sitting down in the middle of the road, her head slumped on her shoulder. Ricardo looked at Steven as if he expected him to slump over like her.

"You could have just told me, what the hell?" Steven said. Then he noticed the hilt of a knife tucked into Ricardo's shorts.

"Maybe you'll understand now," Ricardo said.

"Understand what?"

"Most people come here and see what they want to see: the sun, the sand, the stars, happy people living on an island."

Ricardo twitched his head nervously, as if looking to see if anyone was around, then kicked the sandy road.

"People here are angry, I'm angry," he said. "We get our lives wrecked by every passing storm."

Steven quickly glanced at Ricardo's hands, then back at his face.

"The sun and the sand. You take that away and we have nothing. Your friend Matt didn't understand that. He always had America to go back to. He wasn't willing to do what needed to be done, and the hurricane claimed him."

"Ricardo," Angie yelled from the road.

Ricardo looked at Steven, shook his head, and turned away toward Angie.

"You are lucky tonight," he said. "The storm is gone and I have a girl waiting. Things could have gone a lot worse for you."

Ricardo walked to Angie muttering under his breath. Together they headed back toward the Lazy Iguana. Steven stood in the graveyard. There was so much he wanted to know about Elise that he had hoped Matt would tell him. Now, there was no chance at all.

THE NIGHT MARCHERS   Daniel Braum

Steven followed the path through the old stones toward the water. A few lonely boats rocked in the lagoon, attached to a private dock littered with cans, crates, fishing poles, fishing sling spears, and pails.

Steven registered movement on the dock from the corner of his eye. He walked a few yards to see better. Flicks of rain hit his face. Geckos chirped frantically. The moonlight on the lagoon illuminated a pair of yellow eyes just above the water.

At the edge of the dock, a girl was tied between two docking posts. A woman stood before her, raising her arms to the sky. Their shapes blurred like an inky thing from the deep.

Steven ran to the dock. The wind rushed past his ears, drowning the jungle sounds. The dock's planks rattled beneath him.

Gypsy Woman stood at the edge of the dock, before the frail girl. Steven recognized her as the young girl from the boat. Her hair spun in swirls, as if in the grip of tiny storms. Wind rushed around and the air felt heavy, full of moisture.

"Go away, man from the boat," Gypsy Woman said with a fierce calm. In the night, with her face in shadows, she was more than the exotic woman from the boat, more than the mourner in the graveyard.

Behind her, the girl slumped between the two posts, barely straining the bonds. Welts covered her wrists where the ropes bound her. Her eyes were blank and a slight mist rolled off her skin, as if she were taking in all the moisture and could hold no more.

"What the hell is going on here?" Steven asked.

Elise filled his mind, her hair swaying in the water as she drowned.

A line of water trickled from the corner of the girl's mouth. The air tingled with the kinetic energy of the moment before a cloudburst.

"I'm untying her," Steven said.

Gypsy Woman moved, blocking his way.

"You don't understand! The sea must have her!"

HURRICANE SANDRINE

For an instant they were close, closer than on the boat, close enough to kiss. He didn't want to hit her; perhaps he could push her out of the way.

Pain radiated from his shins and his legs buckled as she swept his legs, sending him crashing into the fishing rods. He hit the planks and the pails fell off the dock with a splash. Lights from the house flashed on. Something hard hit him. Her elbow? Her knee? He put his arms up to defend himself.

Instead of hitting him again, Gypsy Woman lunged for the girl. Steven threw himself forward and grabbed the back of her calf. She fell and her own momentum sent her sliding off the edge into the water.

Steven stood up and began to untie the girl's restraints. Mist poured off her as if she were dry ice. Her wet hair hung in front of her eyes and stuck to her face.

Gypsy Woman yelled from the water. "Don't let Sandrine be free!"

Steven picked up the girl and carried her onto the boat. He placed her inside the small cabin, untied the lines from the dock, and started the engine.

The wind blew fiercer and rain spilled from the sky as the boat pulled away from the dock into the rocking waves.

The boat neared the reef when the rain began to come down hard. Steven wasn't sure what to do, so he stopped.

The girl lay on the floor among a length of fishing line and a few empty beer cans rolling from the swell. Her features were Mexican with a bit of the Mayan nose, though she was thin and lanky. Mist continued to pour from her skin, as if from her pores and her cuts. Inscriptions and characters in black marker or grease-stick ran up her arms and around her neck. Steven recognized one, spiral arms around a circle, the icon for a hurricane.

Steven watched her for any slight rise and fall of her chest. If she was breathing it was too faint for him to tell. He took a deep breath and realized the boat was perfectly still, the wind quiet and the rhythmic lap of the waves gone.

The boat's lights flickered, then blacked out. A faint glow emanated from the girl like moonlight on mist. Steven sensed movement in her, then a gust of wind blew from inside the room, stirring the beer cans.

The girl sat up. She turned her bruised body as if to see the room better, then held out her hands and looked at them. A sound like the wind through palm trees escaped her awkwardly moving lips.

She rubbed her arms, erasing some of the markings.

"Something is very wrong for us to speak this way." Tendrils of thin, almost transparent mist wafted from her nose. Her hair lifted from the growing wind around her.

"I do not mean to hurt, yet I care not if I do," she said. "I need to blow, to move, to pour. All I know is to storm."

Steven heard Gypsy Woman's voice in his head, yelling to kill her. Despite the moisture everywhere, his throat was dry and constricted. The mist rolling off her looked natural, almost beautiful, yet he knew he looked upon something not meant for him to see, not meant to even be.

The girl shuddered. She looked at her shaking hands. Slowly she curled her fingers, stopping short of a fist. As she did, her neck tensed and the shaking moved to her jaw.

"This is so strange," she said, fluttering her fingers slowly. "It is time to go. Already this experience fades."

Steven pictured rubble and wrecked houses, all the people on the island, the headstones beneath palm trees stripped of leaves.

HURRICANE SANDRINE

The girl fell back to the bench with a soft thud. The faint glow from her skin faded. Mist rolled off and away from her. Steven put his hand over her mouth. No breath. He searched for a pulse and found nothing.

As Steven checked her mouth again, a steady exhalation of moist air left her with a hiss like air leaving a balloon. He put his head to her chest and heard movement in her lungs. The hiss became a whistle, then a roar.

Wind rushed from her open mouth, blasting out windows and pushing Steven to the wall. Steven saw the girl thrashing about like an airborne scarecrow as the storm escaped her body. The boat lurched as if cresting a huge wave and Steven slid across the floor and slammed into the other side of the cabin. His ears popped from the building pressure. He felt blood drip from his ear and roll into his hair from the wind.

Mist streamed from the girl and whisked out of the windows, then in an instant all was still. The girl dropped to the floor, limbs splayed. The lights flickered and came on. He stuck his head out of the window. Above, moonlight streamed down from the clear sky. A ring of clouds raced away from the boat.

The storm was taking form around him. The boat bobbed in the calm, in the gentle eye. He pictured the destructive spiral arms, like the symbol on the girl, moving over the island.

He heard Gypsy Woman's words in his head, "The sea must have her."

He picked up the lifeless girl, took her out of the cabin, and tossed her over the side. She seemed to tumble gently, head over heels, as she disappeared into the depths. Steven hoped the sea, or whatever forces wanted the hurricane, would be satisfied with her, or her empty shell.

He tried to speak but could barely move the air out of his throat. "Stay away from the island, please," he managed to whisper.

THE NIGHT MARCHERS Daniel Braum

Steven started the throttle. He hurt all over and needed to get to shore to warn everyone; the nameless tourists, the young girl on the swing, all the divers, Ricardo, his kid helper and Angie. There was no high ground to run to.

He steered the boat back to the main dock where he had arrived in the morning. The water level had dropped so much that the dock was above his head. The boat bottomed out with a screech. Fredrico's words echoed in his head, "We didn't stick around to see the water come back." The storm and inevitable tidal wave were coming.

Steven jumped out and sloshed through the last fifty feet of knee-deep water to shore. Front Street was empty. He ran to the lights of the Lazy Iguana. He could hear the reggae and the sound of the crowd.

The wind beat against the roof, ripping up brown fronds.

He reached the stairs and pushed his way up, knocking a beer out of a laughing diver's hand. At the top, Steven yelled, "Take cover! The Hurricane is coming!"

Those near him who heard, laughed. A man pointed to the fronds swirling like out of control kites in the strong wind.

Steven leaned over the railing and saw a wall of water rolling over the reef. He watched the man's drunken smile leave his face as he saw the water racing towards them.

The man yelled and ran to the bar. Within seconds the blasting music was cut and the catwalks and stairs filled with people running. Steven could hear the rumble of the water above the screams. He stood still. There was nowhere to run.

The wave rushed over him, pushing him into the frame of the Lazy Iguana and tossed him about with the dirt and palm leaves, uncaring, as if he were a stick. It forced itself down his throat as he tried to breathe. As the air left him, he thought it was a fitting revenge for depriving the sea of its prize that it should have him.

HURRICANE SANDRINE

Despite the turbulent thrashing, he felt calm, the calmest he had felt since losing Elise. He saw her face in front of his, in the spinning water. She kissed him and he wondered if he were still alive. He saw her eyes—swirling green and blue and black, like the ocean, as he lost consciousness.

Steven woke up on the beach to the shining sun. The remains of the seaside graveyard and the Caribbean Paradise's cabanas littered the shore. The palm trees were stripped bare and a few coffins jutted out of the ground. The white cross marking Gypsy Woman's grandfather's grave defiantly stood. Steven looked up. The Lazy Iguana's thatched roof was gone but the twisted framework somehow still remained.

"Ha! Hah!" a voice said. "Bob has protected this place."

Steven rolled over. A few yards away sat a diver, who he recognized from the party, trying to light a water-logged cigarette with a lighter that wouldn't spark.

Further down a half dozen people walked along the shore, apparently looking for survivors among the debris. He recognized Gypsy Woman's long hair and sparkling rings even from far away.

One of the men saw Steven and the diver and yelled.

Gypsy Woman came closer, stopped, then ran to Steven.

"You," she yelled and began hitting him. Her blows were wild and had no force. She turned her head to the white cross and began crying.

"Go slow," the diver said. "We'll rebuild."

It seemed a hollow consolation but then Steven realized it is all you can do when everything is washed away. In his mind's eye he saw himself painting the Caribbean Paradise with flourishing palm trees, and white cabanas with new roofs. He closed his eyes and saw Elise, not drowned, but diving deep in the blue where she was happiest. Kicking her fins gracefully, she descended from the blue, into the black. When he could no longer make out her form he opened his eyes to see Gypsy Woman's tear-soaked face.

"The world works in strange ways," Steven said, aware he was feeding her own words back to her. "Who are we to think we can interfere or understand?"

"I hate it. I hate it," she said with her last punch.

Steven inhaled, grateful that the gentle humid air not the turbulent ocean filled his lungs. Like a spirit given substance he felt the air's unseen bond. The same air he took inside him, had been or would be inside Gypsy Woman and all the others. He pictured it in his painting, swirling colored lines from everyone's mouth, meeting and mingling in the palm trees. He exhaled. Sandrine was gone. The only certainty now was the sun and sand, the wind and waves, and his next breath.

MYSTIC TRYST

Bright tropical fish circled the coral head picking at colorful fans swaying in the current. Through the crystal water I saw my favorites: the lemon-yellow butterfly, the tomato-red clown with three black-lined white stripes, and the little iridescent green one that shimmered pink and orange in the light. Seeing them again felt good, like I was back with Kendra but before all the fighting. Clouds of darting fish broke up and reformed in syncopation to my heartbeat. The three fish just floated and stared.

I knew from hours of watching the little guys that they had only one expression, a cute almost-smile. Now, from how they regarded me, mouths eerily opening and closing, they actually appeared distressed and unsettlingly aware.

Go on. Pick at some nice seaweed, I thought, and swam closer. The shadowy crevices and caves in the coral were full of murky dark shapes. One of them shifted and I felt its hunger. My heart raced, jolting out of time with the rhythms around me. I swished at the fish in warning, but they weren't concerned. I felt myself lifting and I rose through long streaming beams of grainy sunlight. The sandy bottom receded, the fish tiny flitting dots. I floated up and up, the presence in the cave watching me. The lap and burble of the waves above grew louder and louder...

THE NIGHT MARCHERS   DANIEL BRAUM

I followed the fountain's murmur from somewhere in the depths of sleep to that eyes-closed-half-awake state. I could still feel the dreamy warm water and sun on my back. I blissfully re-settled into the couch. The session from hell wasn't till eleven and I had no intention of waking or even thinking about the drums until I heard my watch-alarm's nasty little beep.

A familiar tingle bloomed on the back of my neck; the prickly feeling I was being watched, by the cat no doubt about to wake me with a gentle paw to the face.

I reached for her and opened my eyes but she wasn't next to me at all. She was with Kendra, in her new place across the park, along with the juicer, the bread maker, the salt-water tank, plasma TV, our bedroom set, and the Pilates machines.

Dim streetlamp light filtered in, keeping the long sparsely furnished room in haze and shadow. The heat hadn't come on for the year yet and the late September nights were already foreshadowing the cold to come. As my eyes adjusted, I wondered where my new kitten, Nicholas was. I got him a week after Kendra and I split. I had kept the apartment, which, along with peace of mind and my share of the Lotus songs' rights, was what I wanted.

I clinked my nails on the empty Heineken bottle on the coffee table, a sound he couldn't resist. I could squeeze in another twenty minutes of lounging before I had to get ready. "Nikkie," I called, surprised he hadn't come running.

I spotted the little devil across the room, standing in the corner next to my cymbal bag, his paws all perfectly tucked in. His tail twitched like he was tracking a fly.

I clinked the bottle again. He acknowledged me with a chirp, and went back to watching whatever he was watching.

MYSTIC TRYST

I propped myself up to take a look just as the phone rang. Was I late? I'm sure the corporate record company puppets they called a band these days wouldn't care, but Morty was producing and he had always done me good. I fumbled for the phone.

Kendra's number flashed on the screen and a pang of fear hit me.

Why would she call? The papers just became final and it'd been about a month since our last rendezvous, after the big Zildjian party.

I thumbed talk. "Hey. Is everything alright?"

"You took them," she said.

She sounded okay. Pissed, but okay.

"Took what?" I asked. What the hell had I taken? She had everything she wanted. Nothing of hers was here anymore.

"You know," she accused. "It's our destiny. Every wrong I try to right you throw a monkey wrench into."

I pictured the moment I saw her at the party. Black slacks and a sheer top hugged her tall, lean frame. Her long hair was back in a single braid, streaks of natural brown growing in beneath the last bleach job. A simple turquoise choker brought out her deep green eyes. She stared at me when I entered like the night we first met backstage on the *Mystic Tryst* tour. Two hours and three times that many drinks later, we were back at the apartment ripping our clothes off like it was twenty years ago, feeling the exact opposite of what I felt from her now.

"I'm half asleep," I said. "And I gotta get ready for a session, for Morty. I'm going to hang up unless you tell me what you're talking about."

"The fish," she said. "They're with you."

Funny, I was just dreaming about the fish. Kendra was incredibly smart and had killer instincts, but this time she was just plain wrong. I had watched the movers take the neglected and green-crusted thing myself.

THE NIGHT MARCHERS   Daniel Braum

"You have the tank," I said as calmly as I could, though I was getting heated. Despite all her yoga and enlightenment business she could really sock it to you when ticked off. "We just can't keep going back and forth like this. What about our clean break?"

I braced for her to remind me that I hadn't been clamoring for a clean break after six cocktails courtesy of Zildjian.

"Joe, don't hang up," she said. Her voice resonated like the long decay of a thick hand hammered earth ride. Using my real name caught me off guard. She was the only one who did. Even old Morty still used my stage name.

"I'm not wrong about this," she said. "Look across the room."

She was crazy. Beautiful. Impulsive. Complicated and crazy. But when the smoke cleared she was usually right. Usually.

I rubbed the sand from the corner of my eyes and took a look. Nicholas was still there. What the hell was he so fascinated with? I waited a bit and saw nothing.

"And..." I said.

"You don't see them?" she asked.

"See what?" I called the kitten again, but he didn't even turn his head.

"Turn off the lights, and try again," she said.

Every wishy-washy pie-in-the-sky thing Kendra had ever done sprung into my mind. The Feng-Shui consultants. The astrologers. Chakra readers. Aura aligners. Where had it gotten us? Split apart and across the city. My stomach shifted and I felt woozy. I had walked around feeling nauseous and dizzy like this for months after the split. I wasn't looking forward to it returning.

"Kendra, I gotta go." I slammed the phone down, hunched back into the couch, and tried to relax. Maybe I could recapture a few minutes of my dream before I had to get ready.

MYSTIC TRYST

I shimmied into position and let my eyes close. The room blurred into a hazy, soft focus.

Nicholas chirped, and I opened my eyes for one more glance his way. Shimmering in the dark above him was a glowing ball. I squinted and it came into focus. A puffer fish. Exactly like the spotted one I bought Kendra for our anniversary two years ago, except it was a washed out, almost translucent white like an underexposed black and white image. I sat up and saw the corner was crowded with glowing shapes. The seahorse. The lemon-yellow butterfly. The tomato clown. The little green one. Every fish we had ever tried in the tank was there.

In the shadowy, cave-like corner, something floated. A two foot distended blur emerged from the darkness: the big spike-finned lion-fish. It was the first fiasco; how could I forget? I paid four hundred bucks for it and when I brought it home it wouldn't eat. Kendra was furious (*"The money doesn't matter Joe it's the thought of the energy of a dying, starving fish in this house"*) and she sent me back to the store. The guy had told me that's what happens with the more exotic ones taken from the sea, but gave me a refund anyway 'cause he thought the first half of *Mystic Tryst* was the perfect album side.

The spindly apparition hovered above my cymbal bag, silent, ominous, and hungry as it had been in life. I never believed in Kendra's mumbo-jumbo, but unless someone was pulling an amazing trick on me, this changed everything. I picked up the phone and dialed her. I had to apologize. I had to tell her.

"You see them now," she said without me saying a word. "Don't bother, I forgive you."

I said what I had said to her so many times before, in the fragile, quiet moments after our many storms. "So, what do we do now?"

"Meet me at the diner by the park."

I quickly dressed. On the way out I looked at my cymbal bag. Morty was going to kill me, but he would have to wait.

THE NIGHT MARCHERS   DANIEL BRAUM

The diner patrons looked lost and lonely, right out of the lyrics of
Eleanor Rigby. I could hear the steady cello strokes driving the song
forward despite the lack of percussion. I felt like one of those lost
people, hoping for a second chance at a dream that had already
failed. The papers had come. It was official. This would be our first
encounter since. I bumped past some cops and a drunken group of
men in old suits at the door and then I saw her, radiant and angelic,
sitting in one of the big booths along the front wall.

She waved me over and I sat down. She smelled of neroli and
vanilla. I missed that smell. Her hair had grown out and she hadn't
re-dyed it. Streaks of silvery gray mingled with her natural straw-
brown. Her facial features seemed stronger and more defined, even
the tiny spider web lines at the edges of her eyes looked good.

"How've you been?" she asked.

"Not bad," I lied. I didn't know what I was doing. Hanging
around with Morty again, listening to the tracks of the unfinished
album over and over, running around with a girl half my age. I said
none of this, she hated when I was negative.

The waitress came over with coffee and I dramatically encouraged
her. We laughed, long and easily.

"I saw them," I said and took her hands in mine. "I can't believe
I saw them."

She smiled knowingly.

"Why? Why are they here now?"

"There has to be a reason," she said. "Otherwise you wouldn't be
able to see them. And if you didn't see them, you wouldn't believe
me. Then it would be much harder to get them back."

I hated how her explanations were always circular. But maybe
it was something I just didn't understand. I always thought all our

disagreements and fights were all her fault, just another symptom of her incomprehensible ideas, until today.

"They're yours," I said. "But why is it so important?"

"It's my burden. My responsibility. I let them die."

If they died under her watch, they died under my watch too. It was just as much my responsibility.

"That's it?" I asked.

"That's it," she said. "Don't change your mind on me."

"So what do I do? Scoop them up in a coffee can?"

"Let's go. I'll figure something out."

Suddenly it didn't seem like such a good idea to have her back in the apartment.

"No. Wait," I said.

"Why? Is the flavor of the month waiting there for you, naked?"

"No it's just…"

I didn't want it to end up the way it had after the Zildjian party. I wanted so badly to hear her breathing in my ear—to feel her against me slick with sweat. But, the pull was so strong I was afraid I'd break down and beg her to reconsider.

"Just what?" she asked, her deep green eyes accusing me.

"Just nothing," I said. "Let's go."

———

I swiped the fish with the little green aquarium net I found in a box of junk in the back of the closet, but it passed right through them.

Kendra watched disapprovingly. She took the net from me and sat down cross-legged on the floor. She closed her eyes and muttered what sounded like a yoga mantra.

"There," she said.

She stepped into the corner and swiped around. The net passed through the glowing shapes just like before.

"Damn," she said, and scooted up on my speaker cabinet. It looked so natural, so right to have her sitting there, kicking her legs in frustration. "What does a fish want anyway?"

"Bait," I said and scooped her up and lifted her over my shoulder.

"Not now," she yelped. "We have to figure this out."

I carried her toward the bedroom.

"Stop. Stop. Stop," she yelled. "Look!"

The fish had moved from the corner, trailing us in a glowing line across the living room. Nicholas swatted at them.

I gently put her down.

"Turn out the lights so you can see them better," she said.

I walked to the wall and flicked the switch.

"They didn't follow you," she said focusing on the glowing line. "How about me?"

She walked the few steps over to the couch. The fish stayed in place.

"Pick me up and carry me again."

I did. The fish followed us all the way to the bedroom.

We flopped down on my bed, clouds of fish hovering above us and we laid side-by-side staring up at them like they were constellations of stars.

"I should have known," she said. "They want to go home."

"Okay. To your place it is." I put my hand on her leg. "But I'm so comfortable right now."

"No. To the ocean. The Caribbean. That's where they're from."

"How do you know?"

"I just do."

I groaned.

MYSTIC TRYST

"Think about it," she said. "The fact we couldn't make it work hurt only us, mostly. But *we* failed them. They were *our* responsibility. They couldn't go to the store and buy food or get water from the toilet like Sasha if we were gone for days."

"Couldn't they float over to a map to make it clear?"

"Stop it. We have to make this right or it's always going to be hanging over us, no matter what the divorce papers say."

She sprung out of bed and went into the room off the living room we once had used as an office. I heard her clicking away at the computer.

"They're just fish," I called.

The lionfish hovered in the corner away from the rest. I wished it didn't look like it was waiting for food. I was so late. Morty was going to kill me.

Kendra emerged in the doorway. She held the frame with her strong thin arms and looked at me the way I always wanted—a mix of contentment, respect, and lust.

"We're on the next flight to Grand Cayman," she said. "Four thirty, tomorrow afternoon out of Newark. If we're lucky, we can get a couple of hours' sleep in." She turned out the light and crawled into bed next to me.

I wanted to stay. I wanted to wriggle out of my clothes, tell her we were going, and lose myself under the covers. But I rolled away. In my head I heard Jack singing the haunting, lush refrain of Mystic Tryst *(...one more mystic tryst, one more earthy tide and yet you're still here with me...)* He always knew the right thing to do, the right thing to say, and he made it look easy. He was a rock star walking on water until his early end. I felt dizzy as I picked up my cymbal bag. Everyone was waiting on me and I had to go.

THE NIGHT MARCHERS   DANIEL BRAUM

Morty met me at the door with his client, the wispy haired, high cheek-boned lead singer of the latest big budget, teen-angst band.

We embraced in an over exaggerated, back-clapping hug.

The corporate rock boy beamed. Just the look of him reminded me why after every session I swore no more favors. Somehow Morty always found a way to remind me that he landed the first Lotus record deal back in '69. I just wanted the session to be over fast so I could go back and deal with Kendra.

"I really love your work," corporate rock boy said as he clasped my hand. I'd seen his face somewhere but didn't remember his name.

One of the bulbs flickered and a spindly shape lowered from the ceiling. The lionfish had followed me. I awkwardly shuffled up the hall to get away from it. Mort and the kid followed.

"If you asked me if I'd ever get to meet *the* Casey James I would have said you're crazy," the kid blathered. "And now, to have you play on my disc, it's more than I ever dreamed of. It's gonna rock."

Mort had played me the demos. It was going to take a lot more than me to make this rock. As for his ass kissing, I knew he had asked Steve Smith and Terry Bozzio before me and they had both turned him down.

A cute brunette in a busy patterned top and too much eyeliner entered the hall and demanded Rock boy follow her to hair and make-up. I had to fight to keep from laughing. Mort stole a glance at her as they left then ushered me to the lounge behind the control room. He poured me some coffee.

"So, what happened to the drummer this time?" I asked.

"Rehab. Heroin, I think. He'll be back for the tour," Morty said in that callous, chipper way of his.

Being here reminded me my album I'd been "working on" forever, or at least since things went bad with Kendra, was horribly stalled. Perfectly recorded rhythm tracks filled the reels, but the spark was missing. I wasn't looking for a comeback or anything stupid, I just wanted—I needed to hit it square on and nail it. Like Jack would do if he were here. I struggled to remember the syncopated rhythms of the motion of the fishes in my dream.

Thin spikes emerged from the wall above the coffee machine and the lionfish drifted through the wall. Stupid fish found me. Maybe if I ignored it, it would go away.

"Kendra called," I said, to take my attention from it.

"So much for your clean break," Morty said in an I-told-you-so singsong.

The lionfish had moved to the center of the room. Light passed through it disconcertingly and I couldn't keep my eyes off it. I kept thinking if I turned away it would become corporeal and sting me in the back of the head with those sharp spines.

Morty slurped his coffee. "Ready for hair and make-up?"

I stood up. "I told you I don't want to be attached to this. No photos."

"Calm down," he said. "It's just a segment for that 'Making of the Song' show."

If I said no, he was going to remind me again of the good old days and all. I just couldn't stand it. I'd give him this. Maybe use it to throw in his face if I actually took off with Kendra. Maybe I could use a couple of days.

Two minutes later I was in a chair with the cute brunette spraying my hair. I noticed her small diamond ring as she powdered my face. I thought of Kendra's two-carat platinum-set rock on the day we split. It was the quietest moment of my life, looking at it sitting on the kitchen counter top.

"All done," the cute brunette said, and ushered me into the big sound room. The techs had set my cymbals up correctly, at least Morty was good for that.

THE NIGHT MARCHERS Daniel Braum

Tripod-mounted cameras loomed in the corners. I sat behind the kit and slung the headphones on.

"Sorry, Casey, over there with the rest of the band," Morty said. I looked at the control room window. Morty was pointing to the side of the studio where the rest of the band leaned against the wall.

"What the hell," I mouthed to him.

"We're gonna do some takes of the vocals along with a click while he's still fresh," Morty said.

I pushed off the headphones and stomped over to the corporate rock peanut gallery.

Morty's client entered, followed by a procession of cameramen and producers.

Were we just going to stand here for B reel? It was all ass-backward.

I stood around for a half hour while they took a million different angles of the kid singing the opening lines of a song that didn't even exist yet. He was just going to have to do it over anyway once the music got laid down. Morty was a lot of things, but he knew how to make a record. If this was what he wanted, then fine. I just wasn't going to stand around waiting. I walked over to the drum mike to tell him.

I bent down to test if the mike was on. The lionfish appeared out of nowhere, its beady black eyes and splotchy spikes right up against my face. I swatted at it, lost my balance, and fell forward onto the kit. Cymbals crashed and the toms toppled as I tried to stand. Morty burst through the doors.

"What the hell," corporate rock boy said.

"Get the cameras off," Morty yelled to the laughing cameramen.

I picked myself up and headed for the door.

"Casey, wait," Morty said. But I kept walking. Screw it. I was going to the Caribbean.

MYSTIC TRYST

Mercifully I didn't see the fish on the plane but Kendra assured me they were there. We checked into the Blue Heaven resort in the middle of the night. Kendra sat down in one of the lobby's rattan chairs while I went to the front and deposited her ring in the hotel safe with the manager. When we returned he escorted us to our low-rise suite on the beach.

After a few hours of sleep, we ordered breakfast and watched the ocean from our patio while we waited. Endless shades of blue stretched to the clear sky. A young couple held hands and leisurely picked shells at the rolling surf while a team from the hotel spread out a bright red chute for parasailing. Soon, the staff arrived with a lush spread of exotic fruit, caviar, fresh breads and juices.

Kendra held a crumb up. "Not long now," she said.

I couldn't see the fish well in the light like her, but I could feel them watching.

Kendra slid out of her chair and kissed my forehead. "I'm going to make the boat arrangements."

While she was gone, I picked at the pineapple and thought of Nicholas. My assistant would be feeding him, but cats were creatures of habit; he'd miss me and his ghostly playthings. Morty however, was just a creature; he was going to kill me.

A half hour later, we were riding the wind away from the hotel dock in a catamaran. I sat on the net in the front and Kendra sat under the sail, covered in big sunglasses and a batik wrap. She flipped through a book on fish from the hotel gift shop.

I breathed deeply, taking in the salt spray on the wind. Breakfast had been exceptional and Kendra looked like a dream. I was sorry that back home I had forgotten how to truly live.

THE NIGHT MARCHERS   DANIEL BRAUM

The driver, an old weathered guy with kinky gray hair and a quiet authority about him, stopped the boat over a shallow spot. I could see the sandy bottom and the coral heads below.

"No," Kendra said. "Not here."

"Ma'am. This is the best place," he said. "My personal spot. No one snorkels here."

"It's not right. Over there..." she said, and seemed to arbitrarily point out to the water.

"Dangerous out in the open," he said. "Currents are bad today."

"I don't care," she said.

The driver made a face and tacked the boat a hundred yards away. I thought I could make out the long spikes and black eyes of the lionfish among the rigging.

"What the hell does he know?" she whispered angrily.

I felt that things were about to get out of control like so many times before. New Years nineteen eighty popped to mind. Morty had scored us front row seats to the Zen Squires show at the Fillmore, and Kendra had insisted they were better than my back stage access. She danced away, her usual wild self, much to the delight of a rowdy bunch of bikers who wouldn't leave her alone.

"Got a boyfriend," Kendra said.

"So why ain't he dancing with you?"

"Fuck off! He's Casey James."

The current had taken me and I was up in that biker's whiskey-stinking, bearded face. The rest was pure chaos. We came out of it bruised and battered, but okay. I felt that same nervous electricity now, except the lionfish hovering over me made me think things weren't going to end so well this time.

Before I could say anything, Kendra was at the edge of the boat unpeeling her wrap, revealing a bright orange bikini. She rolled off the side with a sploosh.

68

MYSTIC TRYST

"It's so warm," she said. "Come on."

I grabbed our masks and snorkels and followed her in.

The coral teemed with fish. Kendra was right, again. This spot was just like my dream.

"Hold your breath and dive with me," she said.

Pressure built in my ears as we descended the fifteen feet to the coral head. I could faintly make out our fish among their flesh-and-blood counterparts.

After a few seconds we went to the surface for air then dove again.

The butterfly, the clown, and the little green one were picking at the coral when we returned. I could barely see them. They were fading away and I had to go up for air.

We surfaced farther from the boat. The current had either taken us, or the boat.

"Come back," the driver called but Kendra didn't listen. Her feet disappeared beneath the waves. I held my breath and followed.

Looking down I could see I was already being pulled away from the coral head. I spun and saw Kendra kicking—struggling for the bottom. The water darkened, as if the sun were blocked out. I kicked harder, hoping to catch up, but I lost sight of her in the increasingly turbulent water.

In the sandy murk the specter of the little green fish appeared at my mask for an instant, then was gone. Out of breath, I broke for the surface. Clouds had moved in obscuring the sun. The tropical rain I'd heard so much about poured down. I bobbed at the surface. It would have been almost pleasant if I didn't feel myself being pulled farther out into the ocean.

I looked around and saw the catamaran a hundred yards away. The driver was fishing Kendra out of the water. Good, I thought. She was safe. I waved and yelled, then remembered the catamaran had no engine and would have to tack out to reach me.

THE NIGHT MARCHERS   Daniel Braum

I put the snorkel in my mouth and tread water. I could keep it up for a while. I stuck my face in the water. The lionfish was right there. I felt a strange kinship to it. Its simple life had been interrupted, all control and certainty taken away.

The current pulled me faster. The catamaran grew smaller by the second. The waves, the rain, the racing of my heart all beat their chaotic rhythms. There was nothing to latch onto. My leg exploded into a burst of pain and I jarred to a halt. I had been snagged on a wall of coral. The current dragged me along it and that same burning spread to my back. I scrambled for a hold hoping the coral wouldn't snap. The ocean wanted to take me, but I held tight. Someone from the hotel would come. I searched the rain for a steady beat, kept my head above water and waited. Floating in the water I saw the patterns of my life—the currents that moved me. A cycle of bliss and chaos. It had always been this way with Kendra and it always would.

———————

Later that night, after the hotel had fished me out, Kendra and I sat in our big tub full of warm, foamy water and soothing aromatic oils. The flicker from dozens of candles reflected off of the beige and white ceramic tiled walls.

"When you didn't listen and went under like that I felt like it was New Years nineteen eighty all over again."

"Things turned out okay then, I remember."

"Today could have been a lot worse," I said.

Except for the welts from the fire coral that saved me, things were fine.

"You made it down, right?" I said. "The fish are home?"

"Almost all of them," she said, and pointed to a small cluster between the candles and a conch on the floor. "I knew it from the second dive. But I saw a shell I just had to have."

It was no use to tell her she could have gotten us killed. I couldn't handle a dose of her circular logic right now.

"A souvenir?" I asked. She knew as well as I the reef was a protected zone.

"Today was intense," she said. "A milestone. It merited it."

"The shell belongs to the sea," I spat, trying to remember something Jack had said to me once while in a haze. "At one time the calcium was part of the earth. So that shell belongs to the sea—to the world. How's that for a cosmic thought?"

"Calm down," she said, unphased by my tirade. "I was reading up today." She pointed at the fish on the floor. "They're called gobies. I'm pretty sure they're from the Red Sea, but could be India or the South Pacific. We're going to have to travel the world together finding out."

Her foot found my leg somewhere beneath the foam.

"I could think of worse ways to spend my time," I said, but I didn't want to touch her. I was thinking of treading water while being carried out to the sea.

"Good. Tomorrow I'll get the tickets to Israel," she said, obviously missing what I meant.

"Israel?"

"The Red Sea's in Israel. I hear Eliat has the best reefs. Good hash and backgammon, too."

"Isn't it dangerous?"

She sat up, creating a wave that spilled over the side, dousing the nearest candles.

"Here we go again. Joe the monkey wrench. We're almost there. Don't ruin this."

The smell of smoke filled my nose. With the candles out, her face was in shadow. The big lionfish floated between us. I smacked it but only hit the wall.

"I'm not ruining anything. You always have your head in the clouds and ignore what's on the ground."

She stood up and stormed out of the tub, the water pouring off her extinguishing the remaining candles with a sizzle.

I dried off, turned the wastebasket upside down, gathered the two conch shells, and drummed.

I started with the cool fade out from *Mystic Tryst*. The part that was cut too soon on the record. The little gobies scattered, and reformed their school on the ceiling. Soon I had recaptured the rhythm from my dream, the beat of the circling fish dividing and reforming their circling schools. It was so locked in I shouted, and shouted again in time. I chanted and pounded on the pail and shells till my hands were raw.

Then I slid into the tub and sat in the tepid water counting fish.

When I couldn't stand it any longer, I quietly crept back into the room. Kendra was passed out, draped over the bed peacefully.

I laid down on the couch. It was long into the morning before I slept.

―――――――――

I woke up and Kendra was gone. Just like when we split the first time, gone in the night without so much as a note.

Just as I sat up, the door clicked. Kendra walked in holding a big covered tray.

"Done with my workout, sleepyhead," she said without looking at me. "I saved us a spot at the pool and I'm going to have a shower. I brought you breakfast."

MYSTIC TRYST

She placed the tray on the table, put an envelope on the bed, and disappeared into the bathroom.

When I heard the water running, I went over to the bed and checked the envelope. Plane tickets. To Israel.

I pulled my suitcase from the closet and threw my stuff in it. I stomped around and decided to just leave it. I threw on some clothes, grabbed my passport, phone, and wallet.

I opened the bathroom door and thought I was going to yell at the top of my lungs. She was in the shower. The water streamed down on her silhouette behind the smoked glass. We'd never be happy together. Or at least she'd never be. I was happy in my looping patterns. Circles of misery moving closer to and farther away from happiness with every encounter with Morty, with every affair, with every unfinished then completed beat, track, and project. She'd feed into me, like the endless tide, and I'd be satisfied in a way she'd never be. She was beautiful, mysterious, complex as the boulders at the beach, as the reef. I was drawn to her as she was drawn to me, like earth to water as she would say. But ultimately, I'd wear her down, slowly but surely batter her to sand. She didn't belong with me.

I took one last, long look at the water cascading on her slender form and closed the door. The last fish would find their way. Just as she would. Maybe they wouldn't. But I was going home. This was where our paths branched, for certain.

In the cab on the way to the airport, I called my assistant. Morty had called.

"I'm coming home," I said.

He asked me about the weather but I was watching the propellers of a seaplane in the channel along the road sputter to life.

"If Morty bothers you again, tell him to screw himself. I'll deal with it when I get back."

THE NIGHT MARCHERS Daniel Braum

Morty being pissed at me suited me just fine. I was going to be real busy for the next few months with the album.

I looked around for the lionfish. That feeling I was being watched was gone. It'd probably be back again. I had a lot to do yet before I joined Jack in rock star heaven and was sure I'd mess up plenty.

The plane leapt from the waves into the sky. Soon it would be me up in the air and I'd be out of here. I could already feel myself rising.

A GIRL'S GUIDE TO APPLYING SUPERIOR CAT MAKEUP AND DISPELLING COMMONLY FOUND SURBURBAN DEMONS

HALLOWEEN, 1985.

I unfold the note Jenny passed to me in Math and write my response.

Tonight's the best because it's okay to walk around acting out our dreams and looking the part.

Dad stops our brown, plaid station wagon at a red light and I mess up the last word. I suck at refolding the note into the perfect octagon like Jenny had done. She's going to be a witch tonight, and I'm her black cat.

"Can we stop to get mascara?" I ask.

"For what, Faith?" Mom asks.

"Whiskers," I say.

"You already look enough like a cat without putting anything on your face, young lady," Mom says.

"Aw, come on, Mom. I want to."

"Don't push it," Dad says. "Not if you ever want to go out again before your fifteenth birthday."

"Yeah, don't push it, Faith," Benny says.

I want to punch him in his smug, twelve-year-old face, but then I see him looking out the window in amazement at the bigger kids walking toward the arena in their homemade costumes.

He's half-cute, half-pathetic in his hockey jersey that is much too large.

"Be good and listen to your sister, okay," Mom says. "Don't make it hard for her."

Which translates to: "don't say annoying things to people and make your sister have to defend you."

I've already been suspended once for punching the last kid in the face who decked his books and took his food from his lunchbox, and I don't want to miss anymore basketball practice.

"Don't worry," Benny says. "I'm a hockey player. Hockey players don't have time to talk. Unless to ask for candy."

"I don't think there's going to be any candy," I say. "It's not like that."

"The box office opens at nine a.m.? Right?" Mom says. "Jenny Thompson's mom is dropping Jenny and Bill and the boys too?"

"Yeah. I'm meeting them. Don't worry. I have dimes to call in case of emergency."

"The ticket-money is safe in your sock?"

"Yes, Mom."

A GIRL'S GUIDE TO APPLYING SUPERIOR
CAT MAKEUP AND DISPELLING COMMONLY
FOUND SURBURBAN DEMONS

Mom fixes her lipstick in the visor mirror. Dad's wearing cologne. They are going out to dinner after they drop us on the line. I know they want a night alone together, that's why they let me sleep out, but only if I brought Benny along. Benny could care less about Jimmy Brett songs, but Mom loves him. She used to listen to him back when she was in school. So we're going to go to the show as a family.

Benny's staring at the kid wearing a white goalie mask as a costume. I don't think he gets it. The kid is holding hands with a girl dressed as a witch; her short black skirt shows way too much of her thighs. A few blocks away the round monolith of the concert arena looms over the swath of parking lot and the one and two-story houses of the neighborhood surrounding it. A crowd is already waiting outside to be the first in line when the box office opens tomorrow.

"Think he'll play 'Chinese Restaurant Blues'?" Mom asks.

"She's just buying tickets. How's she going to know," Dad says.

I hate his dismissive tone. Mom's eyes go far away. Is she thinking about when Dad used to be nice to her? Or when she saw Jimmy Brett in college, with a boy that was not Dad, before she met him. I can't remember her ever looking at Dad with excited eyes like in their wedding picture that hangs in our living room.

The light changes. Dad rolls forward. On the side of the road is something dead. A big cat or small dog? Maybe a possum from the meadow by the arena. Then I see a twisted wing.

"Gross. Dead owl," Benny says. "Look."

I've never seen one, but I've heard their sounds in the night. As a little kid I was deathly afraid of them.

"I love owls," Benny says. "Whoosh. Mice never see them coming."

"Kittens either," Dad says. "An owl once got one of your Grandma Phyllis' kittens."

"Daaaad. Ew. Stop," I say.

"Guess something saw that one coming," Mom says.

THE NIGHT MARCHERS   Daniel Braum

Exposed on the side of the road, dead like that, it doesn't look so scary. It just looks…broken.

Dad turns into the sprawling lot. He manages not to hit anyone wandering around and pulls to the curb and stops. Benny and I get out. Rows and rows filled with cars surround us. The line stretches around the arena. I can't see where it ends or the ticket window where it must begin. People are in costume so I'm glad I sorta wore one.

"Okay, dolls," Mom says. "See you tomorrow for breakfast. Love you."

Dad can't drive away fast enough. Then I'm free, besides being there with Benny, but that's okay. I'm a cat and it is Halloween.

The "line" is a mob, a suburban street wide, stretching around the arena and into the concrete ocean of parking lot. Little, round portable grills for tailgating are fired up. Charcoal and lighter fluid-tinged air chills my face and I'm glad I'm wearing leggings and a turtleneck. There are no rules here, outdoors. There is nowhere else where we, where all of us can just "be." Kids from school and their older siblings are here, old people Mom and Dad's age too, only they don't dress like Mom and Dad; they look like they are at a concert or bikers I see on Sunrise Highway. Gathering like this will be harder until spring; suburbia is going to sleep for the winter. Until then there is tonight, a night of freedom, a night of possibility with permission for everyone to be what they want to be, who they want to be, granted from their costumes and it being Halloween.

"Hey, Faith."

It's Billy Thompson. The gang has already planted themselves in a spot on the line. Benny runs over to him and his lacrosse team buddies. They're dressed up as the lacrosse team. Dopes. I like them anyway because they're kind to Benny.

One of Billy's friends is telling a story about a giant pig balloon he swears some band floated around during a concert once. The people next to us are talking about a movie where people boarded themselves in a mall to hide from things who eat people. The boom box nearest us is blasting a Jimmy Brett tune. Another Jimmy Brett tune is playing on a different box a few yards away. Some long-haired guy is sitting on a milk crate playing a Zeppelin song on his acoustic guitar as if he doesn't hear the overlapping tunes.

"Where's Jenny, Billy?"

"Don't know. Said she went to look for you."

His breath smells like beer.

The sound of us, all of us, "the line," echoes against the concrete arena. The sound of our passion and restlessness and dreams fills this corner of the night before escaping past the hotels ringing the arena and dissipating into the boring world. Benny's got a lacrosse stick from somewhere and he's throwing a lacrosse ball back and forth with Billy.

Someone taps me on the shoulder. It's Eric Schwartz. I hadn't noticed him but there he is, his hair messed up or just standing up, as always. He's in his green, collared Lacoste shirt and Members Only knock-off jacket, as always.

"Um, hey, he says. "Jenny's not looking for you, she's off smoking a cigarette and didn't want her brother to see."

His eyes linger on my chest as he stands there thinking of something to say, then something behind me catches his eye.

A tall, lean girl in a tight, black cat costume is walking past. The lacrosse ball drops to the ground. Someone whistles. The girl extends her arm and flips her middle finger without looking or breaking stride. Billy and the dopes turn their heads.

THE NIGHT MARCHERS

DANIEL BRAUM

Cat ears poke from the girl's mane of long dark hair. Whiskers and a nose are drawn on her face. I can't tell if her powder-pale skin is naturally alabaster or just great makeup. Her wedge of a skirt reveals legs just as white. Her low cut top shows her defined collar bones and the V of the cords of her neck. She twirls car keys around one slender finger. She's leaving? Where could be even cooler than here? Is she just going to get beer? Or to a party with her girlfriends? Or to meet a boy who isn't a dope like Billy's pals? Someday I'll be as grown up as her. And have a cool costume too. A car to drive myself anywhere I want. I'll have places to go. People to go there with.

A man is walking a few paces behind her. He's following her path exactly, tracing her steps, but there's something wrong with the way he walks. Maybe he's drunk but he's not quite staggering. I feel like I'm watching an old movie with missing frames that was cut and put back together all wrong. The girl walks into the dark rows of cars, no one says anything about the man following her. No one says anything, but I can feel everyone lost in their individual thoughts of her as they're watching.

"You wanna go smoke a clove?" Eric asks. "I got a pack."

"Uh, not now, Eric. Which way did Jenny go? I got a note for her."

Eric points into the lot.

"Hold that thought. Be right back."

I look and see Benny's okay with Billy and the guys, then I walk into the shadow of the arena towering over us.

The line seems even more of its own planet having stepped outside it, our noise, our breath, the warmth of the grills and our bodies is an atmosphere tangible and real. Shadows of cars and the steel light poles cast by the moon form layers of overlapping darkness.

A GIRL'S GUIDE TO APPLYING SUPERIOR CAT MAKEUP AND DISPELLING COMMONLY FOUND SURBURBAN DEMONS

I pass some sloppy drunk guy pissing on a car. The sound of it hitting the metal hubcap is gross. Some dopes are laughing. A few cars away, some older girls are passing a smoke around.

At the end of the row I see Cat Girl's unmistakable silhouette. Curves define her tall, lean shape. She's standing in the center of the lane, one hand on her hip.

The wrong-looking man is next to her. He's shorter than her. Nothing special about his shape. I can't make out words, but I hear fighting. He pushes her. She staggers. I realize she's in high heels. He pushes her again. She falls back onto a car hood. I move closer. She's cursing. Her words are slurred. The dopey guys stop laughing. The tink of the drunk guy pissing on the hubcap fills the sonic void. Everyone sees. Why isn't anyone doing anything?

I don't plan on getting into a fight. I don't plan on hitting anyone. I don't plan on getting my fist bloodied like when I smacked the kids pushing Benny around. I run.

Up close the man is bigger than I thought. Much wider and heftier than me. He's in a white tank top undershirt, showing muscles despite the cold. The feeling of being outside in the meadow at night, afraid of strange sounds that I never thought I'd feel again, returns. His mouth is a grimace of grit and rage; nothing like the easy-to-crush bravado of the chumps at school who'd never been punched in the face until messing with me. This guy looks like he has most certainly been punched in the face before and he's not going to go down from just one punch or run away if his nose bleeds. I don't like that he's not wearing a costume, only a pair of red devil horns, with no strap, that must be glued to his head.

Punching him isn't bravery. Its reflex. One second I'm standing there. Watching how he's got his waist and chest pressing her to the car and is wriggling her pants down with his arms. I see her thigh bone and concave belly and white skin exposed, then I feel my hands pounding on his back. He turns. Too slowly. The motion is all wrong. Missing frames. My fist connects with his face with an awful crunch. There's the sound of something ripping.

The side of his face is caved in where I hit him. Did I do that? His skin is broken but there's no muscle or guts underneath, only... blackness. Blackness in the shape of a face. Darker than the shadows. It's the blackness of the night sky. The gaps between the stars in space. Looking at it I'm alone. Like I'm somewhere upstate, outside with only the big, dark sky and the emptiness of space and I'm filled with the awareness of being really, really small. I once dreamed I was hiding under covers and woke up in a dark cave, then I woke up from that dream into the absolute darkness of my room. I cried out but no one came. The blackness of his face that's not a face is worse than that. Worse than thinking something's going to swoop down from the trees and get me. I hear an owl cry. And I'm just a little girl again afraid of the night.

He pushes Cat Girl again, and the sound of her against the car hood snaps me out of it. I back away, tasting the crisp, barbeque-and-smoke tinged night air. I feel my heart working and my breath and my sweat. He's off the girl and moving for me. Straight at me. Like a boxer. A boxer about to kick the shit out of me.

I hate his expression. Not afraid. Not gloating. Just... nothing. Just, 'I got this.'

I put my hands up like I think a boxer should. I've never put my hands up before. Grandma Phyllis once told me her Uncle Freddie taught her how to fight. One time she tried to teach me and I wish I'd really listened.

Fear blooms on the man's face. From my hands? From me pretending to know how to fight? No. His eyes are on something behind me.

A GIRL'S GUIDE TO APPLYING SUPERIOR CAT MAKEUP AND DISPELLING COMMONLY FOUND SURBURBAN DEMONS

I turn. A woman is at the end of the row. Walking toward us. A grown up. Looks sort of like… Mom? Grandma Phyllis? No… like…me? Like me, yeah me. How I think I might look when I'm grown up. The woman strides past barely glancing sideways at me as she does. Her skin is old. Taught over the bones of her face. The skin on her hands is covered in overlapping scars, white lines of knit flesh crossing each other again and again and again. The man runs. The woman dashes over to Cat Girl and whispers in her ear. Then she chases after the man and disappears into the dark.

The drunk has stopped pissing.

"Holy shit. You see that?" one of the dopes says.

"What, dude?" the drunk says.

"She smashed the shit out of him," one of the older girls says and then takes a deep pull off her cigarette.

Cat Girl slumps on the car hood. I run to her. She clutches my arm with both of hers.

———————————

She takes her heels off and hands them to me. Even without them she towers over me. She doesn't let go of my arm as we walk. I wouldn't walk here in stocking feet. Her doing that makes everything even more surreal. She smells of burnt sugar and cigarettes and fancy salon shampoo. The sour reek of alcohol seeps from her pores and something else, something that makes me think of overripe strawberries about to spoil. She's so drunk if she let's go of me she might fall.

Her cat makeup is smudged, but even messed up she looks so, so cool.

"What happened?" I say.

I don't understand what she is saying. Her words are so slurred. Something about Jimmy-fucking-Brett.

Her eyes are brown. Her lower lip is thinner than her plump top lip. I noticed the curved lines in them. The tiny hairs along her chin are visible in the dim moonlight.

"That lady. What did she say?"

"She said never take off the costume," she says clearly and lucidly and doesn't sound drunk at all.

"What? What does that mean?"

"The way a girl fights commonly found demons is to never take off the costume, no matter what you are wearing."

Then she hugs me and kisses my cheek in a thank you sort of a way and she's back to clutching my arm. I ask her again what she means by that, but I only get slurred words and more Jimmy-fucking-Brett. I don't ask her where she was going or where she wants to go now. I know she wants to stay with me. Close to me. And that's just fine. That's what I want too.

———

I show up back at the line with her clutching my arm like that. Benny is asleep on a beach towel next to a charcoal grill. Billy and the dopes are holding beers, staring at us. Jenny's there, not even hiding the cigarette that she's smoking.

I feel the weight of everyone watching. Looking at her, looking at me, looking at us, two Halloween cats back from the night. I don't know what they are thinking but the silence and the stares do not feel good.

"Great makeup," Jenny says.

"Thanks," Cat Girl says, trying not to slur her words and failing.

"How'd you do it? You should do hers," Jenny says.

Then, just like that everything is okay. Everything is in place. Everyone knows how to perceive what they are seeing. Billy moves the half empty beer next to him on the ground away from Benny. I see, but I don't care as long as Benny doesn't puke and Mom doesn't find out. The dopes twirl their lacrosse sticks and resume their game of catch. I see them steal glances. We're all part of this micro-city, this planet, and the atmosphere is comforting and exactly what I want. What happened moments ago is still replaying in my mind. But I'm here. I'm okay. We're okay. We're together, we're all together, and anything in the night will be kept at bay as long as this is true.

———————

I learn a lot about Jimmy Brett music. How to get mascara on just right and how to blow smoke rings from Jenny and Cat Girl. The night is full of laughter and barbecue and drunk guys screaming Jimmy-fucking-Brett way too many times, but faster than I like morning threatens to reclaim the sky.

Without the darkness of night, something about the line has changed. People are hugging tighter to the arena. Packing up lawn chairs. When had it stopped being Halloween? Not at midnight, for sure. Sunrise is coming. I don't want it to change us back into what we were. The line had its own semblance of order and courtesy and sharing, and I can feel that dissolving in the dawn. Then people are running. Just running. The guys next to us grab their shit and make a mad dash for position near the box office window.

I try to wake up Benny, but he's fast asleep. Jenny and I each grab one of his arms, lift him and drag his scrawny hockey-jersey-clad self into the crowd with us. Everything is a mass of elbows and pushing and cursing for a few minutes. The sun has come up and we're on the newly re-formed line for Jimmy Brett tickets—tightly packed with people in sight of the box office window around the bend from where we started. Benny yawns.

"Is it breakfast, yet?" he asks.

I look around for Cat Girl. She is nowhere to be found.

With the cloak of night gone, all the trash, empty beer cans, broken bottles and bedraggled faces looking worn for wear are revealed. I look around for Cat Girl each time the line moves and we take a step forward. We're closer to the front than I ever thought we would be. An hour later I have tickets in hand.

Me and Benny and Jenny and Billy and his sorry looking pals are standing at the curb, all of us a mess, when Mom and Dad roll up. "Chinese Restaurant Blues" is playing in the station wagon. Dad looks like a goof trying to be cool, drumming on the steering wheel. He's chipper and smiling.

"We brought bagels," Mom says.

Everyone piles into the wagon. The boys are all stuffed in the back, but the bagels and cream cheese get sent around and we all manage to eat.

"How are the seats?" Mom asks.

"Good," I say. "Actually, we got great seats."

Cat Girl's exposed white midriff springs into my mind. The man wriggling her pants down. The sound of her slamming onto the hood of the car.

"It was good, Ma," Benny says. "But there was no candy. Is it too late to trick-or-treat?"

"There's always next year," Dad says.

Will fifteen be too old to dress up and trick-or-treat, I wonder.

"How was it sleeping out," Mom asks. "Was it cold? You have fun?"

If I tell her the truth I know it means no more nights out. I'd seen something. Seen through something. Through the life Mom and Dad think they are giving Benny and me. Where we live isn't safe. No matter what Mom and Dad think. Night or day. Seen or unseen, there is…danger. Things not even the light will stop. I lost something in the rows of cars and I don't want Mom and Dad to lose that too. I'll take care of Benny. I'll watch over him. And Cat Girl if I see her again. And Jenny, of course.

Next year maybe I'm going to dress up like that woman I saw. The woman who scared the devil-horned man away. Or maybe just in a better cat costume, with mascara.

I'll wear a costume every day, not just for Halloween. Cat or grown up who scares devil-horned men away, I'll dress up and pretend, or just pretend. I'll keep pretending until I am what I'm pretending to be, who I want to be, what I want to be, and I'm never going to stop.

ACROSS THE DARIEN GAP

Where Central and South America comes together lies a 54 mile stretch of rainforest, the only missing link in the Pan-American Highway—the 16,000 miles of continuous road stretching from Alaska to South America."
—from Butler's *Guide to the Darien*

Distorted reggae chords blare into the jungle from a tiny Marshall amp in the corner of Johnnie's Video Bar. I watch a blond-bearded, dreadlocked American chuck chords on a beat up, blue, Fender knock-off guitar. His buddy, crammed in the corner behind him with his drum set, hammers out a sparse but steady beat.

Alexa shuffles on the dance floor with the seven others we're traveling with. Her long black hair is coated in sweat and Costa Rican grime. She smiles and for a moment I can believe she is carefree, despite all our running and fear.

She keeps her distance from a short Indian man who is spinning in circles with his arms extended and eyes closed. A big, almost toothless grin spreads on his wrinkled old face. He's definitely had a few shots of guaro too many.

I picked up the seven others between here and San Antonio to bring us to nine. Makes us easier to mask. Harder to scrye. Now we look like just a bunch of nobodies heading to the gap, leisurely. Not in a beeline. Nothing that will call attention to our pursuers.

Alexa laughs and drinks beers and guaro with the rest, the bunch of them oblivious to the burnt-out look on the faces of the musicians, a look born of too many years of living lean. I know it too well. They don't notice how the bass player, a Costa Rican, stands away from the transplanted gringos, probably once hippie students from Boston, avoiding direct eye contact as they play. They don't yet have the wisdom to realize that every face, in every place we have passed, was not placed there for our amusement or education. Except for Alexa.

My old pal Johnnie himself stands behind the bar smiling as he serves a beer. A video screen behind him plays an American rock video with the sound off. He smiled big and greedily when we stepped into his gringo heaven in-the-middle-of-nowhere bar. He wouldn't be smiling so wide if he knew that unlike the hippie hold-overs in the corner who are probably running from themselves and their perceived sins of the world, the horrors I'm hiding Alexa from are dangerously real.

Tomas hired me to take her across the Darien into Columbia. Told me she's the daughter of some big time mystic, but not who. Told me her Pop's enemies want her dead, but not why. I'm guessing a lot of people don't want her to grow up big and strong like her Daddy. Now she's got some bad stuff on her trail.

You can't run from these things, Tomas said. *They'll keep coming forever. Her Dad is gone and we are all she has. Her only hope is to stay ahead of them long enough to get her across the Darien Gap, onto my ground. My hemisphere. I'll stand a real chance of hiding her there.*

ACROSS THE DARIEN GAP

I don't know why he chose me. Probably 'cause I'm small-time enough to slip under the radar and not be noticed. I know just enough arcane tricks to make a living, keep me alive out here, and to piss a lot of people off.

The band stops so Boston-Dreadlock man can tune up. The din of peeping frogs, chirping lizards, and pulsing hum of insect night sounds fills the lull. The Indian keeps spinning, his hands almost slapping Alexa. The group laughs at him. Alejandro and Rita indulge in yet another public kiss. "Get a room," David taunts. Alexa rolls her eyes, then notices me. A glowing smile grows on her beautiful face. She walks over to the window.

"Nate, get in here and dance with me," she says.

I screwed up right from the start and used my real name. Some instinct in me mistakenly reacted as if "she and I" were real, and not just another job and fear born fling.

She tosses her freshly-showered, long, curly hair. She smells like soap and flowers.

I flick my cigarette and lean in. "In a minute," I say, trying to manage an earnest smile, hoping it hides the sick feeling I get thinking about all this running. I walk across the dirt road to check the wards I placed in the edge of the jungle.

The leaves on the cibolas and ferny underbrush still lean south as I directed. Nothing has disturbed my "barrier". Tomas said these simple wards would fool Alexa's pursuers. Magical masks, he called them. Nothing outside will detect anything magical inside. Anything stronger will announce your presence for miles, like a flare. Keep it simple, and safe.

I walk along the barrier to check the next ward point.

A faint blue glow shimmers in the darkness. Something has walked into the barrier. Blue mist peels off a man-sized form, its pointed ears tight along its bald head. It turns, revealing stunted

THE NIGHT MARCHERS   Daniel Braum

reptilian features, on an almost human face. Its eyes are the solid milky-blue of a snake about to molt. It moves its arms and legs slowly, deliberately though its wiry frame looks built to run.

I freeze. What the hell did Tomas get me into?

It keeps moving, apparently unaware of me. The bent plants all flip direction as it passes.

I didn't bargain for this. Just figured I'd cast some wards, baby-sit some kid, and return home six months ahead on the rent.

The ward works. Simple and safe.

It circles an ancient strangler fig a few times, then steps out of the barrier—mist wisping off it as it disappears. Tendrils linger and settle on the ferns before dissipating.

I stand motionless, hoping it is gone.

A twig snaps. A dark shape close to the ground moves toward me. I release the breath I can hold no longer. It freezes. A black feline head regards me with intelligent yellow eyes. A jaguar. What is it doing this close to shore? A few heartbeats pass then it lifts a paw, slowly then gently puts it down.

Nostrils flaring, it crawls closer, its belly pressed to the ground, and I smell its musky stink. It paws the air in front of me, opens its mouth, baring its thick sharp teeth, releasing a low guttural growl. I hold still, thinking of what to do, but it crawls away in the direction the blue demon headed.

I stand still until my body is convinced all threat is gone. The adrenaline stops flowing. My heart slows. Beads of sweat roll down my face.

I backtrack to the bar. Juan is standing outside watching the five who have gravitated to the beach. When we met in Guatemala I hired him to be a lookout and some muscle, but more importantly to be our ninth member. I wouldn't trust him with my girl, but I trust him not to run if things get out of control. David asked him about his scarred up arm. Shark bite, he said and they all believed him.

ACROSS THE DARIEN GAP

"Everything good?" he asks.

"Yeah, everything's still in place. But I'm getting tired. Double duty tonight. We'll sleep well tomorrow."

"Check," he says.

Inside Johnnie's, the band is packing up. Alexa, David, (who keeps hitting on her), and the Indian guy are the only ones left on the dance floor, moving to the sound from the video screens.

I want to get between them, but don't. Keeping our secret serves me better. He'd get pissed and maybe leave. We are nine and I want it to stay that way.

The Indian guy abruptly stops his spin and turns to me. He brings his hand into a claw and rakes the air. "Meow. Grrrowl. Meow," he says through a mouthful of laughter.

How did he know?

"Don't bother the paying customers," Johnnie says, pushing him to the exit. "Time to get out of here."

"What's with him?" David asks.

"He's nuts," Johnnie says.

David yawns. "It's dead in here, anyway. Let's hit the beach."

"I'll bring you drinks," Johnnie says.

Alexa's eyes protest. I can read her well. They say you're not going to dance with me after all.

I stare back. I'll see her in her cabin, later. Like always.

We join the rest of the group, standing in a circle at the edge of the water smoking cigarettes under the stars. Balls of heat lightning flash on the horizon, slowly rolling closer.

"Come on," Alexa says to me. "Take your boots off. Let's go in the water."

I take off my shoes, roll up my pants, and wade out into the shallow water with her. It's only knee deep for a half mile out to the barrier reef. Hordes of tiny phosphorescent plankton float on the surface. We leave glowing trails in our wake. I light a cigarette and try to relax. We're warded in all directions. Except from the water. Can I even place a ward on water?

After a minute David follows. I glance at Alexa's half submerged legs. I don't blame him for his persistence. Alejandro and the others leisurely wade out to join us.

A big orange and purple cluster flashes in the sky.

"What was that?" David asks.

"Ball lightning," I say.

"But there's no rain."

"Doesn't have to be. Friction of front on front."

"I don't care what it is. Just look at it," Alexa says.

"Beautiful," David says.

As always, he adds one word too many.

"I mean, it's the power of nature," he continues. "Makes you think all the nature worshippers and animal lovers have it right sometimes."

"Not really," Alexa says with disdain.

I think of the things searching for us in the jungle and the malice needed to sic them on us.

"If you could be any animal in the world what would you be, Nate?" Alexa asks, mockingly.

Something that hides, I think. Something that scavenges, crawls around on its belly. A crab. I don't say it aloud.

As much as I can't stand him, I need David to stay with us and keep our number nine so I encourage him with an inquisitive nod.

"I guess a fox," he says. "Maybe a wolf or something."

Half of Alexa's face is lit by the stars. I can see the green plankton glow reflected in her brown eyes. I follow the taut line of muscle and cords from her neck to where it disappears under her t-shirt. Her smooth skin is perfectly tan.

ACROSS THE DARIEN GAP

David is still talking, but I'm not listening. Alexa yawns and stretches. Her shirt rides up revealing the coffee colored skin of her flat stomach. She wades back to shore. In a few minutes I will follow.

———————

A humid wind blows through the thatched roof of the tiny cabin. The murmur of lapping waves serenades us.

Alexa is staring out the open window. Johnnie chose a great vantage point of the beach for his cabins—a little rise nestled at the edge of the jungle. I gently press my hand in the small of her back to move her away.

She arches reflexively. I take a deep breath, stifling my desire. I haven't double-checked all the wards yet.

"You gonna stay?" she whispers.

"I gotta check on everyone."

"You're always checking on everyone. Stay with me, just this once."

"I'll be back. I promise."

"Hurry."

I check the wards I set around the four cabins. Muffled cries and groans from Alejandro and Rita's cabin join the night sounds. In the dark of the night, when we are alone in each other's arms, Alexa talks about the life we are going to have in Columbia. A villa. A ranch. Lazy days in the sun. It helps me believe that I'm special, that *this* is special and going to last, though I know it won't. It can't.

I imagine her cool, slender hands moving over my arms, to my shoulders. I check the last ward and hurry back to her cabin. I quietly slip through the door.

The room glows orange from the smoldering end of a mosquito coil. Alexa's in a long tank top, staring out the window again. Geckos skitter on the walls, feasting on tiny spiders and nocturnal ants.

"Hi," I whisper.

"Hi," she whispers back. The back of her tank is wet from her hair. "Shower was nice, but cold," she says.

"Sorry I missed it."

She's quiet. Been waiting up for me.

"What are you thinking of?" I ask. I expect her to turn, say something soft and breathy with passion in her eyes, kiss me as if breath depended on it, and slip out of her clothes.

"The Indian at the bar," she says. "He made me sad. He was so out of it. The others were calling him El-Capi-tan."

She never ceases to surprise me. "What does that mean?" I ask.

"I don't know. But they laughed it up."

"Maybe they're the fools, you ever think?"

"Of course they are," she says quickly, "but he was probably just running away—drinking down his sorrows."

Like me. I'd love to run away with her. Live the life I never had.

"Maybe he was laughing at us," I say. "Maybe he just came out of the jungle to have some guaro, spin to the beat, and look at pretty gringas like you."

She thinks about it for a second. "No, he was just lost and they were just being mean." She looks away. "Everyone wants to make a side trip out to the island," she says, her sadness apparently purged by voicing it.

"You know we have to keep heading south."

"You always stick to the plan?"

"Always," I say. "But for you, anything."

"Are there really no mosquitoes on the island?" she asks.

"Really," I say. "Only a lot of crabs and monkeys."

"You wouldn't lie to me," she says playfully.

"Never," I say. But I would. I have a hundred times already. To keep her safe. To keep my distance.

ACROSS THE DARIEN GAP

"Let's go," she says, her voice dipping low with an excited tremble that drives me crazy. "Just us. It'll be so good."

"Not now," I say. Too dangerous. Gotta stay with the wards.

She frowns. Did I snap at her?

"Tomorrow, silly," she says with a slight laugh, but she meant now. I can tell. I laugh with her, relieved I haven't shaken her good mood. But when this is all over and the sun and good food and gentle wind are gone, she'll tire of me, realize my nervousness doesn't come from watching this stupid group. I'll bark at her one time too many and she'll be gone, too.

"Listen," I say. "I'm going to hit the bathroom then I'll ask Johnnie if I can use his boat."

She smiles.

I go to the bathroom and splash cold water on my face. All at once, the six geckos that had been leisurely hunting insects scuttle frantically through the cracks in the walls. Above, the roof rustles with movement.

Alexa screams.

Up. I didn't ward from above. I burst through the door.

Snakes and frogs are raining down on her from a tear in the ceiling. I dive, but don't reach her in time. She is bitten. Again and again.

I yell a word of banishment but the thing inside the snakes is strong and only half of them disperse. As the frogs hop away, disappearing through the window and under the bed, the snakes rear in an unnatural unified motion. I take a step back and they strike her neck as one. She gasps. Gurgles. Flaps her arms. Red frogs hop on her face and roll on her lips, spreading their poison.

Outside, a jaguar cries, a screech like glass breaking. The snakes freeze, drop to their bellies, and slither away with the fleeing frogs.

I brush a straggling frog off her, drop down, and rub poison from her lips. She's stopped breathing and her eyes are rolled back. Her neck is swelling.

THE NIGHT MARCHERS   Daniel Braum

I scramble to my bag, hunting for the stuff Tomas gave me.

Alone, these are inert, he said. *Combine them. Combine them again and you may be able to command her back.*

Bring her back? I asked.

From the void. Catch her if she's falling. But only once. I told you this is dangerous work, if you're not up for it...

I'm up for it, I said.

Should it come to this, get ready to run. My enemies and every demon they have sent will see it like fireworks in the night. Then they'll come for you.

I combine the green and brown herbs and force the earthy reeking stuff down her throat, caressing her swollen neck.

I speak the words Tomas told me.

Alexa's eyes open and bulge. Her chest rises with a sputtering breath. Her back arches, violently. She gags, spraying poison and herbs.

She sucks in air, face taut, neck muscles flexed. A look of fear plastered on her face. Did I snatch her back in time?

She struggles to breathe. Her chest falls and with a hiss she succumbs to the poison. Again.

It's not fair.

She lays in a slick of frog guts and blood, her neck puffed and blue. Her life squelched before it could blossom. She had real compassion. And with the power they say she would have had, what a waste.

I feel a scream welling in my gut. There's nothing in my bag that can save her now.

It's over. She's gone. I grab my pack and run.

I hand Juan a fistful of cash and tell him to take the others north.

"Where?" he says.

"Anywhere, away from here," I say. "Alexa and I are going to the islands."

"The islands," he says to himself, scratching his chin suspiciously. He knew the plan. He knew we'd never go. He's wondering what went wrong.

"This is what I hired you for. Go."

He pockets the money.

I dash back to the video bar. Johnnie waits with Alexa's body where I left it, in the garbage pit behind the kitchen.

He sprays a half can of lighter fluid and dumps the jug of kitchen grease on her. He pauses with the matches.

"She not gonna like this," he says. "We're gonna make one angry ghost."

He's right. But it's my only choice.

Don't let them get her body, Tomas said. *Burn her. Smash her bones.*

Her spirit? I asked.

She will go where she can not be reached.

I stuff the rest of my cash in Johnnie's front pocket and remind him of a dozen things I have on him from over the years.

He throws the match and she goes up in flames with the trash.

I want to wait around to see that he does it right, but what I've done has lit me up like a beacon in the night. So much for simple and safe.

I've got to run. Find somewhere to hide. Find some help. My best chance is Chandra about twenty clicks down the coast. She used to conjure luck charms and shark wards for the rich surfers on the circuit.

The kitchen grease sputters. Johnnie counts his money.

"Vaya con dios," he says.

I wish I knew the way.

THE NIGHT MARCHERS

The aroma of strong coffee and fresh banana bread makes my stomach buckle with hunger. I stumble up the steps of Chandra's wooden hut. The surfers eating breakfast on the deck hush and turn as I push past to the screen door.

Chandra almost drops the tray of scrambled eggs and juice as she runs into me. The lines around her eyes and lips have deepened since the last time I saw her. Her red hair is in two long ponytails tied with ripped blue bandanas.

"Nate! I never thought I'd see you here again. You're a wreck."

I steady myself between two rickety tables, pulling off the batik tablecloth. Sugar and habanero sauce clatters to the ground. Chandra grabs me under the shoulders. Though past fifty, she is still lean and strong. A Costa Rican man in an apron rushes from the door behind us.

"It's okay, Manuel," Chandra tells him. "Go outside, check on the tables." She leads me into the kitchen, through a door into the back room. Batik tapestries line the walls. Bronze and wood statues, bottles of oil, and crystals crowd the top of the wooden dresser. Lingering odors of frankincense and sandalwood mix with the smell of eggs from the kitchen.

"I'm sorry, Chandi," I say. "I did wrong by coming here. Something bad is on my tail."

"Sit down," she says. I collapse onto the small bed. I see the concern spread over her face. Can't tell if it's for me or for the trouble I'm bringing.

She regards me with her piercing blue eyes. Her left, almost violet one, stares off into space.

"You've been working way over your head," she says. "You're lucky there's anything left of you."

"I need your help," is all I manage to say.

She disappears through the curtain door and returns with a glass of juice. "Take this and sleep. We'll shake what's tailing you when you wake."

"Please don't let me sleep for long."

I wake and Chandra is sitting on the edge of the bed. Shadows from tall pillar candles dance on the thatched ceiling.

I picture it bursting into a rain of snakes.

"I gotta get to the Darien," I say.

"Easy, easy," she says. "You look better. Strong enough for this."

She takes a bit of salve from a mortar and pestle on the bedside table and dabs it on my lips. She then rubs some on her eyelids and the center of her forehead.

Her strong hands close around mine. She hums and murmurs in her rich voice. The candle flames dim.

Her hum trails off and her face contorts like she swallowed a bad shot of guaro.

"Oh, Nate," she says with disgust. "That poor girl. It's so horrible."

I picture Johnnie sifting the ashes and smashing her teeth like I instructed.

The candles flare. "I know what you need to do," she says. "You're not going to like it."

Chandra releases my hands.

"She hasn't crossed over."

It's like I feared.

"The things in the jungle will come for her, and you until she does."

"Why won't she go?" I ask.

"She's too mad. You failed her. Pretended she mattered. Then threw her in the trash. Like you would have one way or another. Her anger is all she has left."

"I've got to get her to cross."

"It's not going to be easy." She calls for Manuel. He's through the curtain fast. "Go into the jungle and find me a snake," Chandra says. "A small poison one. In the morning, go into town and pick out the bravest boy, for real, not just the loudest, and see if he is willing to earn good money to go with my friend to Panama."

The road ended miles back, and this is the end of the packed earth that continued in its place. Twisted mangrove roots dip into the murky salt water and stagnant mud. Across these waters is the other side of Panama, and South America beyond.

Alexa's phantom, pale and white—a frozen image of her at death—hovers where the dirt meets the water, inches above the sanctuary I failed to bring her in life. Just like Chandra said. I can feel her rage, tangible like a coming rain, certain as a disturbed hive of bees about to swarm.

She's angry with me. Angry I lied to her. Angry I let her die, and then ripped her back once she did.

"I have a boat waiting at the docks," I say. "We can go for our boat ride now."

Alexa doesn't budge. A long shot, but I paid the fisherman anyway.

"Who you talking to?" the kid asks.

"Nobody. Don't worry." I give the boy the bag with the rest of the stuff from Old Tomas. "You remember how?"

He nods his head, yes.

I take out the small canvas bag holding the snake.

ACROSS THE DARIEN GAP

The blue stain on Alexa's neck darkens.

"You want to see me suffer," I say.

I can tell she's listening.

"You want to hurt me."

Alexa's ghost vibrates with an unsettling intensity.

I nod to the boy. I hope he stays brave. I take off my left boot and sock. I wriggle my big toe in the mud.

I open the bag and grab the young snake behind the neck. I force its jaw open. A drop of venom drips from its small fangs. I stab the curved tooth into my toe.

Pain shoots through my foot and radiates up my leg. My mouth goes dry, my head throbbing with each racing heartbeat. Everything goes black, and then I see the boy as a blurry ghost. Alexa is vivid and clear. Her face locked in the ghastly expression from when I ripped her back.

The poison has me. I don't have much time so I move to her.

Alexa lifts her hand, slowly bringing it toward my face. I think of her ashes in the jungle mud behind Johnnie's. I can still see the beauty that once was. She'll never grow to be a woman like Chandra.

"I'm sorry," I say. I open my arms to embrace her.

She clenches her fist and swings, connecting with my jaw. The blow is solid. I've traveled far.

She hits me again. Right. A left. She swings her arms wildly overhead. I hear her saying, "stay with me" over and over, but her blue lips don't move. She always wanted me to stay. To share one restful uninterrupted night. I never did.

With each blow her body is less substantial. She drifts back, reaching for my hand.

"Come," she says. Her eyes, dark in life, are black as the void.

I should go with her. It's only right. I squeeze but my fingers pass through hers. She fades until the faint blur of her gossamer outline melds with the darkness.

A throb in my foot jars me. I open my eyes, gag, and spit out the rancid tasting herbs.

The world snaps into focus. Her phantom is gone. Safe. Beyond anyone's reach now.

The kid did well. He's nowhere to be found. Maybe if I hurry I'll catch up with him on the road.

I picture one of the reptilian demons clawing its way through the jungle.

They have seen. They have felt me return. But with their quarry gone there is nothing left for them, except vengeance on me.

I try to stand, but I'm too woozy.

I never made it across the gap. Part me of me wanted to believe in Alexa's dreams for us on the other side. I'd like to think we are together, lounging forever at some lazy villa, in the endless moment of her last pleasant thought before dissipating into the void.

A howl sounds in the jungle.

Maybe a jaguar will watch over me. Or the little guy from the bar.

"El-Capi-tan," I call for him. I cough out brown leaves, struggle to my feet, and run.

SPARK

I'm not like the Red River guy. Not at all. He was a sicko firebug and a murderer, and they did right for sending him on a one-way trip to spark city.

My hands shake as I turn the gas can over. I can't wait for the sweet stuff to pour. I run outside, trailing fluid all the way, strike the match, and boom! The night blossoms into glorious orange and red.

"Where are you?" I call into the dancing flames.

A slender leg emerges from the tongues of fire. I follow the strands of red hair up from her ankles to where two glowing eyes shine in the flames that form her face.

Fire Girl turns, her burning form disappearing into the flames and emerging again. Her mouth moves, but I hear only whispers and the crackle-pop of searing wood. I reach for her, singeing the hair on my hand and arm.

"This won't do," she says. "Give me a bigger, hotter flame."

I extend my arms, presenting her with the burning farmhouse.

"What about all this? Please stay. Talk to me..."

"It's not enough," she says.

"Why?"

THE NIGHT MARCHERS   Daniel Braum

I want to listen, to stay and beg her to reveal her secrets, but I think I hear the distant whine of sirens. I have to be free to be able to give her what she wants.

Speeding away in the car, I see her dancing after-image in every red light.

A bigger flame. That's what she wants, that's what she'll get. I slide my hand between my legs and picture her spinning in the fire.

My phone rings. The car swerves while I fumble for it. It's Nadja. I bite my lip, loosen my tie, and take three long breaths to get it together.

"Hi, honey. I'm on my way home. How are you?"

"You sound out of breath," Nadja says.

"Just frustrated from the traffic."

"I was hoping you'd be home by now. Long day of presentations. I hate the art director on this campaign..."

The tailpipe of the car in front of me drags, throwing sparks onto the road. I bite my lip. Harder this time.

"Burn," Fire Girl's voice says along with the sound of metal clanging on pavement.

"...and we're out of milk for the coffee. Can you pick some up?"

"Sure thing," I say and hang up half way through her rote "love you".

Michelle's name and number flashes on the screen.

"Where are you?" Michelle demands in her rich alto voice with that trace of a southern sizzle that drives me nuts. "I need you to meet me. Now."

I gotta get home. The wife is gonna kill me, is what I should say.

"I'm heading down Ninety-Five. Where? The Riviera?"

"No. My place. John is in Connecticut till tomorrow. You can stay all night."

"Gimme a half hour."

SPARK

I imagine huge pillars of flame streaming into the sky. My next burn will be bigger. Higher. Hotter. I'll stay longer and be able to hear Fire Girl's voice loud and clear.

I picture firemen pulling blackened crisps of bodies from charred wreckage. I'm not a killer. How was I supposed to know kids would be partying in an abandoned sawmill? I'm a good guy. I know I can pull the big one off without anyone else getting hurt.

The morning sun hurts my eyes. When I rolled into bed late last night, Nadja didn't stir. The family portrait of Allie, Nadja, and me greets me accusingly as I enter the office, like it always does. The happy-go-lucky smiles of me with Jonas from the golf outing seem obscene next to it, but I can't bring myself to move either of them.

"Good morning, Mr. Raycivik," my assistant says. He places a Fed Ex (from Refron I hope) and my coffee on my desk.

I tear into the box. It's full of keys and pass codes to Refron's refining facility in Jersey. My number-one-facilities-manager-man, Ken Lauman, came through for me. Good thing a little greasing of the palms still goes somewhere nowadays.

Someone knocks on the door.

"Not now, busy," I chime with a healthy tinge of stay-the-hell-out-of-here. If it was Jonas, he'd order me into his office from the intercom instead of getting off his fat ass.

The door opens and Michelle slides in, all done up in that red business suit I love.

The intercom buzzes. "Sorry, she got past me," my assistant says fearfully.

"I needed to phone her before my nine-thirty anyway," I say in my best "no problem" tone, then slam the receiver.

"What, are you crazy?" I say to Michelle. But I'm thrilled and she knows it.

"Thought you'd get a little rise out of seeing me here," she says, locking the door. "I didn't get enough last night. You stole away so fast."

"Michelle, this is nuts. Everyone here knows Nadja."

She grabs my hand and licks my fingers. "A little sugar with that coffee?"

"I can't. Not here."

She grabs my tie and musses my hair.

"Tonight," I say. "I promise."

She stands on the desk, removes a stainless steel Zippo from her jacket pocket, and holds it under the sprinkler.

"How about a little alarm to empty out the building, then you and I get lost for a while in the shuffle," she giggles.

"Go ahead," I say as seriously as I can. I'm dying for her to spark it. I can almost hear the hiss of *her* whisper. I straighten my tie and pat down my hair, but I hope she does it.

She sits down on the desk. "You really are a party pooper." She flicks the lighter absently. Glittering, ephemeral, sparks fly off the flint. A beautiful, thin flame bursts into being. For an instant, I glimpse those ruby eyes I yearn for.

"I'm waiting," Fire Girl whispers. "You can do better than an abandoned farm house."

I'm on Michelle like a blaze that can't resist dry wood. I know I should stop, but I'm hiking down her skirt, whipping off my belt, grabbing her shoulders. I push her down on the desk. She slides a leg up and around me, then exhales a familiar sigh of pleasure. I know our kindling moves well. The rest is different every time. Like a good flame.

I close my eyes and see an inferno jetting into the sky.

SPARK

Pressing against her, my eyes meet the framed photos on my desk. I'll create the biggest blaze ever. I just have to work it so no one gets hurt.

———————

Trying to leave the office early, I tell Jonas I have to jet off to another dinner meeting to butter up the Refron boys. Just my luck—in the lobby I bump into some suit from accounting whose name I can never remember.

"Hey Raycivick," he says. "I read they fried that bastard. I just want to say sorry, again, about your daughter," he says. "You must feel some relief now."

"Thanks," I say.

"How's your wife?"

I'm not going to tell this bozo that Nadja doesn't touch me anymore. Does he really want to hear how all our heat is gone? That she acts as if any closeness will lead to passion, which will lead to the act of creation, which the world has proven always ends in bright flames that will burn out into ash and be gone, like Allie, leaving only emptiness and pain. What the hell is he going to say to that?

"Nadja's fine. Listen, ah, Fred, right? I got a dinner in fifteen, so I gotta run."

I immediately head upstate, though I'm supposed to meet Michelle, Ms. Insatiable, at six at the Riviera and then be back home for dinner with Nadja at seven-thirty. No way any of it is going to happen. Not tonight. I have to see *her*. Just a small one to tide me over before the big burn.

The highway gives way to the back roads, and I pull into a little shit of a gas station, the kind without a security camera. I pay the kid a twenty and fill the three gas cans in my trunk.

THE NIGHT MARCHERS   Daniel Braum

After a half hour the car lights thin out and I turn onto State Road Seventy-Eight. Gravel flies as I zip around the turns.

Finally, I reach the abandoned milk facility. I discovered it while antiquing with Nadja on one of our futile attempts to take our minds off Allie. And I've been saving it for an emergency like this.

The sun is low in the sky, but I can't wait till dark. I skid around to the back of the factory and run the car into the old loading dock. I pop the trunk and haul the gas cans inside. Pouring gas all over, I stumble and gasp for breath. I'm too excited—moving too fast. I slow myself and look at my watch. One breath per second.

"Anybody here?" I ask.

Two-one-thousand.

Three-one-thousand.

"Good."

I fumble for the matches and drop two before the blessed sulfur smoke wafts to my nose.

"This won't do," Fire Girl whispers from the tiny flame. "Give me heat that will melt glass. You know where…"

"Last chance. Anyone?" I call.

Outside, a familiar engine whines and turns over.

Shit.

I snuff the match and glimpse Michelle's little red Mazda pulling a U-turn out of the lot.

What the hell is she doing here?

I stand with the withered match in my hand, the sweet reek of gas everywhere. I'm so close. I can almost see her. But I've been sloppy and didn't realize Michelle had followed me. I should have called and made up some excuse.

I rush outside calling her name. Her tires spin on the gravel and she peels out onto the road.

SPARK

I bolt to my car, gun it in reverse, then slam on the brakes. I jump out and try to erase my tire tracks with my hands. Michelle drives like the wind. I have to come back for this mess if I'm gonna catch her. I hit the road leaving my tracks and un-sparked flame behind.

I push the car close to a hundred miles per hour, yet I can barely keep her taillights in my sights.

I need to hear *her* voice. Even for just a second.

I push the cigarette lighter in and fumble for some gas receipts. I touch the flimsy paper to the glowing hot coil.

"Who is she?" Fire Girl whispers. "I thought you want only me?"

Her voice fades as the paper crumples into ash. I light another one.

"Does she understand the need to burn?"

"I guess she doesn't," I say.

"Then you know what to do with her."

I fumble for more paper receipts, but all of them, and Michelle's taillights, are gone.

———

Nadja turns the gas on the stove down. The water boils over and drowns out Fire Girl's whispers.

"Damn it, Bill. Just stand there and stare, why don't you?" Nadja says.

Breakfast used to be a joyous madcap rush to get Allie to school, Nadja to the office, and me to my first appointment. One match from a sicko firebug changed all that forever. In his request for clemency, he said he thought he was just setting fire to the Red River bus yard and didn't know that a child would be sleeping, overlooked, in the back of her school bus. Neither of us have sat at the table since.

I pour the water into the sink and fish around for the boiled egg.

111

THE NIGHT MARCHERS Daniel Braum

"Screw it," Nadja says. "I'll grab something on the way." She storms out of the kitchen. "And there's still no goddamned milk around here."

I stare for a while at the empty place where Allie used to sit. Then I turn to the stove burner. I want to light a little one in the sink, but I have to find Michelle. How much did she see? Where did she go? Her car wasn't at home last night when I drove by. I'm late for my first appointment, but I don't give a damn.

The doorbell rings. Nadja probably forgot her keys.

I peer through the window to find a uniformed cop at the door. I feel the sweat drip under my shirt. Very bad timing. My trunk is full of charges and igniters for the big burn. How much does he know? Probably enough. He's here.

"Come in," I say in my calmest no-pressure voice. I can sell this guy. He's a good overworked civil servant buying peace of mind.

"Mr. Raycivik," he says, looking at a clipboard. "I was expecting the Missus. Sorry to hear about…"

Everybody knew the Red River case. It changed everything. Day after they put the monster down, I woke up a new man.

I watched the closed circuit screen showing them strap him into the chair. I hoped the bastard was thinking of me—that my pain was the last thing through his mind before he fried.

The lights flickered and sparks flew from the connections on his temples and wrists. For a second, I just knew he was thinking of me, that he heard me damning him to hell. Besides, Fire Girl was there. She told me so. That night I went to the saw mill outside of town with some newspaper and a lighter and—

"You okay? I hate to catch you at a busy moment," the cop says.

SPARK

Probably just lulling me into making a mistake. I wipe the sweat from my forehead and wish my tie wasn't so tight. I may have to take him down. Bring him out back. Get the gas can and…

"It's that time again. The annual Police Benevolent Association fund drive. Last year we counted you for…"

I picture the withered match falling to the gasoline-soaked floor at the old milk house. Our tire tracks, my footprints, and god knows whatever else is still there. I have to hurry and light the big burn. First I have to find Michelle.

I drive by her house twice, check the Riviera and Le Gran Paradise. I even swing by her gym and favorite day spa. At five to four, I hit gold and catch her right where she is supposed to be, walking out of the shiny green glass doors of her office building in White Plains, an hour before quitting time.

"Bill. What are you doing here?"

"Thought you'd get a rise out of seeing me," I say.

She walks faster, her heels clicking on the pavement.

I move next to her, match her stride. I throw my arm around her waist.

"My car. I'll drive," I say.

"Uh, Bill, I gotta go. John's waiting for me."

"Come on. It's been two days. I owe you."

I open the door, holding her with the other. Her legs fold like matchsticks and she collapses into the front seat.

I hurry around the car, slide behind the wheel, and start the engine.

"What'd you see? Who'd you tell? The cops? My wife?"

"Bill, I don't know what you're thinking. I didn't see anything. I didn't talk to anyone."

She's looking to buy a dose of things are okie-dokie, normal as can be, so I give it to her.

"I just *needed* to see you," I say.

She relaxes a bit, but all the heat between us is gone. I speed up.

"Where we going? The Riviera's off Ninety-Five."

"Somewhere else."

I hit the Taconic so I can do ninety and avoid the traffic and speed traps.

I turn off after a few exits and pull into a place called Jerry and Ginny's Cabins and Campsites. I'd been there with Nadja and Allie once. Six cabins. All a nice walk and out of earshot from each other.

"Bill, we gotta make this fast. John's expecting me."

"Since when did you give a damn?"

"Calm down. You don't look so good."

I try to pull it together. I don't want to hurt her, but I don't see another way. I have to pull off the big burn and nothing can come in the way.

I open the trunk, push around the wires and charges and grab a bag of coal, butane, and some two-by-fours. I toss them into the barbeque pit.

"Bill, what the hell are you doing?" Michelle says.

I ignore her, flip open the can of butane, and catch the sweet smell. I squeeze the can, coaxing all the fluid from it, and flick the match. The crisp wood takes with a satisfying hiss. The paper and leaves crackle and fold into themselves, disappearing into the hungry line of glowing orange.

I look through the wafting black smoke for *her*.

"Where are you? What do I do?" I ask.

"You're more messed up than I thought," Michelle says. She kicks off her heels and bolts into the woods.

SPARK

The flames sputter and gain a hold on the wood. I can faintly make out *her* flickering face.

I could catch up in seconds. Wrap my hands around her neck, then let the flames eat the evidence. But the big blaze has to be lit. Nothing can jeopardize it.

"Let her go," Fire Girl whispers.

"But she'll tell someone. The cops."

"Go. You are so close. Nothing matters now but the flames."

She's right. I have the keys and pass cards. No one can stop me.

I leave Michelle in the woods and head for the Refron plant in Jersey.

I set the last charge onto the side of the giant fuel tank with a thunk and fix it in place with a ragged strip of duct tape. With tens of thousands of tons of compressed gas and all the raw sweet crude around here, things are going to get real hot. I'm going to see her clear as day. Hear her voice loud and strong. Maybe be able to touch her.

I clomp down the steel stairs and hurry to the next massive storage tank.

Wheels rumble on the metal flooring. A scruffy janitor pushing his cart waves to me. I hold up one of the pass cards and spit out an improvised line. "Inspection deadline."

He smiles feebly, his mouth full of broken and yellowed teeth. "At least I'm not the only one working late," he says.

"Anyone else here?" I ask.

"You mean Burt? He covers zone two and the front. He's always late."

I picture the fireman pulling bodies from charred wreckage. Does it matter if a couple of janitors get fried? The thruway is only a hundred yards or so away, the cars will be safe enough if this whole place blows. Won't they?

I should just go home. Take a cold shower. Think it over. Make sure. I *have* to hear her. Will *she* wait?

I dial Nadja. She'll know what to do.

"Bill?" she asks, then whispers. "It's him. It's him."

Voices murmur in the background.

"Where are you?" she asks.

"I'm okay, honey. I just don't want anyone to get hurt. I'm not like that monster. I'm different. I'm so close now. I can almost hear her."

"Who? What? Never mind. Just come home, honey. Everything's going to be fine. I can get you help."

"I'm sorry I haven't been home for dinner lately. For everything, really. I just have to do this, then everything's going to be okay."

"Bill whatever you are thinking, don't do it. Just come home, everything will be fine."

She's right. Everything will be fine. Crisping a couple of shit sweepers doesn't count.

"Remember, I didn't want to hurt anybody."

"Bill, I love—"

I hang up the phone, hit the timer, and run.

I don't stop until I clear the maze of tanks. I stand in the fueling lot among the jumbo tanker trucks where I have a great view. Any second now.

A plume of red shoots into the sky. A glorious burning pillar reaches for the heavens.

Flames blossom everywhere. Tanks explode. A chain of deafening bangs and booms moves closer.

Heat washes over me and I choke my last breath as the inferno robs the air of oxygen. A roaring wall of fire rushes to the fuel yard. Yellow. Orange. Then nothing but red.

SPARK

———

"Tell me. Tell me," I beg. The pain is gone but I burn, just a thin finger of flame in the inferno.

Fire Girl laughs. She isn't slinky and slender anymore. She looks sort of like my little Allie.

"What do you want to hear?" she asks. "Should I call you Daddy and say I want you to burn like I did?"

I feel myself flickering out. Any second now there will be only black.

I fight for focus. "You're not my daughter, and I'm not like the Red River guy," I say.

"No. You're as different as can be. Right before the current fried his brain and I asked him where the spark would jump, he thought of you, right away. No fighting at all."

I just want to burn. To merge into the red. To fold into the yellow and orange. "I'm a good guy," I manage to say. "I don't want to hurt anyone."

"You're almost spent now. One more thing left for you to do before you go. Show me where the spark will jump next."

"You're not Allie. Why don't you dance, like before? Tell me why? Why did all of this happen?"

She cups her breasts, flicks her tongue, and bursts into the slender silhouette of flame I knew.

"She was such pretty fuel," she says.

I've been sloppy. Bought what Fire Girl was selling. There is no why. Fire simply burns because it can. Because it must. I picture Nadja buttoning up her white blouse for the family portrait. The day I beat Jonas at golf. Michelle when she was just an admiring colleague. I try to banish them from my mind, hoping the spark will end with me.

Fire Girl smiles, her ruby eyes glittering and kinetic.

"It never ends," she says. "They'll always be fuel to feed me."

I see Michelle running out of the woods. She's at a gas station. The attendant is calling the cops. He rips open a pack of smokes for her from behind the counter. She lights a cigarette. Fire Girl is there in the flame.

I feel myself slipping. Losing focus. Losing fuel. The black cinder at the end of it all is close now.

THE
GHOST DANCE

A crow bobbed its head, fluttered its wings, and took flight from its perch on the roof of the nightclub. A patchwork of hand-made band posters covered the wide glass window. The crow squawked and flew over a circle of hundreds of dancers crowding the sidewalk and street.

The briefing said there would be crows, Erin thought. The bird's presence made this different, more real. Erin scanned the crowd: mostly teenagers, not just from the Rez. The last rays of the late summer setting sun cast a red glow on the closed stores of the strip mall and the circle of dancers crowding its streets. No sign of the suspect. No lucky break today.

The dancers' feet lifted and dropped in unison, then in syncopation with the pounding bass and low grumble of guitars audible outside the small club. It smelled wrong.

No pot. No beer. Not a single one smoking a cigarette.

Her partner, John Avenco, got out of their unmarked Ford Taurus. Together they walked toward the circle of dancers and the nightclub.

THE NIGHT MARCHERS   Daniel Braum

"You believe it's really him?" Avenco asked.

Erin shrugged. She didn't know what to believe. Two days ago, agents from Squadron Thirty Seven had apprehended the girl called Sitting Bull, along with a beat-up van full of guitars and amps. All the recent chatter indicated something big was going down— tonight. Something big enough for the director to have almost every agent scouring the Reservations and every rock and roll club in the country for the suspect, Crazy Horse.

Avenco looked around, amazed. "I never even heard of this dance thing till that first clash with the National Guard in Houston."

Erin pictured the image she saw on the news: a giant circle of dancers, much like this one, surrounded by lines of Guardsmen in riot gear.

"I know my history, but come on."

Erin held her tongue. The Ghost Dance, the desperate pro- test movement of the Native Americans, had been outlawed over a hundred years ago. Since the fated massacre at Wounded Knee, it was rarely seen outside ceremonial gatherings. Its resurgence along with the rebellious and unified talk of the tribes spooked her. She couldn't expect Avenco to know all this, but now, after the briefing, he had no excuse.

"I mean, what the hell?" Avenco continued. "Even my sister's kid in New Jersey is doing it."

The government today wouldn't condone shooting into circles of mixed-up suburban kids, would they? Erin hoped she wouldn't be expected to.

"That's rock and roll for you," she said, not wishing to voice her concerns to Avenco. "You were a kid once."

"Yeah, of course," Avenco said.

"Let's just clear the place, confirm he isn't here, and be on to the next one," she said.

THE GHOST DANCE

"Yeah, I heard the briefing. But rock and roll, Wounded Knee, and reservation teenagers pretending they are dead Indian heroes. It doesn't make sense."

Erin agreed. At Wounded Knee, hundreds were slaughtered by American soldiers when they refused to stop dancing the Ghost Dance. The dance itself would not bring back the buffalo and herald the downfall of the invaders, like they claimed, neither then nor now. So why the Bureau-wide alert? Why all the fear?

"Rysing Trybe," Avenco said, shaking his head disdainfully.

Crazy Horse's band. Erin looked at a sun-faded poster: a silhouette of a mohawked figure, guitar slung around his back, stood in front of a rough, sketchy buffalo.

Rysing Trybe. Tonight. First set 9 pm. We shall live again.

The y's in Rysing and Trybe connected.

Problem was, intelligence reported over a hundred bands called Rysing Trybe booked all over the country. The big rock clubs in New York and L.A., county fairs, and lots of smaller clubs like this one, in sleepy downtown Phoenix. Even with the help of the local sheriffs, cops, and highway patrol, the Bureau couldn't cover them all. This was probably a dead end, Erin thought. Most of the manpower and resources were focused near the big gatherings. The news had reported that fifty thousand were expected in the Black Hills. Twice that in San Francisco and New York. The director had said these estimates were low.

They reached the edge of the circle of dancers. A big man all in black stepped out of the door and stood, arms crossed, watching them. The dancers' feet moved up and down in unison like a huge single-minded animal.

"Glad this is all supposed to be peaceful," Avenco said. Erin watched the blank expressions of the dancers as they circled past.

She knew the Ghost Dance was non-violent, but she sensed a fury, beyond the years, in the young faces.

"I'm heading 'round back," Avenco said, his voice echoing in her ear, as he disappeared 'round the corner of the club.

"I copy," she said into the tiny microphone attached to her small black earpiece.

"Too bad we couldn't just bag this guy at home." Avenco always chattered when he was nervous.

"Too bad," Erin agreed, and she meant it. There was surprisingly little intel on Crazy Horse. Besides the CD they weren't sure of anything.

The music inside the club stopped. The dancers in the street continued to circle, eyes distant, as if moving to a rhythm from an unseen drum.

"We shall live again," a girl near her called out. The rest answered with a low murmuring moan. The crow cawed from somewhere overhead.

Erin sighed. "All right, I'm going in." She stepped up to the black-clad, muscular native man. A small white stone carving of a buffalo hung around his neck on a simple black cord.

"Next set's in 20 minutes." He looked past her at the circle of dancers. "If you're not dancing you better leave."

Erin squared her shoulders, feeling the comforting weight of the Kevlar vest beneath her suit. She pulled her badge and ID out of her suit pocket. "Federal agent. Step aside," she said.

The bouncer didn't move. She looked up at him, at least a full head taller than her.

"What sort of post-nine-eleven fascist bullshit is this?" he asked, looking at her badge. She pushed her wispy blonde hair out of her eyes. The white streetlight and red neon cast two shadows of his bulky frame, one a red penumbra of the other.

THE GHOST DANCE

"Federal agent, step away from the door," she said louder. She tried for that emotionless "I'm all business this is my job and I'll kill you if I have to" look she'd seen so often on Avenco.

The crowd stomped. The crow cawed. The big guy didn't move. "Crow's got a message. Aren't you listening?" he said.

Her training told her not to listen, but his words had a seductive pull.

"What message is that?" she said. She wanted to say, *step aside or you are under arrest.*

"Dance the ghost dance. Clear your heart. Focus your prayer. Join us to praise the birth of the white buffalo."

For an instant it all made sense; dance, believe in peace, and the return of the buffalo. All she had to do was dance and join the power of her belief to the group.

"You in yet?" Avenco radioed in her ear, snapping her back to the moment.

Erin blinked her eyes and took a second to orient herself. Seeing the bouncer staring at her she moved her jacket aside, revealing her gun. She reached into her pocket and held up the warrant.

"I'm in," she said to Avenco.

"Fuck you," the bouncer said, and stepped aside.

Erin walked into the smell of smoke, sweat, and something earthy and herbal.

The girl collecting cover just inside the door gasped upon seeing her badge. Erin's adrenaline kicked in, her eyes scanned everywhere for danger—for the suspect. She glanced at the girl: Rysing Trybe t-shirt, cigarette behind her ear, spiked belt, roll of cash in her hand. No weapons.

Erin walked through the narrow hallway and entered the club. She stood at the edge of the hardwood dance floor, opposite a raised stage about a hundred yards away. Thin wisps of smoke curled around metal scaffolds and colored lights which hung from the high ceiling. Small lights inset into the old paneled walls by the tables on the left provided the only illumination, besides the small stage lights. Spinning, stomping dancers filled every inch of available space of the dance floor; big, human, concentric circles turning within each other. The sweat, moisture, and that earthy smoke, sage maybe, was much stronger. She coughed as she angled into the crowd.

Someone bumped her—a dancing girl, eyes closed, face stern yet somehow blissful in the shadows from the low light. Erin brought her hand up in front of her face instinctively. She reached for her gun. Easy, she told herself. These are kids.

With the smoothness and grace of a yoga pose, the girl raised her hands above her head, her shirt lifting just enough to reveal the tattoo of a sun surrounding her pierced navel. Hands in the air, she swayed like a reed, all the while maintaining the driving staccato rhythm with her feet. The girl opened her eyes and stared, oblivious to the gun.

"You don't stand a chance against my prayers," she said. Her body didn't break its hypnotic motion.

"Step away," Erin said.

"You don't stand a chance against my love," the girl responded in a breathy voice.

Erin edged past her as the girl danced in place, hands twirling patterns in the air. Erin craned to see over the crowd. Across the club, on the stage, a lanky teen with no shirt adjusted the rack of toms on a shiny red, silver, and chrome drum kit. He looked up and wiped a sweaty lock of long thin hair out of his eyes with his tattooed forearm as she approached. Recognition flashed in his eyes—the look of a deer before bolting.

"Curly! Cops!" he yelled to someone on the side of the stage.

THE GHOST DANCE

The suspect's childhood name according to the bio. The ancient sepia toned picture of Crazy Horse, a grizzled but regal old man, entered her mind's eye.

Erin turned to intercept the group of people bustling away from the stage. Girl in black jeans, CD in hand. Guy in leather jacket holding a guitar. Guy in vest, white t-shirt. No weapons. No suspect.

They orbited around a short, hefty native teen as they moved toward the sales table. He looked at least three hundred pounds, wore big wide leather pants, a studded spiked belt, and wristlets like an eighties metal star. A single long braid snaked from his close-cropped hair. It was him. She remembered his voice from the CD—deep and guttural, an angry bear growling over heavy, dark cadences.

"Heads up," Erin said to Avenco. "I see him. He might make a run. Notify HQ, I have a positive ID."

"Got it," Avenco said. She pictured him waiting outside the back exit, grim, zen-like expression on his face.

"Federal agent, step away," Erin said, pushing a dancer aside. "You," she said to the suspect, watching his hands, "Slowly now. Hands above your head."

Oblivious dancers circled past, their mutters and mumbles bouncing off the old wood paneling.

"Get in here, Avenco," she said into her microphone.

"Coming," he said. "No response from HQ or Squadron Thirty Seven."

Erin focused on the suspect. She felt like she was trying to arrest a queen bee without alerting the hive.

"Carrying any weapons?"

"No," the suspect murmured.

"Where's your ID?" she asked, patting him down.

"Don't got none," he said slowly. His voice was soft, nothing at all like the disc.

A white guy in a leather blazer, dirty red-blond hair slicked back, the manager probably, pushed through the crowd. "What the fuck is this?" he demanded. His smoke-stained teeth and lines under his eyes stood out after looking at so many kids.

"Federal agent," Erin said. "Show's over. Clear everyone out of here," she said louder, waving the warrant.

"Like hell." He took a step in.

"Step away, now," she yelled. "Unless you want to come with him."

He backed off. The dancers began to chant, as if reacting to a silent or unseen cue. The suspect smiled.

Erin took out her cuffs and snapped them around the suspect's fat wrists. He smelled of leather and sage.

"Tashunka Witko. You are under arrest for conspiracy to overthrow the United States government. You have the right to remain silent, anything you say…"

The manager laughed. "Don't worry, Grandfather, we'll have you out in no time," he said.

Grandfather. Erin noted the term of respect for an elder.

"I'm not worried," the suspect said, as Erin tightened the cuffs. "I'm sad for her. We will break her chains."

"Just don't say anything," the manager said.

"I want to talk. It's all supposed to happen this way."

Avenco pushed through the dancers, badge drawn, alert green eyes scanning the crowd. A stray strand of dirty dreadlocked hair swung at him. Avenco batted it away. Erin recognized that rigid and tight let's-get-out-of-here look on his face.

"All good?" Avenco asked.

Erin nodded. She saw his recognition of her fear in his eyes.

"Let's have some house lights," Avenco said to the manager.

THE GHOST DANCE

The manager spoke into his radio. The house lights snapped on with an electric hum. The suspect looked even less imposing in the harsh light.

"Let's go, Mr. Witko," Erin said and pushed him through the spinning circle of dancers. He moved with no resistance.

"My name is Crazy Horse," he said softly.

Erin steered him toward the door, Avenco covering her. The dancers danced on, their hair and flowing arms looked less mystical in the light, but still disturbing.

They weaved their way to the mouth of the narrow hallway leading to the exit only to find the door girl blocking the way. She smiled emptily, revealing a space between her two front teeth.

"We shall live again," a soft voice said, though the girl's lips didn't move. A thin line of drool hung from the corner of her mouth.

"You OK?" Avenco asked.

"Fine. Hearing things. Let's get him out of here."

She placed her hand on the girl's shoulder to move her. The waify girl felt solid as a tree and didn't budge. The door opened. The big bouncer from outside and a dozen teens from the street poured through, choking the hallway.

"Move," Avenco yelled, his face reddening. Erin tapped her pocket, feeling for her spare clip.

Erin pushed the girl again, but she didn't yield. The line of spit broke and fell.

"This war will not be fought with guns," the suspect's soft voice said from behind her.

On the word "guns," the dancing stopped with a resonant stomp; the final united footfalls echoing despite the crowd. Feet planted, the teens swayed in place, like tall grass rippling in the wind. Whispers and the hum of the lights filled the void left by the absence of pounding feet.

Erin jerked her head, looking for the source of the scratchy whispers. She saw only empty stares and Avenco's cornered animal look.

"Damn," he said, tapping his earpiece. "Try yours, I'm not getting through."

Only white noise. She shook her head.

Crazy Horse looked at her. "You hear the voices. You see me for who I am. You even think of me with the name I earned from my father."

"What the hell is he talking about?" Avenco said. He looked as if he could start shooting any second.

"Stay calm," she said to him. "Squadron Thirty Seven will realize we are out of touch; they'll come."

"You must not cry when your friends die," Crazy Horse said to himself in that steady low voice. A bead of sweat dripped from his nose.

"When your friends die," the dancers answered. Their voices echoed and blended with the murmur of whispers.

Avenco pushed the drooling girl. The big bouncer stepped forward and pushed back, sending Avenco stumbling.

"You must not hurt anybody. You must not fight," Crazy Horse continued calmly.

"Always do right," the dancers answered, "We shall live again."

"Your world is falling. Way is being made for the return of the buffalo," Crazy Horse said. "The victors of war write the history books—this time the true story will be told."

"And what war is that?" Erin asked.

"This tale will be written in the sky with the wind," Erin heard a chorus of voices say, though no one's lips moved.

"I'm going to read him his rights again, if he's gonna talk," Avenco said.

THE GHOST DANCE

"The tribal leaders have united. We will dance, focus our faith, and free the land you have enslaved. The Buffalo will return to the land, a signal of great prosperity for our people."

"Anything you say can or will be used against you in a court of law," Avenco interjected. "You have the right to an attorney. In the event you cannot afford an attorney one will be appointed to you. Do you understand these rights?"

Crazy Horse looked at Avenco as if he was a slow child. "I understand that I live again. I know my name is Crazy Horse, like my father before me. My circle is strong and full of medicine."

The dancers swayed left, then right, as if moved by an unseen breeze.

Avenco drew his gun. "Your circle is under arrest for conspiracy to..."

"Easy!" Erin yelled.

The dancers nearest to Avenco opened their eyes and grabbed him with the speed of snapping turtles striking. Avenco struggled and fired his gun, taking out a light with a pop and a crackle. Erin listened to her instincts and froze, as glass rained down on her and Crazy Horse. The dancers knocked the gun from Avenco and held him by the arms, legs, and around the waist. He convulsed and jerked but did not break free.

"Our father in the sky remembers who are the savages. This war will not be fought with guns and bombs," Crazy Horse said. He then walked over to Avenco gracefully, despite his meaty hands being cuffed behind his back.

They stood face to face, patience to fury.

"I will show you," Crazy Horse said to him. "Even you can join us. It will not be long now."

Crazy Horse leaned forward, touching his forehead to Avenco's chest.

"Terrorist," Avenco spat.

"You don't stand a chance against our prayers," Crazy Horse said.

His voice echoed in whispers. Erin thought she felt a breeze moving the moist smoky air. For an instant she saw a tall blurry shape in the place of the short wide kid before Avenco. The old sepia-toned picture of Chief Crazy Horse flashed in her mind.

Avenco went slack. The dancers let go of him and he slumped to the ground.

"This war will not be fought with guns," Crazy Horse said. Erin noticed something different in his dark eyes. Wisdom, patience, and indignation.

"Give me your gun," he said.

Erin put it down, aware of her second weapon in her shoulder holster.

Crazy Horse looked at her kindly.

"He was not ready to join the dance," Crazy Horse said, nodding at Avenco. "But *you* are."

Crazy Horse stepped up to Erin, close enough that his face almost touched hers. She felt her lungs expand and contract, conscious of the taste of sage and smoke in each breath.

"Join us," he said.

Out of sight, in the distance, a single drum pounded four steady beats, then the rhythm of hundreds of pounding feet joined in as the circles of dancers resumed their dance. Erin heard chanting, clearly, like the whispers but louder and in focus. The harsh house lights overhead dimmed and changed to a soft filtered quality, like the first rays of dawn.

Crazy Horse's face appeared different, older, an amalgam of the fat native teen and the grizzled old man Erin knew from the picture. As he swayed—keeping his eyes directly in front of hers—the young boy seemed in focus, with the image of the old chief trailing behind just long enough to blur.

THE GHOST DANCE

"It's not too late for you," he said, young and old lips moving. "Not everyone is strong enough to believe."

She glanced at Avenco, motionless on the floor.

"But I don't believe," Erin said, noting the echo of her voice was gone. She sounded as if she were outside. The walls looked hazy and insubstantial as if she could walk through them.

The circles of dancers widened, each dancer an arm's width from the next. A blurry human form trailed each dancer, an impossible upright shadow. Erin made out feathers and fringes on their torsos.

A crow cawed from overhead. Erin could only see its shadow pass over her, then the circle. The cawing made sense, she could almost hear words in the patterns and rhythms.

"Caw-caw-caw, caw-caw." Stomp. Stomp, from the dancers. Boom from the drum.

"We shall live, a-gain." Stomp. Stomp, from the dancers. Boom from the drum.

Crazy Horse smiled. "We're almost there. Soon the buffalo will return. Dance with us."

She felt tall grass tickle her.

"I don't want to dance," she said, her voice sounding slurred and delayed in her head, but her body moved to the drum. Something inside her yearned to guide it and insisted that she dance. She lifted her foot and brought it down in between beats.

As her foot touched down, the floor and walls faded. Erin could see a grassy field. She didn't notice when the ceiling disappeared, but now hundreds of dancers moved in a field beneath a sky tinged orange by the rising sun. She moved with the circle, her eyes on fringed shirts with tassels and beads.

An animal smell, heavy and musky, reached her. Shadowy shapes of the teens now trailed the dancing, chanting natives. Now, she understood the words.

THE NIGHT MARCHERS   Daniel Braum

"You must not cry, when your friends die,
You must not fight. Always do right.
They have no chance against this prayer.
They have no chance against this love."

Her feet moved with the beat. She threw her hands up and traced circles in the air in front of her. Crazy Horse smiled and reached out his hand.

"Dance with me," he said.

Though his lips moved, she could not hear him over a deafening static and crackle.

"Say something to me if you're still alive in there," a strange new voice said in her earpiece, then faded to crackling.

"Agent Erin DiNafro?" the voice said, "This is Squadron Thirty Seven. We have the premises surrounded."

She wanted to say, *He's here. I have him in cuffs, I'm close enough to take a shot*, but her heavy lips said, "You don't stand a chance against my prayer."

"Agent? Stay put, we're executing suppressive measures before moving in," the voice said, then the static returned.

Erin's stomach dropped as if she were in an elevator racing down from a skyscraper. Wind blew across her face. The lights flared, then dimmed, blacked out completely, then flashed and dimmed again. A big American flag waving in the wind appeared in her mind, then the clean-shaven, beak-nosed image of the President.

"God Bless America," the President said. "Land of the Free, Home of the Brave."

Erin coughed and spat, tasting the stale, sweaty air of the club. Ceiling, walls, and teenage dancers surrounded her. Dozens of them fell to the ground, their dancer shadows gone. The remaining dancers on their feet held their ears and foreheads. Erin watched a girl thrash as if in a seizure and then fall.

A figure in black fatigues and a thick black flak vest slowly stepped through the door, an agent from Squadron Thirty Seven. A shiny black helmet and reflective visor hid his face. The big bouncer rushed him, then fell to the floor, holding his head as he came within six feet.

Walking slowly, and carefully, the agent walked into the club. Erin saw images of the American flag and the President in the black visor.

"America is the land of the free. The reservations are your homes. You are free to worship the Great Spirit in peace," the image of the President spoke.

Crazy Horse and a small group of dancers backed away from the approaching figure. They formed a tight circle in the center of the club.

More black-clad figures walked slowly through the doorway. Erin watched them enter as if watching a dream. They fanned out forming a circle around the circle of dancers still standing, still guarding Crazy Horse.

Silently and in unison the Squadron Thirty Seven agents took a step closer, closing the circle. The faces of the dancers grimaced in pain. Blood trickled from the nose of a young girl. The Squadron took another step closer. A dancer thrashed wildly, and spun out of the circle. An agent grabbed him and two others ran up to wrestle him away from the formation.

The voice of the President was louder, the message repeated faster and faster. She saw no source for the sound, but knew it originated with the agents. Something they did broke the focus, broke the unity of the dancers. Besides the riot gear, the Squadron's agents wore no equipment she could see that might disrupt them. No stun gun, no tazers. Was the disruption coming from the agents themselves?

THE NIGHT MARCHERS DANIEL BRAUM

Crazy Horse stood defiant in the center of the last six dancers standing.

"The suspect is getting away," a voice echoed in Erin's head. "He has resisted arrest, fled from a felony and a federal crime. Respond appropriately."

Erin knew the suspect was not getting away. Crazy Horse was surrounded. Erin wanted to tell the voice, there is truth to their cause—why are you arresting them? You should be joining them—every dancer counts—everyone who believes counts and brings them closer. But instead, she took her gun out of her shoulder holster.

Though she struggled, she started to lift the gun.

A Squadron Thirty Seven agent moved next to her. She turned and stared into the black visor. She saw her face, but it was wrong—as if she was looking at her academy graduation photo. Then the image of Crazy Horse, like the sepia photo but in full color, filled the visor. Red coppery war paint adorned his skin. His eyes narrowed. Images of Indians killing settlers in an ambush flashed, then an image of Crazy Horse being led away in chains, then an image of thousands of dancers in a huge circle.

"The Ghost Dance has spread from the reservations to our cities, to our youth," another strange new voice in her head said. It sounded like the President. "The suspect is a clear and present danger to the United States of America."

Erin raised her gun and centered Crazy Horse in her sights. The hefty teen looked at her. He stood upright and unflinching, his hands still cuffed behind his back.

I don't want to do this, Erin thought. This man is unarmed, restrained, and surrounded by dozens of agents.

"Do your job," the voice commanded. She felt blood trickling from her nose.

THE GHOST DANCE

"I forgive you, sister," Crazy Horse said. "What you do makes no difference. This time your soldiers are few and we are many."

Erin pulled the trigger and watched the bullet fly as if she were watching a movie. Crazy Horse's body jerked back. He fell onto a dancer and slid to the floor.

I just shot a cuffed suspect, Erin thought.

No, you were only doing your job, the voice answered.

From the corner of her eye she saw dozens more Squadron Thirty Seven agents pacing the club. She realized she was the only non-helmeted figure left standing.

Flashes went off. Who was taking photographs? A black helmeted figure stepped in front of her. "Lieutenant Fetterman, Squadron Thirty Seven," he said. She recognized the voice as the voice in her head.

"I don't believe what is going on here," she screamed. "I can't believe what I just did. You made me do this. How?"

"You served your country well. It is time to rest now." She suddenly felt tired and wanted to sleep. "You're going to be all right."

A dry breeze swept over her. For an instant she saw Old Chief Crazy Horse and a band of dancers in the grassy field. A buffalo lay on its side in the grass. Crazy Horse bent down and picked up a writhing little beast. A newborn. He wiped the blood off it, revealing white hair and skin. A white buffalo. Crazy Horse smiled.

Lieutenant Fetterman grabbed her hand and the image disappeared.

Fetterman led her out of the club. Erin found it hard to walk, hard to keep her eyes open. Dozens of Squadron Thirty Seven agents stood motionless and silent among the fallen teens in the street. Fetterman was careful not to step on any bodies as he led her across the street to a personnel carrier.

Helicopters hovered overhead. On the far side of the street, camouflaged marines dragged bodies to somewhere outside her view.

Fetterman gently pushed her into the waiting arms of a marine inside the personnel carrier. Inside she could hear a little better over the choppers' mechanical whir.

"This her?" the Marine asked.

Fetterman nodded and walked away, toward the club. Erin could barely keep her eyes open. She felt her memory fading, her thoughts confused.

"What happened in there?" the Marine asked.

It is beginning, Crazy Horse said in her head.

"This war will not be fought with guns," Erin mumbled. The crow cried from somewhere overhead. Erin understood its message.

"The buffalo have returned," she said. "We shall live again."

THE GREEN MAN
OF PUNTA CABRE

The weathered cross atop Mount Cabre shakes like a tattered scarecrow, and the can of paint I was going to touch it up with rattles and hops. The soft ground of Juan Haberno's cornfield below ripples like the muscles of a horse trying to throw an unwanted rider. The poor farmer throws his arms out trying not to fall. Another aftershock from the big one last week. I pray for the Lord to spare me, though I know he never hears. If he were to call me home now, then I would know his face. I could beg for forgiveness for ever doubting that he was always looking down on us. I grip the gray peeling wood and steady myself. A wave of buckling earth tears across the field leaving a wake of turned-up rock and dirt. As if Juan hasn't suffered enough. The awful groan and rumble of rock fades, and with a jerk that sends the paint can flying, the quaking stops. White paint oozes from the upturned can and seeps into the soil.

After a moment of deathly quiet and still, the flutter and tentative chirps of birds return to the jungle. Juan looks at the three-foot wide trench newly cut through his field and yells something I can't hear. Even in the face of this, it's probably a joke, as usual, like "How about that one, Padre?"

I pick up the almost-empty paint can and walk down the hill to my little church at the edge of Haberno's farm. Two years ago, when I first arrived, I put up the cross, thinking it would be a beacon of faith, always visible to the village. The way they welcomed me and my work filled me with hope. That was before I learned that to them Jesus is just another name for one of their ancient gods, and every Catholic Saint and holiday has its own Maya counterpart.

When I reach the bottom Haberno waves. "God's plowshare," he says with a laugh. The aftershock just destroyed a chunk of his field, yet he still smiles. Bless him. I'd be thinking of all the work needed to fix it in time for planting.

Ignacio Rivera, the local brujo, darts from the jungle at the edge of the field and joins Haberno at the rocky trench. He surveys the damage with his dark eyes, closely set above his flat, wide Mayan nose. His short, wiry frame bears signs of his old age but also of strength, like a jaguar past its prime yet still capable of the kill. "God don't like the new corn," he says and regards me with a scowl, like he always does.

Punta Cabre's fields once boasted nineteen distinct strains of corn, passed seed to seed, father to son for generations back into the time of the Maya. Two years ago the infiltrating strains arrived. Resistant to heat. Resistant to bugs, but bland and genetically dominant. Soon all the corn will be the same and there's nothing anybody can do. Not even the misguided fools up North who thought themselves smart enough to tamper with the work of the Lord.

To the people here, corn is more than just a livelihood. It is a symbol, a bridge between the many levels of worlds they believe in. The corn's roots reach into the world below, and bring the cobs and energy of life into our world. I wish I could rid them of these notions, but given their history and way of life I don't fault myself for my slow progress.

I shuffle up the three rickety steps to the church. My predecessor kept it full of Mayan images and statuettes of sun gods, sky serpents, spirits of smoke and rain and dozens of others. Yet, somehow, he was respected by the Cardinal and the people both. I never understood how he was so full of faith. Certainly not by making his church into a jungle shrine, as Ignacio would have me do. No idols or false gods rest under my roof.

"Padre! Padre!" a young voice cries. Marco, Juan Haberno's son, is running down the dirt path along the field, cradling a ragged bundle like a giant rag doll.

"It's a man!" he says, his chest heaving. The skinny, dark-haired boy looks up at me. With his flat nose and coffee skin he is a true child of Punta Cabre, Maya through and through. With the honest and kind smile I so closely associate with him, he places the bundle at my feet, as if for approval. An ancient, crumbling blanket covers the corpse of an old man curled in a fetal position. Brown mummified flesh is stretched taut over his thin bones and face, placid with a gentle expression of sleep. Twisted hands clutch a small bag, a seed bag, in a death grasp.

"Marco Haberno, where did you find this?" I say. "You know to stay away from the ruins."

He's a good kid, though more interested in futbol than my Bible class. It would ruin me to see him chopped up by the rebels, displaced Zapotistas, who regularly loot the archeological sites to fund their hopeless fight for rights in the corrupt Government.

"I know," Marco says, "I've been good. I found him in the crack that opened up in the field."

"And you brought him to me?"

Marco shrugs. "It didn't seem right just leaving him there. I thought you could give him a proper burial."

If there is hope that this child will grow up with Saint Mary being Saint Mary and not the Chac of Rain, then there is hope for all. Does this child see faith in me?

"You did a good thing, Marco," I say. "We'll give him a proper funeral." Though I wonder how.

After he leaves, I wrap the body in a white shroud and place it under the palapa in the graveyard. The mummy has been brought here for a reason. A test. A test of my faith. I hear the chitter and caw of conures in the trees above. I look, but see only black myna birds fluttering into the jungle.

———

The townspeople crowd the graveyard in a half circle around the open grave. Juan Haberno left work filling in his field, and even Ignacio Rivera put aside his dislike of me to pitch in and help dig the hole. Eduardo, leader of the young rebels, non-descript and ordinary without his mask and rifle, has come. I hope the eyes of the government soldiers are elsewhere. An attack now would be disastrous.

The mummy lays under the palapa in a simple wood coffin. Ignacio Rivera leaves a plate of fruit and a bundle of herbs alongside it. Each of the mourners follow, one by one. Soon, a mound of red hibiscus and bougainvillea blossoms, corn bread, coins, tortillas, glass candles adorned with Catholic Saints, incense both lit and unlit, cakes, and cookies has accumulated. Marco drops his offering last, a steamed tamale wrapped in corn leaves. This is not going as I wanted. The aroma of chicken and spices mingles with the smell of fresh, upturned earth.

I fold the shroud over the body and slide the plank closed.

THE GREEN MAN OF PUNTA CABRE

"He came from the ground," Ignacio Rivera calls out, "put him back that way."

The murmurs from the crowd tell me I cannot refuse. I take the body out of the coffin, carry him to the open grave, and place him next to the mound of earth. All I wanted was a good Christian burial for this man. He was probably just a simple farmer like Juan Haberno. The adults lower their heads, and a few of the boys look around curiously.

During my short service I tell them that this burial shows even their ancestors have found Christ. From the abundance of offerings and Maya symbols and statutes, I can see my wishful falsehood is of little consequence to them. What is Marco to think? What will he grow up to believe? Even the rebels know, beliefs shape our world and are worth dying for.

Eduardo helps me lower the body into the ground. He places the first shovel full of dirt into the hole.

"May Jesus Christ protect you," he says softly.

They all line up for a turn to shovel some earth.

When all is done, and the last of them has gone, I sprinkle holy water into the hole and begin filling it in.

———

"Good morning, Padre," Juan Haberno says, leaning on his shovel. "You don't look so good today."

"Didn't sleep so well. Woke up early to prepare the cinder. It's Ash Wednesday. I'll see you in church?"

"Yes, see you in church," he says and twirls a little canvas bag on its drawstring. The seeds inside rattle like a maraca.

The sound brings last night's dream back to me. A tiny old man was curled up inside a fibrous, green ball in the buried mummy's heart. Tubers, roots, and runners grew from it, pushing down through the body to drink and up to find the sun. I woke just before the rustling creepers broke the surface.

Juan Haberno trudges into his field. Strong morning sun bakes the fresh earth of the grave. A myna bird swoops down and grabs a brown lizard. After school, Marco and the other town kids line up at the church doors to receive the ash on their heads.

What Mayan day or ritual this coincides with I don't know. Some god of smoke, maybe. The children accept the ash uncaring of any symbolism or my religious explanation. Saint or smoke god, they just want to be done with it and play ball.

With sweat-slicked ash on their foreheads, the bunch of them run from the church, kicking a ball back and forth. A wild kick sends the ball into the graveyard. When Marco catches up with it he lets out a cheer. "Come look, everybody!"

I run.

He is pointing to a healthy, foot-high, three-inch thick, green sprout poking its way out of the soft earth where we buried the mummy yesterday. Is it a weed? A sign? Whatever it is, it has risen unnaturally fast. Faster than anything I have ever seen.

The kids look at each other with confusion and joy. Then they let out a unified cheer, and Marco kicks the ball high into the air.

"Please, please don't step on the graves," I say to the people gathered to see the bulbous cornstalk that has shot up in the graveyard.

It has only been two days, and already the stalk growing from the fresh grave is higher than the wooden crosses and stone slabs marking the resting places of those who have died since my arrival, mostly rebels. Visitors have come from nearby Mechalu and Saint Cristobol.

THE GREEN MAN OF PUNTA CABRE

The Haberno family gladly sells them tamales, proudly pointing out it was their son who found the man buried beneath the stalk.

"Wish all my corn grew that fast," Juan Haberno says. "It is a miracle."

"It truly is a miracle," an old lady in the crowd echoes. Is this the Lord's apology for the quake? A reward for their faith? Surely it is a form meaningful to them. I want to hush her, but looking at the pile of offerings surrounding the stalk, I realize it won't do any good.

"A miracle." The words fly from every mouth.

"Please, please," I say. "This is holy ground. All altars must be outside the graveyard."

In my dream, vines and tubers snake from the stalk and bury themselves in Haberno's field. They pulse, carrying dark ichors away from the rows of corn to the mummy, who is sitting atop one of the gravestones. Black dribble runs from its mouth and nose. I move closer and realize beneath the fresh earth and green fungus its face is mine. I wake with a start to the resonant bark of a gecko chirping on the tin roof.

Visitors have come from Chiapas, Guadalajara, Mexico City, the small towns of Guatemala, and everywhere in between. The sick, the dying, the blind, the crippled, the old, and the religious pilgrims all want to touch and pray at the miraculous corn stalk. I roped off the graveyard with twine and fishing wire to keep them from knocking over the grave markers.

Ignacio Rivera sits in front of the palapa, self-appointed caretaker of the now six-foot plant. He shows visitors in one at a time, pointing out the face of Jesus he and the people of Punta Cabre have seen in the bulge in the stalk's center.

"See, there," he says to an old woman clad in traditional bright orange Guatemalan garb. The husk is dark green and thick like a palm frond. Raised veins run through it.

"Like the Sacred Twins present at the dawn of the first world, the Green Man is gonna come through into our world," Ignacio Rivera says. "He's gonna make the corn okay again."

"The white-faces up North want one kind of corn," a farmer in the crowd says. "They'll try and stop him. They'll send men in suits, with big trucks, guns, fancy poisons, and even demons."

"They'll have to come through me first," Ignacio says. "I'm gonna sit right here till the Green Man comes and when he does, I'll be here to greet him. I'll watch over him as he sucks out all the bad from the fields and praise him when he brings it back up North where it belongs. Look, you can see his face now."

I sometimes think I see things in the patterns in the wood grain of the pews. Faces maybe, but never that of the Lord.

No look of recognition dawns on the old woman's leathery face. I have not seen the face in the plant either, no matter how hard I try. Perhaps the face they see is really one of the Mayan Chacs I will never recognize or am I precluded from seeing because I doubt?

How can they think something holy would manifest here, like this? The only divine aspect I can see in the stalk is that it is a test. A test to see if I have the will to take away this false idol. It gives them such hope.

"Out of the way! Water for the Green Man!" Juan Haberno calls, weaving his wheelbarrow through the crowd of waiting pilgrims.

He dumps a barrel full of water on the mound of earth around the stalk and goes back for more, pushing past Eduardo and some other rebels I recognize. I see a familiar face, Padre Christopher, making his way toward the front. He parts the crowd, walks past Ignacio Rivera with a nod, and hands me a letter.

"From the Cardinal. Arrived yesterday," he says. "They're sending an Inquisitor from Mexico City to investigate your *miracle*."

———

The Inquisitor's blond-haired, blue-eyed angelic face regards me coldly, like a cherub all grown up and weathered from too much time in harsh, earth-bound places. His heavy black boots shine impossibly, as if he stopped in the jungle just outside of town to polish them. An ivory cross, white and pure, hangs around his neck, the only white accent on his perfectly-pressed black garb besides the starched collar. I see no sweat stains under his arms.

He looks at my simple cloth poncho and my wooden cross. "Why do you not wear your collar, Father?" he asks.

"The heat," I say with a smile. "Besides, everyone knows me."

I extend my hand. He doesn't take it.

"I'm Inquisitor Morgan."

"I was expecting you, just not so soon," I say.

"With the urgency of the matter, I made haste."

"What urgency?"

He mutters to himself and looks at the altars ringing the graveyard. "What are these?" he asks.

"Altars. To the plant," I say.

"And you permit it?"

"How am I to stop them?"

"You could begin by wearing your collar. Perhaps you have lived too long around these pagans."

Is this what has happened? Have I sailed too far from one shore and not close enough to the other?

"You don't believe it is a miracle?" I ask. I want to believe. But I see nothing. Only a strange, unsettling jungle plant.

"We'll see," he says.

"What if it is the face of the Lord?" I ask.

"We'll know."

"But what will happen?"

"I'll have the child document his experiences, begin the long path to Sainthood. The Cardinal will designate funds to build a church here. A real one. He might take interest and want to see it."

"The Cardinal, here? In my church?"

"Of course not. We'd take the plant to him."

Why would he want a miracle destroyed? Ignacio Rivera would never permit it. But at least the responsibility will be off my shoulders.

"What if it's not a miracle?" I ask.

"An abomination, then. Most are," he says, his eyes lingering on my simple cross. "We'd have to cut it down. Salt the ground. Cleanse your church. Either way, whatever it is, it's coming with me."

"They won't let you," I blurt, surprising myself.

A brief laugh escapes his lips. The hollow sound is the first emotion he has shown. I am convinced he doesn't care if he is right or wrong, he just wants his prize.

"They always try, and always fail," he says.

I lead the Inquisitor through the maze of crosses, altars, and piles of offerings to the palapa, its sides now curtained off with bright, striped blankets.

Ignacio Rivera stands in front, a stern sentinel in contrast to young Marco excited by the crowds.

146

THE GREEN MAN OF PUNTA CABRE

"Just because you're from Italy doesn't mean we gotta let you in," the old brujo says.

"The Vatican is not part of Italy, and I am from Mexico City. If your claims are true, the plant is clearly the responsibility of the Pope. Today, I am his sole representative here," the Inquisitor says.

"So what," Ignacio says. "You're still not going near it."

I gently usher the Inquisitor away to defuse the situation, then hurry back to the old brujo.

"If the Lord chose to reveal himself to us, then cooperating is going to make it easier to bring his message to the world," I say.

"This town doesn't care about the will of your Pope," he says. "They just want to plant their corn in peace. Like their families have always done, and they can barely do that anymore. Now the Green Man has come and he's going to make it right, so I'm going to protect him."

"I won't let anything happen to it. Just let him look, for a minute. Marco brought the man to me. I put him in the ground. That has to count for something."

"All right, Padre. I don't trust your church, but you've always been good to my town."

I wave the Inquisitor over, and Ignacio reluctantly lets us pass.

The stalk is several feet taller than yesterday. It brushes against the top of the palapa and bulges midway, as if pregnant with a giant cob.

The Inquisitor bends down and collects some of the moist, brown soil in a round plastic container. Ignacio grumbles under his breath. The Inquisitor moves his hand along the bulge, examining it as he might a woman with child. Then, he produces a syringe from the front pocket of his robe.

"No," Ignacio yells, but Morgan jabs for the stalk—a viscous fluid dribbles from the tip of the needle.

Ignacio pushes him, causing the strike to miss. The Inquisitor quickly gains his footing and slams the brujo in the chest with his open palm. The movement is clean and graceful. Efficient and precise. Ignacio stumbles back and falls hard on his behind, rasping for air.

I feel the force of the strike against his chest reverberating in my own. I have seen the aftermath of violence in the corpses of the rebels buried here, but never so close.

"Stop this!" I yell. "At once! These are church grounds!"

What kind of a priest resorts to such violence? How is he capable?

Marco, followed by a horde of pilgrims, rushes inside to the fallen brujo. "Somebody help!" he calls over the commotion. "He can't breathe!"

The Inquisitor pushes his way toward the plant but the sheer number of bodies keeps him away. He weaves among them stepping closer to the plant, his eyes like a wolf among sheep, deciding which ones to cut down. I fear for them.

Ignacio sits up with a roar, a seed bag in his hand. He throws the open pouch at the Inquisitor's face. A cloud of seeds and dust hangs in the air around him. For a moment, the Inquisitor's pristine face becomes twisted and ugly. He rasps for air then holds his neck, coughing violently.

Ignacio falls back down, the fire leaving his eyes. The Inquisitor drops the syringe. It breaks and the liquid bubbles on the ground with a hiss. The Inquisitor backs out of the palapa, against the current of people rushing in.

In my dream, lines of raised earth move from the stalk toward my church. Everything changes and I am in a modern farmhouse far away. The thick vines tunneling beneath burst from the ground,

148

each tipped with a razor sharp thorn. They slither through the windows, push up the floorboards, creep into my room, and wrap slowly up the bed. They pause above me before forcing their way into my ears and down my throat. The tendrils converge in my heart. I wake, coughing and clutching my chest.

The town has come to my church again, this time to pay their last respects to the old brujo. Eduardo and some of the rebels have brought food and money for his weeping family.

I think of the white can of paint seeping into the ground, the syringe of some unknown, but certainly potent, poison meant for the stalk. Such bad things have come to this town, the rebels and the soldiers that pursue them, the bad corn, and now this. Ignacio was their protector and sadly was more of their spiritual leader than I have ever been. Why can't these people have peace?

An old Mexican priest enters and totters over to the coffin in front of the altar. He leaves a bundle of flowers, drops some cash into the box, and regards me with a kind smile.

"Sorry for your loss," he says. His hair is matted with sweat. Deep lines run in the leathery skin of his face. His moustache, full of yellowing hair, not quite gray, hangs beneath his nose like the whiskers of a manatee.

"Samuel Morgan, Inquisitor from Mexico City," he says extending his hand. "I take it I'm expected."

His eyes are clear and truthful. Why would he pretend?

"Yes," I say. "It's just that you've already arrived. Or a man claiming to be you."

His face crumples into a frown, making his wrinkles look even deeper.

"I was afraid of that," he says.

"Father Samuel," a woman cries. "You've come to see the miracle." Her recognition confirms my instincts. It is he, not the other, who is the real representative of the church.

"We need to talk, Padre. Privately," Samuel says. "Where is this Imposter?"

"Eduardo spotted him at Senor Rolon's abandoned farmhouse at the edge of town," I tell him. "He killed this man, our local healer."

"He is capable of far worse."

"Is he going to hurt the plant?" Marco asks.

"The plant, yes. Let's have a look. Straight away," Samuel says.

Eduardo sits on a stool outside the palapa with a rifle on his lap. He looks at us grimly, but lets us pass. The stalk almost reaches the thatched roof. The bulge is almost wide enough to hold a man. Samuel runs his hand along it. He places his face to it, as if listening for something within. He steps back, and after squinting for a moment his sad, tired expression changes to elation.

"Oh, I see. Right there," he says.

So quick? So certain? Perhaps it is only I who can not see. Does the Lord refuse to show himself to me, or do the others see hope where I see only texture and lines?

"What?" I ask.

"A miracle. For certain," he whispers.

"What are you going to do?"

"If it is not the work of God, the Cardinal wishes it destroyed."

"You said it was a miracle..."

"And it is. Corn doesn't grow like that. Just what do you think is in that pod?"

The Green Man. Marco brought him to me. I put him in the ground. He is the hope for this town.

THE GREEN MAN OF PUNTA CABRE

I search the lines of the plant for the face. My mind's eye only delivers the cherubic visage of the Imposter. Cold and stern. Like a statue chiseled by one who never truly knew what a priest should be.

"Who is he Father?" I ask.

"Who, I am not certain. Though I have seen those like him before. He seeks to do harm. Who sent him is easier. Those up North did. Those who tampered with the work of God by making the bad corn."

"What will you have me do?"

"This is your church. These people are your charge and they are in need. Stand with me. Stand against him."

"But you said the Cardinal's wishes are to…"

"The Cardinal may get his wish soon enough."

I picture a gaping hole in the graveyard and barren desolate fields.

"Ask yourself what these people want and what they need. I will ask only that you be strong and certain, because our enemy will return with the darkness. What relics do you have here?"

"Only what you see," I say. "My predecessor kept all sorts of things, idols, dolls, trinkets in the church. I destroyed them and keep my church free of it."

He does not look pleased.

"Your predecessor kept these things in his church for a good reason."

"Are you telling me there is power in their icons? Meaning in their ways?"

"They would say so. In these ways are where their beliefs are. And there is power in belief."

"And you, Father? What do you believe?"

"I believe today we must deal in power."

Perhaps there was good reason after all for Ignacio's pestering me to follow the ways of old, and to let the church be the jungle shrine he desired.

"I have nothing. The nearest church is Mechalu," I say.

"Mechalu. Yes. The Saints," Samuel says. "We can call upon the Saints. If we hurry we can return by nightfall. We must."

"Do we dare leave the plant unattended?"

He leads me outside. Marco stands at attention next to Eduardo. "If he returns we will fight," the boy says and Eduardo nods, grimly.

I don't like to see him near the gun. Samuel looks at the rifle and frowns. "I pray that it will be enough. Our hope is that our enemy is still licking wounds inflicting from your dear, departed brujo. But, he will return. Ready your horse, and a mule, we must ride right away."

———

Soldiers stop us outside of town and ask about the rebels. I tell them we are men of the cloth, and they look at our mule suspiciously. They warn that if we aid the rebels there will be a price to pay. An attack to rid the town of rebels is coming, they say.

We ride till we reach the bustling market crowding the square in front of Mechalu's church. Vendors in close quarters wrap meats, pack fruit, fold blankets, and handmade shirts. People just like the townsfolk I know purchase candies, flour, handmade dolls and trinkets, to sell to the crowds back in Punta Cabre.

Samuel buys a caged chicken and a single egg from a farmer unloading his rickety wagon. We clop through the market and tie the horses and mule. The smell of fresh pine greets us as we open the heavy hardwood doors.

There are no pews. No chairs. No altar. The floor is covered in a thick coat of fresh pine needles. Along the walls, encased in glass in their own alcoves, are the Saints. Two feet high, each wears traditional clothes and a small, round mirror hanging around the neck. Those along the east wall glow with the late afternoon sunlight streaming in from windows high above.

THE GREEN MAN OF PUNTA CABRE

A young couple clears the needles beneath the Saint in the corner. Red fabric pokes out from underneath the layers of traditional blue clothing the figurine wears. Thin red and yellow candles are stuck to the floor in pools of wax.

"Saint Figueroa," Samuel says. "Granted Sainthood in 1914. Patron Saint of Children, also the Maya guardian of newborns."

He leads me to a Saint midway up the wall. Layer after layer of clothing wraps the doll. He clears the needles beneath it.

"Has it been ten years?" he mutters. "Your red poncho suited you better."

"If they treat the people well, the Saints stay for another *tun*—a Mayan cycle of time. They get new clothes, but the old ones stay."

Like the temples built on temples in the jungle. Did I do wrong to the town by clearing all the old out of the church when I arrived?

"This is Mother Eloisa," he says. "It is said she cured a great sickness brought on by a demon living in the boat of a prominent fisherman who sailed too far from shore. Though the symptoms were closer to chicken pox, her potency is not in question. You can see from her clothes she's been here a while. She is associated with the Maya spirit of Purity. She will cleanse you."

"What have I done?"

"The Imposter has clouded you. I need you clear and focused. It is your church where the plant resides. Your church that will be assaulted. Your will, your prayer will be the most potent protection. You will see this bond better after Mother Eloisa has lifted the veils from your eyes."

I had the fragile hope we were coming for crosses or blessed statutes of the virgin. But I knew better. Though I trust the old man, I know not to what strange shore he is sailing.

The young couple scurries out of the church. Samuel closes the door behind them and walks back to Mother Eloisa.

"Kneel, Padre."

I drop to my knees. I lift my hand to cross myself. Samuel stops me. He takes the egg he bought, passes it over me, himself, and then Mother Eloisa. He brings it over the candle flame and holds it there. For an instant, I see the silhouette of a wriggling, misshapen chick, then it is just an egg again, red from the flame beneath it. Reflections of the candle flame dance in the mirrors of the Saints.

He drops the egg, and it splatters. A puddle of yolk and white spreads toward the needles.

Samuel opens the cage door and swiftly grabs the chicken by the neck. He lifts the struggling bird into the air and holds it over my head in a flutter of feathers and clucks. He passes it over the Saint, and with a quick swish of his other hand, its neck is cut. Blood drops mingle with the egg.

I feel a gentle patter all over my skin, like the first fat raindrops of a downpour. The dull ache of the day's ride washes from my legs.

Samuel lights a white candle.

A scarred, sunburned face, with broken teeth and stringy, thin, disheveled hair, jumps into my mind's eye. The man is clothed in dirty linens, as I would imagine a leper from the Bible.

"He is horrible," Samuel says. "But, he can't hide his true face from the Saints."

He points at three other Saints in quick succession. "Take them from their alcoves. We bring these four to Punta Cabre."

———————

Joseph of the Angelic Flame and Peter the Revealer stand in their glass cases in the two far corners of my church. Mother Eloisa and Mary Elena of the Golden Fields rest atop the altar.

THE GREEN MAN OF PUNTA CABRE

Samuel affectionately pats Mary Elena's glass case. He lights a cluster of green and black candles and sticks them next to the offering of dead frogs slit up the middle that are piled in front of Saint Joseph. The graveyard and the jungle beyond is silent. The thatched roof of the palapa bulges where the cornstalk is pushing through.

I close my eyes and can sense the positions of the Saints, like compass points. My shoulders tingle with energy. I feel it coursing through the room, alive and kinetic, a power absent even on my best days and most inspired sermons. Ignacio would be pleased.

Eduardo enters. He holds a black mask and ammunition is slung over his back. "My men are in place," he says. "They have warned most of the pilgrims away."

"Thank you," Samuel says to Eduardo. "Beg them to stay inside and keep their children close. It is almost night."

With the haze of evening, a man comes. He walks the deserted dirt path and stops at the edge of the graveyard. His sunburned face is coated in sweat and grime. His hands and neck wrapped in filthy linens and bandages. The air around him ripples like a heat mirage. I think I see the cherub-faced Inquisitor, then his ragged visage returns with the putrid odor of a filthy port street in summer.

"I've come for it, Samuel," the Imposter yells, his hoarse voice cracking. "Stand aside."

"You are rot," Samuel yells to him.

"And you are alone among the faithless in the jungle. You cannot win." The Imposter steps into the graveyard, gingerly at first, as if testing the ground. Satisfied, he plows forward.

Samuel lights the thick wads of incense sticks bound together and stuck in the soil.

"Your prayers, now," Samuel says to me.

I speak the first words that come to mind, "Our Father, who art in heaven…"

Samuel grits his teeth, and gestures with his hands—as if wrapping an invisible thread around a ball. Tendrils of smoke waft to the Imposter, carried on a perfectly obedient wind.

The Imposter halts, then struggles to move. His dirty hands clutch the air. I picture them closing around the old man's neck. Then mine.

I speak the prayer words louder. Nothing happens.

Samuel glances to the trees, then lowers his fist. A hail of bullets rain down from Eduardo's men.

My bones feel like they have turned to jelly. I can't bear to see the pulp they have reduced him to.

I open my eyes. Bullets are falling harmlessly at the Imposter's feet. He thumps forward, bullets dropping around him like gnats. Samuel and I inch back until we are against the church door.

I speak slower, enunciating each consonant, losing myself in the words. For an instant, in my mind's eye I see the green bulk of the plant. In the lines of the husk I see an oversize Mayan nose protruding from beneath a tiny eye. His grinning line of a mouth moves, then is gone. Whether it is the face of the Lord or a Mayan Chac I don't know. A sharp pain dances on my fingertips, energy like tiny firecrackers explodes on my skin, crackles up my arms, and settles in the roots of my teeth as I pray. This is my church. These are my people. I will not let him enter.

The Imposter staggers, then takes a menacing step forward.

Samuel glances at me, and a giddy drunken smile spreads on his face. Does he see something I do not?

"Think of the Saints," he shouts and lowers his fist again. Another volley of bullets explodes from the trees.

THE GREEN MAN OF PUNTA CABRE

The bullets ricochet off the Imposter. Dust and incense smoke has gathered around him like a cloak. Only steps away, I can smell his reek, the stench of unclean flesh, and rotten vegetables.

As he moves, the smoke ripples. I see shadows, shapes, afterimages of where he passes.

His filthy hands reach for me and though I punch and kick, they close around my neck.

I choke and cough. My knees threaten to buckle and my vision dims to a black circle.

"You must pass through me," I say, only I think I hear Ignacio's raspy old voice speaking.

All is smoky dark, and full of the putrid stench. I feel one of my blows connect with the Imposter's chest. Beneath the soft flesh, I feel impact with bone—the reverberation moves through me like electricity.

I hear Ignacio's voice whispering in the language of the jungle. I think I see him moving in the smoke. Then I am striking, kicking, biting at that awful rotten neck like a beast.

"You have to come through me," I say. This time I am certain I hear the words with Ignacio's voice, and a deep harmonic echo. The Saints?

I feel strong arms pulling me. I turn to see Father Samuel.

"Get back," he says.

The Imposter staggers, blood oozing from his neck.

Another round of bullets bursts from the trees. This time, the Imposter spins in a gruesome dance, thrashing this way and that, throwing off clouds of dust. The bullets have found their mark. My prayers? Or the power of the Saints?

A red glow, like hot coals burning within him, emanates from his unraveling bandages and robes. He makes it to the edge of the jungle, trailing ash and swirling linens, before falling.

Samuel drops to his knees, exhaustion and relief on his old face. It is so quiet I hear his racing breath. No chorus of insects, frogs and lizards.

Eduardo lowers himself from a tree just as the world begins to shake. Another aftershock. Deep booming reports of gunfire punctuate the terrible groan of rock.

"The soldiers have heard. Hurry," Eduardo says, trying to stay on his feet. His men drop from the trees and awkwardly run on the heaving ground into the jungle. The sound of rifle fire grows near as their unsteady forms disappear into the darkness.

The aftershock passes, and I wait for the sounds of the night to return and tell me it is alright. They do not. Something rustles in the palapa.

"Go," Samuel says. "There is one more thing that must be done."

"Come with me," I say.

"You will finish this," he says, looking to the jungle. "My work is out there. In the fields."

"What are you talking about?" I say.

"When all is done, return the Saints to their home," he says. His exhaustion from a moment ago is gone. Something has changed in him. He turns to the jungle and for a moment his face is a face of leaves and vines.

"Who are you? Tomorrow will another man named Samuel Morgan come to this town?"

"I am a man of faith. As you are," he says, and without looking back follows the fleeing rebels into the jungle.

I want to run after him, and demand him to tell me what happened back there, instead I hurry to the palapa. I can't make sense of anything, but I know will protect the plant. I will not budge, even if the soldiers come.

THE GREEN MAN OF PUNTA CABRE

I'm surprised to find Juan Haberno inside. His hands and forearms are covered in sticky clear sap. The pod is slit open and wilted over. The rear blanket wall has fallen. Whatever was growing inside is now gone.

"Thank you, Padre," he says. "Your god is strong. I'm sorry I ever doubted."

"Juan, what happened?" I ask.

"The Green Man has come," he says in a daze. "I saw him."

Something rustles outside. I catch a glimpse of a man standing just inside the tree line. It could be a trick of the shadow or the dense growth, but he appears to be green, a green as dark as the prehistoric ferns.

Rifle shots crackle nearby. The man disappears into the jungle.

"Juan, you have to leave," I say.

"He said he's sucked all the poison from the corn, and he's going to bring it back up North. He wants the mummy returned to where we found it."

I have no time for questions. Whatever has happened here, the soldiers are getting closer, and I will not have Juan suffer any more.

"Then hurry and help me dig," I say.

I plunge my hands into the mound of earth surrounding the stalk. Thick pink roots sprout from its base. Intertwined within them, near the surface, is the rotting shell of Marco's mummy. It still clutches the seed bag. I pick it up and we run.

The rifle fire is louder. People fleeing town run across the field to the jungle. Bullets fly over us from somewhere in the trees—one of Eduardo's men covering their escape. A man herding crying children bumps into me, and I almost drop the mummy.

Bullets whiz back and forth above us as we push against the flow of fleeing bodies to the trench. The aftershock has widened it, undoing the attempts to fill it in.

Marco is standing there. He is so close to the edge I fear he may fall.

"Marco, run," I yell.

"A quake when we found him, Padre, and quake when we put him back," he says, smiling and proud.

I hear a whiz and an awful crunch, like a bullet hitting a tree, and Marco is gone. The earth at the edge of the trench crumbles. I drop the mummy and dash over. Marco lays at the bottom. A bullet has found his head. I turn to hold Juan back, to spare him from the sight.

Juan has not moved. He stands frozen and expressionless next to the mummy. Crossfire sails above.

"I told him to go with his mother," Juan says.

The morning sun bakes Juan Haberno's field. I use the last of the white paint to coat the old weathered cross. I light a bundle of incense and leave an offering of tortillas and chocolate for Marco. With Ignacio Rivera gone, Punta Cabre needs me more than ever. I will find them a new brujo, or learn about every leaf and every animal myself. Maybe now that this storm has passed these people may return to growing corn.

"Chac, bring the rain," I say. "Juan Haberno's field needs water."

I want to contact the Cardinal, inquire about Samuel Morgan. I'm sure I'll find a name in the records, although who the man is I doubt I'll ever know. Right now, it doesn't matter. It doesn't matter if I was touched by a god of smoke, or some remnant of Ignacio. I don't care if the stalk was a rampant weed or birthing pod of a vengeful spirit of the corn. There are so many bodies to bury. So much to be done. My cemetery will soon be too full.

THE GREEN MAN OF PUNTA CABRE

The Saints can wait a little longer before returning. I have already asked Maria Haberno to craft me a doll and some clothes. After I place Juan's seed bag in its hands, one more will be returning to Mechalu with them. Saint Marco Haberno. Herald of the Green Man of Punta Cabre. Maybe his home will be in my church. I need to fill it.

JELLYFISH MOON

Twin crescent beaches of fine, white sand fanned out from the rocky tide pools at the foot of the steep cliff, a calm and shallow bay between them. Two larger-than-life figures hewn from the rock flanked a wide cave entrance leading into the heart of the island. The seated men had the elongated heads of salt-water crocs, and were said to be servants of Harat, the guardian spirit of the small fishing community turned exclusive tourist haven. Where the beaches thinned and arced together forming the narrow mouth of the bay, San paddled his dugout full of tackle and wire to repair the nets. Bare-chested and barefoot, his dark skin glistened with salty sweat.

The bay was closed off from the ocean with nets. Just as it had been every time this year for generations. San's father, and his father before him had been a net diver. With the growing tourist industry came stronger nets and plastic buoys, but the job was always the same: check the nets and keep the bay free of crocs for the Jellyfish Moon.

San paddled close to the line of buoys marking where the nets disappeared beneath the water.

Every paddler was on the water patrolling for crocs. San heard his brother-in-law Charlie's deep chuckle. Of course he was happy.

THE NIGHT MARCHERS Daniel Braum

The sun was shining, all was cool and calm, and he came home every day to his wife and children.

"San, you take your head out of da sky and dive down to those nets," his sister, Tal, called from a cluster of paddlers.

Her voice surprised him. She should be preparing for the festival but she loved to wrestle the crocs out of the bay with her husband Charlie and the boys.

"I checked them twice already today," he said.

"Den check 'em again."

"Got 'em," Charlie cried. His rope noose was taut from the struggling of a snared croc below. Tal deftly turned her boat to go help.

"And when you are done, Marika is here," Tal called over her shoulder as she paddled away. "Charlie says one of the boys took her bags up to Ruby Shores."

San's arms went weak upon hearing her name.

It was the worst time, he had so much to do before the dark of the moon.

San put his feet in the water, readying himself to check the rocks at the sea floor anchoring this section of nets.

It had been almost a year since she had left. Only two more days to the dark of the summer new moon, the Jellyfish Moon. Already the round, translucent creatures were flowing in with the tide. The nets were wide enough to let their fist-sized, spherical bodies pass, yet small enough to keep the head of even a small crocodile out.

Feeling the soft creatures against his toes, he gazed at the huts and viewing platforms that had already been set up for the rich tourists at the distant edges of the beaches. Normally these were the least desirable places to sunbathe because of their distance from the palm tree shade and the outdoor pavilion of shops and vendors on the other side of the Temple. Soon they would be the most desired spots to view the yearly return of the invertebrates and the ceremony and festival that followed.

San thought of the sunset parade; the locals, his friends and families selling aqua-fresca, roasted nuts, fresh baked cookies, chocolate and fruit brownies, and the frosted coconut cake he enjoyed so. Marika had loved that cake.

"Come with me, San. Lets watch together from the Temple."

"I have to go and check the nets. It's my job to keep the crocs out."

"But it's the festival."

"I love you Marika. You know I was a diver long before you came. It's who I am. Who my father was."

"I'm your lover. I'm going to be your wife."

"Don't make me choose."

He didn't have to. That night she left without a word and had not returned.

He still couldn't believe it. Though she was an outsider—born in Czechoslovakia but living in New York, Paris, and Milan since her early teens—San knew she felt the wisdom of wind through palm, of the sunshine on the water, and of letting the outside world of war and strife go to hell. A photo shoot had brought her to the island, and days later she told him she wanted to leave behind her career and the life that went with it. She had been ready to escape the grind of the fashion world and her wealth granted her that luxury.

Tal had told him that no matter how sweet the smile or sincere the words you can't trust an outsider. "All they want is a fantasy, a fling with an islander and island life. Sooner or later they go," she had said.

As the months passed after Marika had left, he had heard word of her through the newspapers and the tourists on his snorkeling boat. He hadn't realized how famous she was. He hadn't cared.

San threw his diving knife at a small croc nosing about his boat. It missed and sank into the clear depths.

THE NIGHT MARCHERS DANIEL BRAUM

Marika, I always wanted you back, but what was I gonna do? Go to New York and fight for you? How? With my diving knife and my tackle?

If Marika really had come back then there was a chance. Maybe she'd see that she belonged here, with him. He'd show her. If only there wasn't so much to do.

———

"He's a big one," Tal yelled. "San, come on over and help us carry him out of the bay."

San stopped his paddling. He desperately wanted to say "no", and run to Marika, but he could feel Tal's eyes on him, just waiting for any indication he would refuse.

He rolled out of his dugout into the shallows and waded over to Tal and Charlie, who along with Lynden and Big Rog were leading the snared croc to shore.

"She's an eight footer," Lynden said. "You think it's Gertrude?"

"Can't be sure till we get her on shore," said Charlie. "Don't complain, back on San Raphael I used to see twelve to fourteen footers all the time."

They wrestled the croc out of the water onto the rocky shore. San didn't think the four of them needed his help, yet he bound the leathery reptile's jaws closed with a roll of silver tape.

They finished taping its front arms and the four of them picked it up. Tal prevented its tail from thrashing.

"Come on now, over to the other side of the island to the nice garbage dump where there's lots of food for you," Charlie said.

She'd find her way back, San thought. They always did. Took them a couple of days. But it was enough time to let the festival go through.

JELLYFISH MOON

Charlie groaned playfully. "What's the point of taking them out of the bay? They just come back anyway."

"How long you been here, sweetie? The bay is to be kept empty and free of the influence of Harat, at least for one night. The jellyfish enter, with the dark of the new moon as they do year after year. The absence of the moon and the spirit of the migrating jellyfish brings purification. Cleansing. The restart of these cycles brings renewal."

"I could use some of that renewal," Charlie said, groping for his wife. "Harat is just a story."

"He's our story," Tal said. "The real reason, of course, is that the big man at Ruby Shores wants the crocs gone. Thinks they'll scare the tourists away, and then he'll have no more money."

Charlie laughed. "Crocs aren't a danger unless you're swimming at night in the garbage dump."

"I know, dear. I know. What are we gonna tell 'em? It was the crocs' bay first?"

They approached the path leading up the cliff to the Temple.

They can take it from here, San thought. "I have to go and meet Marika," he said.

"I thought that was one that would stay gone," Big Rog said.

"Let the man be," Charlie said.

"She's back to suck us dry," Rog muttered under his breath.

"I'll see you tomorrow," Tal said to San. She spoke the words as if they were an order.

San climbed over the rocks to the path. Why did he even bother to help? Now he wouldn't have time to clean up and still have a chance of catching Marika before dinnertime. He wished things could be like those first idyllic months when he woke with her to the morning sun, came home to her after a day on the boats, dined with her on fresh fish on their grill, and drank and walked the beach till it was time to start over again the next day.

THE NIGHT MARCHERS DANIEL BRAUM

San entered the black cave mouth leading into the Temple. Strings of electric lights lit the passage, illuminating tribal ceremonial markings alongside old and modern graffiti. The handrails for the tourists were pitted and rusting from the salt air.

Within a minute he came upon the main chamber. Two croc-men, like the giant pair outside, sat in silence next to the lone, stone slab of an altar.

A pile of incense ash and a bunch of wilted, yellow flowers lay before the slab. Harat was strong, San thought. His people were always fortunate. With the hotels, tourism was booming. But, with the outsiders came many rules and insidious problems. Loyalties were divided and one had to go farther and farther to get a good catch of fish. Many made a better living by working the tour and dive boats. The island was changing. San himself even ran a snorkel boat on his off day. He didn't know what kind of gods the outsiders had, but he hoped Harat was strong enough to wrestle with them and prevail.

He turned the corner, hurried down the passage, and pushed open the door that led to the pavilion.

A dozen hotels and twice that many day spas and restaurants lined a square paved with clean sand colored stones. Stalls and carts spread out like a snail shell from the central fountain: four stone crocodiles, modern replicas in the style of the temple, spurted water on a giant jellyfish in the center. At the edge of the strip, hulking iron cranes lifted the girders of next year's new hotel into place, spewing oily smoke into the clear sky.

A small crowd had gathered around Mr. and Mrs. Henderson's trinket stand. He could hear the old woman yelling, and something told him to pick up his pace. He broke into a run when he saw Marika.

She was sprawled on the floor, one high heel off, her leg twisted. Mrs. Henderson alternated between yelling at Marika and her husband who was taking pictures with a yellow disposable camera from their shop.

San knocked the camera out of his hand and bent to Marika. "You all right?"

"She break. She pay," Mrs. Henderson said. "She no wanna pay."

"I didn't break anything. I broke my heel, then he started flashing that thing at me."

San helped her to her feet. Marika kicked off her other heel and leaned against him.

"You fall and break glass," Mrs. Henderson said, pointing at a few broken jars of expensive skin crème made from the bay water and jellyfish that was popular with the tourists.

"Old lady," San said indignantly, "you should be ashamed. This is my girl. And you let her lay there and don't help?"

Mr. Henderson rummaged through stacks of t-shirts looking for the camera.

"This is my business," Mrs. Henderson said. "I don't go and break your swim masks."

"I tell you what. I pay you for your crème, on payday. I'm good for it. But, I don't want to see none of those pictures nowhere, ya hear?"

"Deal," the old woman said. She waved to her husband to clean up the crème.

San slid his arm around Marika's waist and led her to the hotel. His arm against her back and his hand on her pelvis bone made him shiver.

"You okay?" he asked.

"It's gonna be fine," she said.

A uniformed teenager opened the security gate to the grounds of the Ruby Shores hotel. The palms were cleaned, and the flowering shrubs manicured. Small beach-rock fountains gurgled, surrounded by oceans of thick emerald grass.

"Why didn't you tell me you were coming?"

"You'd only yell," she said. "It's better this way."

Beneath her heavy eye makeup were dark circles from lack of sleep. She'd lost weight. In her fancy sundress she looked like one of the too-skinny girls from the magazines the tourist women read on the beach. Her face was the same. The most beautiful he had ever seen. Her eyes were alert jewels, which despite their striking beauty somehow spoke of sadness.

Marika smiled to the staff who greeted her as they walked through the spacious lobby. When she looked away, San noticed their disapproving frowns. It felt like a long time until the elevator dinged and arrived to take them.

When the doors closed, he smelled the vanilla and spice of Marika's perfume and beneath a hint of her sweat. The smell of her.

"I saw a picture of you and some man in the paper. What is it? You coming here to make sure it's me, not him that's right for you?"

"Something like that. It's complicated."

San looked at her. "You're tired of the big world life again and you've come home to me. I can see it in your eyes."

She pulled on a strand of her thin, sandy hair like she did when she was nervous. "Am I that transparent?"

"No, I know you." San wanted to kiss her and push her away all at the same time. The magnetic pull between them had not diminished with time, yet there was something more. Sex wasn't why she returned.

"I know a lot has happened, but you and the island were always in my heart," she whispered.

She was so close and feeling her skin on his as he supported her was like a dream he had wished for, for so long. He remembered he had also felt the same dreamy sense with her, right up until she surprised him and disappeared.

JELLYFISH MOON

"They say you come down here to have one last fling with me, then you go back to New York?"

"San, not now. What do you want me to tell you? All I know is I'm here now. Isn't that enough?"

Maybe it was. Maybe it was too much.

The elevator halted, and the doors opened to her suite at the top of the hotel.

A cool breeze moved through the simple, elegant quarters. Thin, sand-colored drapes flapped at the big windows, giving a panoramic view of the bay.

Marika traipsed past the sitting area and flopped down on the big bed. The gesture reminded him of the old days. Of the Marika he knew. He yearned to lay next to her. To answer the words left hanging in the elevator by saying, yes you are here, that is enough. He thought of Tal telling him that outsiders only wanted an island fling. This was different. It had to be.

Marika pulled the pillows out from beneath the soft aqua bed-spread, cozied into them, and lit up a cigarette.

"It's good to be back," she said, and took a long pull, causing the orange head to glow strong and bright.

She exhaled a stream of smoke. One of the first things she had done after meeting him last year was quit.

"Why did you come back?" San asked. The soft, carpeted floor seemed so strange to him. Yet Marika looked perfectly at ease with the plush surroundings, an inhabitant of an impossible dream world. He wondered if this was what it felt like to be a rich outsider, a big man. The notion both repulsed and excited him.

She took another disturbingly long pull before answering. "For renewal," she said, her voice wavering. "For some island peace. Yeah, some island peace. But this time to take it back with me."

"What if I want you to stay?"

He bent down next to the bed and kissed her. Her body stiffened at his touch. She pulled away at first, then relaxed and met his lips with the openness and ferociousness he remembered.

Marika's arms found his back, his shoulders, his arms. She turned sideways and pulled him onto the bed. With the soft swell of her breast against him and her leg around his San forgot where he was. He tasted the cigarette smoke on her and for a second he could have been down at the shore with her a year ago. She pressed herself as close as could be to him before forcing herself away with a gasp. The cigarette had burned an ugly hole in the spread. Marika swatted it out and settled back into the pillows in silence.

The strangeness of the soft-around-the-edges place had lost its charm, and San yearned for his place by the sea.

"Come back to the house with me tonight," he said.

"San, I can't."

Her eyes said otherwise.

"It was a long flight. A long day. I need to sleep." She groped the night table for the pack of cigarettes. "And I won't if I'm with you."

San knew she could not be forced. His easygoing way was the heart of their attraction and what she wanted—what she needed right now.

"I'll be up at dawn," she said. "You can take me out on the boat."

He kissed her gently on the forehead, turned, and went into the elevator.

He thought of his favorite spot out on the ocean as he descended. A shallow sandbar where they first kissed. First touched.

The perfect place for our new beginning, he thought.

———

JELLYFISH MOON

San checked that no one was around and placed the extra gas can, two snorkel masks, a lunch of fresh fruits, and a six-pack of Crystal Reef, Marika's favorite beer, in his small motorboat at the dock. He'd take it around to the other side of the island, then walk back to the hotel to retrieve Marika, without anyone seeing.

"Where you going wit' 'dat boat?" Tal said. She stood in the shade of the dock house, holding a plastic bucket full of jellies.

She knew where he was going, there was no use pretending.

"Lynden and Big Rog got da nets for me. They *both* gonna check 'em today."

"They are not," Tal said, punctuating each word. "Get your butt in your boat and go do your job."

The jellies sparkled orange and green in the shadow, creating a glimmering outline of her on the wall behind. She stared fiercely, not just with the authority of an older sister, but with the stern wisdom of an elder, of the community leader she was certain to be.

"I do what I gotta do," San said.

"That's what Charlie used to say, and look what happened to his home, San Raphael."

San thought of the nearby island, full of paved roads, high rises, and smoky cars. It was miserable.

"If everyone did as you do, we'd be another San Raphael in no time. As it is, we are holding onto the heart of our island by just a thread."

The image of the Temple filled his mind. A gossamer net strung between the giant statues scintillated in front of the black cave mouth. He felt as if he were passing through it as he walked past his sister.

"You count," Tal called after him. "Every one of us does. We are different. Our world is not their world. Even though they come together here, we have to remember that. If we lose even one of us to the siren call, soon we all be falling down like dominos."

San started on the rocky path, then stopped and turned toward the way to the pavilion. No sense in hiding or taking the long way now, he thought.

Twenty minutes later he was back, helping Marika into the boat, Tal nowhere to be seen.

The sun had just lifted from the horizon and cast an orange sheen on the rippling cells of early morning waves.

Lynden and Rog were paddling to the nets. They stopped to look as San started the engine and moved away from the dock. Marika smiled and rummaged through her straw bag for sunglasses and lotion.

San cut the engine just before the nets, flipped it up and let the boat coast so as not to get snared. He dropped it back in and veered the boat to the open ocean. Marika lifted her head to the clean breeze, closed her eyes beneath her big rose sunglasses, and untied her hair.

Their wake was full of little jellies propelling themselves toward the bay. San had never given the creatures much thought. He knew there was something special about the water—the temperature, high salinity, and mineral content that drew the jellies as well as the tourists and rich spa-goers to the island. The salt-water crocs were more mysterious. A British research team he had once taken diving had yammered on that they were attracted to the pulsing rainbow patterns the jellyfish made at the festival, though he didn't know exactly how, nor did it really explain anything. Crocodiles and Harat, who wore their reptilian form, embodied the spirit of the island. Leave us to our sleepy, mysterious ways and we don't bite.

Marika interrupted his train of thought by sliding her arm around his waist.

"The world always looks better after a good night's sleep," she said.

JELLYFISH MOON

"The world always looks good here."

San gave the engine more gas and they sped into the blue. Just as the island was almost out of sight, he stopped the boat and eased it onto a green area of shallow ocean, which gave way to a pristine strip of sand.

Marika smiled. "Our place," she said. "I can't wait to go in."

San noticed the thick, gelatinous mass of a man-o-war dipping and bobbing a few yards off the boat. Before he could warn Marika to be careful of its tentacles, a dark shape rose from the depths, a big, old croc. It snatched the three-foot jellyfish in its jaws, and for a few seconds swam with it just beneath the surface, only its back ridges visible. More crocs rose from the depths and fought for chunks of the huge jelly with splashes and thrashes.

Back again, San thought. *Season after season.*

He jumped over the side onto the sand bar then helped Marika out of the boat.

"Don't worry," San said. "They like it better at the mangroves during the day."

She stood in the foot and a half of water, then sloshed away from the edge. "I'm not worried."

San unpacked the sun umbrella and planted it for her. Then he produced the six of Crystal Reef and plopped it in the water under its shade.

"Shame on me," Marika said. "I've forgotten how good life can be."

San watched curious silver fish approach the bottles. Lazy black and yellow striped barbs picked at the sea grass.

"You can have this every day you know," he said solemnly.

"Relax, honey," Marika said. She kissed his cheek. "Forget about tomorrow. We have this day." She kissed his other cheek. "We have this moment. Everything is perfect. A completely perfect moment."

THE NIGHT MARCHERS   Daniel Braum

As her lips touched his, San recognized the words as his own. The very concepts he had taught to her, when she had first met him—a stressed out tourist unable to unwind. He desperately wanted a string of these moments, a series of never ending islands continuing into the future.

He took a deep breath and sat with her in the shallow water. They spent the afternoon eating fruit, watching sea birds, and talking intently about nothing. As the day grew late, a cluster of the small jellies floated past, massaging them with their tiny harmless tentacles and gelatinous bodies.

Marika sprang to her feet.

"I'm here for the festival, San," Marika said abruptly, as if brought on by the touch of the jellyfish. "I'm not going to stay. And I want you to come with me."

San stared at her beautiful face. Squinting from the sun, her lips were parted in a slight, crocodile smile.

"And then what?" he asked. "What happens when you leave me and I am all alone in your country?"

"Have you been listening to them, San? Do you believe I'm an evil spirit here to lure you away? We never have anything more than the now. I'm just offering you the same without this island as your boundaries."

It was easy for her to say, San thought. She had everything.

"How do I know you haven't come here for your island fling, like they say?"

"Will you let me try to convince you otherwise?"

Her kiss smoothed the edges of his fears and brought him back to the moment. He knew the first step towards convincing her to stay was to truly have a string of wonderful moments, so he let the subject rest.

Late that night they returned to San's hut and slept on the beach under the stars like they used to. As the last sliver of the moon shone down upon them, San dreamed of stirrings under the water and great tears in the net. He awoke with words eager to leave his mouth. "I can't go with you Marika. My place is here. It's just like last time."

He thought she heard, but couldn't be sure. He didn't wake when Marika left just before dawn.

———————————

"There you are," Tal shouted. "Sleeping late when tonight is the Jellyfish Moon. Lynden found tears in the net. Get up right now."

San scrambled to his feet. Luckily Marika was gone, the only hint of her presence the imprint on the sand next to him.

"Any crocs get in?" he asked.

"None that we can see. Every paddler is out there searching, to make sure."

Within minutes, San was in his dugout, paddling a load of tackle and wire to the nets.

The cave mouth of the temple was covered with nets and colorful banners. Red blindfolds had been placed over the two statues' eyes.

San stopped by the buoy where Lynden was diving. The water was thick with jellies brimming with the energy of renewal. San could see the crocs on the other side of the net, their bodies weaving in the flow of translucent creatures. He could sense their hunger.

San wanted to see the world, but unlike Marika, it was a distant musing of some far away beauty. His place was here and he believed the world would come to him, eventually. What if he was wrong and his place was with Marika? What then?

He took three deep breaths, filling his lungs, and rolled out of the dugout. With strong, swift kicks, he was ten, then twenty, then thirty feet down. He slowly released small bubbles from his mouth. The net had been ripped in several places and a stone anchor had shifted on the bottom as if something big had tried to break in. There was a lot of work to be done.

San stitched, very aware that only a dozen yards away, on the other side of the thin barrier, crocs swam among the jellies. They rolled and swirled erratically, like housecats on the herb. He reached for his knife then remembered it was gone.

He ascended and retrieved his tools, the tackle, and wire. With a glance to the shore he saw the beaches were already filling. He wished he was there, with Marika.

San took three breaths and descended again. Consciously keeping his heart rate slow to conserve air, he deftly tied the ends of the first tear together with the wire. Out of the corner of his eye, he watched Lyndon struggle to keep his stitching closed. He turned back to his work and found himself face to face with a big croc floating on the other side of the net. Its toothy mouth was open just enough to give the impression of a smile. San kicked for the surface.

"Did you see that big croc?" San said to Lynden.

"Where?"

"Down by my tear."

Lynden ducked his head under the water, then came right up.

"There ain't nothin' there."

"He was right there, staring right at me."

Lynden ducked his head under again.

"Visibility's perfect. Your eyes be clouded by that woman."

Or too many days in the sun and salty water, San thought. Marika has offered me the world.

San went back to work. He and Lynden stitched and wired till it was late afternoon. Lynden didn't have a friendly word. San didn't see the big croc again, though he kept thinking it was just out of sight. The beaches filled with tourists and spa goers. The new-agers were out in force trailing incense and chanting, waiting for Tal and the elders to come to the beach for the festival blessing.

San wanted to go back to his place to wash off the salt of the day and get some needed sleep. But he had to see Marika. He couldn't let her go without seeing her one more time. Then he would know what was right.

He tied his dugout to the dock and walked through the crowd to the Ruby Shores. The pavilion was almost deserted. Most of the vendors had taken their carts and wares down to the beach. He noticed Mr. and Mrs. Henderson pushing their cart away. They were talking to a tall pretty lady in a suit, holding a microphone, who was followed around by a man shouldering a big camera.

Big Rog's son was working security at the hotel gate.

"I'm here to see my wife."

"She ain't here."

"Let me in, I'm telling you she's on the top floor."

"I'm telling *you*, she's at the festival. Left a half hour ago."

The sun was low in the sky. He'd have to hurry and find her before the crowds and darkness made it an impossible task.

Rushing to the beach, San edged his way through rich families, well-manicured couples holding hands, and long-haired, wide-eyed young people adorned in croc tooth jewelry and bright colors that were supposed to mimic that of the nighttime jellies.

The smell of grilling fish, roasting pineapple and nuts made his stomach grumble, but he kept on looking for a glimpse of Marika.

He asked the cake man selling fruit brownies. Big Rog working his grill. He stopped to buy a pack of Marika's favorite cigarettes at the Henderson's stand. Mr. and Mrs. Henderson had not seen her, though Mr. Henderson smiled and clicked a mock photo of him with his hands. Sweaty and exhausted, San patrolled the two strips of beach.

THE NIGHT MARCHERS DANIEL BRAUM

He thought of the smiling face of the croc beneath the water and glanced up to the blindfolded croc-men statues. A female form moved in the shadows of the cave mouth. A slender arm rested on the leg of one of the croc-men. Marika? She couldn't be in the temple. The thought was so absurd. It was irreverent. Exactly the sort of thing Marika would want to do. It was what she wanted to do last year.

The last bit of the sun sank below the waves, and a hush spread over the beaches. Deep drums sounded from the trees. Sparks of orange flickered through the bay full of jellies, mimicking the departed sun as the procession of elders appeared at the tree line. Marchers wearing big paper-mache croc heads of bright orange, yellow, and purple stepped in time. San pushed his way through the crowd. The pungent smell of festival incense wafted above the aromas of cooking food. Flag bearers carried poles trailing green, blue, and red streamers. San knew one of them was Tal. As if in response, the jellies in the bay ignited in a burst of color. Vibrant greens and oranges radiated through the bay like a million submerged fireflies. Bursts of primary reds and yellows and blues spontaneously appeared to the cheers of delight from of the crowd. New-agers edged closer to the shore, anxious for the blessing to be done and to be the first into the supposedly restorative waters.

San wished he were watching with Marika. The waves of color were hypnotizing, and it occurred to him he had never seen it from this vantage. He raced to the pavilion and stole away unnoticed through the door leading into the heart of the temple.

The murmur of the crowd was muted inside the dim passage. The lights leading into the temple chamber were out. He hurried, his hand on the rusty rail, expecting to come upon Marika, sitting a few feet back from the mouth of the cave, smoking a clove, taking solitary delight in her privileged view of the bay. He would quietly slither up behind her and snake his arms around her…

180

JELLYFISH MOON

The thrashing rustle of leather on stone met him. Guttural growls and heavy breathing echoed in the room. It was coming from the center. The altar.

"Marika," he called out, and squinted, his eyes not yet adjusted to the faint light reaching in from the mouth.

He struck a match. In the sulfur glow he made out a monstrous form on the stone slab. A huge, ridged tail sprouted from the back of a man, thrashing side to side as he mounted someone on the altar. Two slender female legs wrapped around his mottled back.

The match went out. Was it Marika and one of the costumed men? The moans intensified. He lit another match. The woman had mounted the croc-man.

San stepped forward to see better, but he didn't want to. As his match sputtered he saw Marika's face. Her eyes met his and she smiled, her mouth full of huge, jagged crocodile teeth.

An animal roar filled the darkness mixed with Marika's cries—no longer of passion, but of rage. San heard the awful sound of fists connecting with flesh, like a butcher tenderizing a fish. The croc-man roared in pain.

He didn't know what kind of gods the outsiders had, but he hoped Harat was strong enough to wrestle with them and prevail.

San ran to the altar and fumbled for another match. He stumbled, dropping matches, screaming Marika's name. He wasn't sure if he should be rescuing her or stopping her. The moaning stopped and the rustle of clothing and footsteps replaced it.

Outside, the muted cries of delight gave way to a horrendous, unified scream.

San struck another match. The figures on the altar were gone. The room was empty. Was he feverish from lack of sleep? He inspected the altar. Dark, blue fluid, like crocodile blood, stained the altar.

He ran to the cave mouth and pushed through the nets and streamers. The new-agers who had waded into the bay were frantically pushing each other over to get out.

The entire bay was alight with rapid patterns of red and fiery oranges, the brightest he had ever seen. Three dark shapes weaved through the jellies. Crocs. Ripples of dark violet and blue jellies in their wake.

White froth splashed at the net line. Hundreds of others were pushing to get in. They breached the waves as if some invisible signal had them frenzied.

Then San saw the cloud of red. Blood. Someone had been bit. He knew he should run down and help, but he had to find Marika.

The apparitions in the Temple had to have been a delusion. But the blood, the ridges on the croc-man's back were so real. Seeing Marika, he would know. The town bells were ringing. The fire alarm was blaring. He could hear the roar of panic from the bay. He ran for the hotel.

The gate to Ruby Shores was open and unattended. San darted in, dashed through the lobby and into the elevator before the lone woman staffing the desk could stop him.

The elevator rose slowly. San jabbed at the tenth floor button over and over. The doors slid open with a hiss. A teenage boy in a Ruby Shores uniform, someone's son that he knew but whose name his frenzied mind couldn't remember, sat in the plush sofa playing solitaire on the coffee table. He looked pleased to see San.

"Finally, you came," he said.

"Where is she?"

"Easy, easy. She ain't here."

"I checked the festival. She's not down there either."

"Don't kill the messenger, mon." He shoved a thick stack of documents next to the playing cards towards him. "She left this. For me to hand to you and no one else."

JELLYFISH MOON

San ruffled through the papers. There was a passport with his name and picture inside. Travel papers. A valid visa. A plane ticket with all exit fees paid for. Everything was paid for. These items were so hard for a man like himself to obtain. He'd wished for them so often when Marika had left last year the memory of the yearning was like the touch of an old friend. He tore open the envelope beneath. It was full of US hundred dollar bills.

"Don't worry. It's all there," the kid said. "She paid me well."

Jellies evacuated the bay with the rising sun and the low tide. The reporter from yesterday spoke into her microphone while the cameraman panned the bay in the background.

Tents were set up under the palms. People scurried to and fro attending to the wounded and shocked tourists as best they could.

"News of this is going to be all over the world," Tal said.

Charlie came barreling down the beach on an old bicycle. He hit San over the head with a rolled up USA today.

He opened it to a big picture of Marika at the Henderson's cart.

"Stuff like this doesn't keep people away for very long. Everyone's going to want to come here now," Charlie said. "You okay?"

San shook his head. "In the Temple, I saw…" He didn't know what he had seen. His tired mind was capable of anything. Perhaps his desire for Marika had finally made him crazy.

"Listen," Charlie said. "I thought I saw a lot of things in San Raphael. Your wife she come to have a taste of native life and then she go. That's all it is. I'm sorry for you, but you've seen it happen all the time."

"It was no costume or paper-mache," San said. "The gods had come alive and had their way with her."

"Or she with them," Tal said. "She is a servant of the gods of the outsiders. Whether she knew it or not, and whether she meant it or not, she came to lure you away. Every one of us could be the lynch pin soul. The one, that if taken away will cause the rest of us to fall."

San riffled through the stack of hundreds. It was more money than he could earn in two seasons. He yearned to see Marika. But if Tal was right and he left now, there might be nothing to come back to. Only another dirty, washed up San Raphael.

"She left me a plane ticket and a fistful of cash," San said.

"Holy smoke," Charlie said. "You gonna go?"

"If I'm gonna catch the plane, I have to head to the mainland soon."

They watched the reporter at the edge of the messed up beach. Debris floated in the bay water.

"She's already left a hole in us," Tal said. "A hole big enough for an old toothy one to swim through. You can't leave now."

"Are the crocs gone?" San asked.

"Big man at the hotel say so," Tal said.

"Which means there are probably dozens and dozens of them still out there," Charlie said. "The nets are ripped up real bad."

The hotel frameworks loomed over the grim scenes playing out on the beach. The shadows of the heavy crossbeams cast mottled shapes over the tents for the wounded. He could leave right now and never see the artificial landscape these skeletal giants would mature into.

"Goodbye," he whispered, then threw a load of tackle and wire into his dugout and paddled for the nets.

Maybe someday Marika, he thought. Maybe someday the tides will bring you back to me. But for now, the moments we had will have to do.

THE NIGHT
MARCHERS

THE BIG ISLAND, HAWAI'I

Steep cliffs rose from the jagged lava rocks that ringed Captain Cook's Bay. Peaks of gray stone jutted from the lush green mountainside, the raw and exposed bones of the island itself. In the almost empty parking lot for the public dock, six Hawaiian teens stood around a weathered red pickup drinking beer. A few empty spaces away, a shiny rental car glared in the late afternoon sun. Across the lot, two younger boys sat on an old stone wall dangling their legs over the water. They faced out, towards the cliffs.

A sarong-clad woman stepped around the snorkeling gear on the dock trying to take a picture of a chubby man climbing from the water.

Max Ke Kumu watched them all as he walked into the lot. The sun shone on his bare back as if trying to coax life into his faded tattoos, angular tribal bars running from the base of his neck all the way down his lean body. When the teens saw him striding toward them they put down their beers and did their best to pretend they weren't there.

"Aloha, bruddah. Whaddsdascoups moke," they nervously greeted him in pidgin.

"Aloha," Max said.

He looked to the beers, then to the boys, then to the cliffs. The boys grinned.

"Hel-lo. Ex-cuse me," the woman in the sarong called in a saccharin sing-song. "Could you take our picture?"

Instead of answering her, the teens turned to Max and wondered if today would bring another tirade or permission to make a buck or two?

The woman walked over and handed her disposable yellow camera to Max.

"With the nice mountains in the background if you can," she said.

Max's face remained expressionless.

"It's going to be beautiful," she said, sliding her arm around the chubby man's waist.

"The bay *is* beautiful," Max said, softly.

The couple held their smile.

"Its name is Kealakekua. Which means pathway to the Gods," Max said. "It is the place where Captain Cook arrived."

Max wanted to say Cook was also killed here, a year later, but the teens depended on these *haole* tourists for money. On any given day he had a hundred reasons to hate the haoles, and some of them good ones. Captain Cook's gunboat diplomacy. The subjugation of Hawaii. That the best land, the royal land, was now mostly resorts for non-Hawaiians. But it was the presence of all these people swimming near the cliffs every day that burned him most. The bones of Hawaii's chiefs rested in hidden caves in the cliffs and it was his charge to keep them secret and safe.

THE NIGHT MARCHERS

The man squirmed and the lady cleared her throat.

Max snapped the photo.

"Uh, there is a small monument to Captain Cook up the road," he said. "The boys can take you there."

The couple quickly gathered their gear and loaded their car. The teens watched and muttered to themselves. Max knew what they were thinking; even though he didn't rant or lecture or scream this time he still managed to scare them away.

Max walked to the two boys sitting on the shore wall.

The brothers, Kenjo and Iwana, had grown since he had first seen them on the streets of Hilo running bump and grabs on locals and tourists alike. Kenjo was now tall and skinny and wore his hair in a long straight ponytail like Max. They were no longer boys but far from the confident teens who drank beer and surfed and vied for jobs at the giant hotels.

"Howzit?" Max asked.

"Good. Dakine," Kenjo said, playing with his pooka shell necklace.

"Did you have grinds?" Max asked.

"Yeah, at da place by the new hotel like you said," Kenjo answered. "Mrs. Nakamura didn't make us pay."

Good, Max thought. Hawaiians taking care of Hawaiians.

"If da snorkelers are gone for today, and nobody else is near the caves, why we still watch den?" Iwana asked.

"Because it's your turn until tonight, when I will come to take your place."

He grows bold, Max thought. There is so much I want to explain but so much to do.

Max rested his big hand on Iwana's scrawny twelve-year old shoulder. "It is an honor to protect the *alli,* your Kings," he said. "You'll understand better when you are older."

"I knew you were going to say something like that."

Kenjo's forehead furrowed. "Do you really think King Kahmehamea is watching us?"

"I know he is," Max said.

Kenjo looked down at the water. They all sat motionless, with only the sounds of the waves and the wind.

They doubt, Max thought. They have experienced nothing to make them believe. Fancy cars and jobs and hotels and satellite TV, these things are real to them, but our Kings and Queens and the system of *kapu*—everything that makes us Hawaiian—is not.

Max wanted to tell him that once he too had rejected everything Hawaiian, that he had once thought that being American was the way to go. He had dozens of stories from his years at the Department but none of them seemed right. His old life had taken him around the world and he had done many things he now regretted. He saw a better way for the boys.

After a few moments, Max stood. "See you tonight."

They are far from old enough yet, he thought. There is no one else. Soon I'll have to tell them more.

———————

Waipio's pristine white sand beaches arced between jagged cliffs in elegant semicircles. The water was calm today, though Max knew the rage it could show. Old timers still spoke of the big tidal wave of Forty-Eight that washed through the valley. Max mourned the loss of life but was grateful that since most of the survivors had relocated to the city of Hilo, Waipio valley was left free of development.

The tall, green mountains cast their long evening shadows into the valley like black lava fingers creeping over the dense treetops. A single trail, the only road in, cut a steep winding "Z" through the green. Max followed it to the bottom. Three dilapidated vacation houses surrounded by giant ferns and moss-covered trees stood lonely where the path led deeper into the valley.

The pungent smell of taro stew wafted from an open window along with the mournful, ethereal refrains of a slow Hawaiian song. Besides the vacationing locals there were few neighbors to hear it. Jack Arake offered Spartan accommodations for backpackers a ways up the trails. Retired Dutch shipbuilders had built a tree house replica of a wooden tall ship and took in a few guests per season. And a few native Hawaiians, like Lakolo Johnson, had renounced their citizenship and come to live in the wild.

The growth rustled and a backpacker emerged from the path. The young man gave a friendly nod and said, "Aloha," as he passed Max.

Max kept walking without responding.

Not all of Hawaii is their playground, he thought. They must understand.

Pink bromeliads and white orchids poked between giant oval rubber tree leaves and ferns competing for space in the dense growth. The trail wound into the valley and opened into a clearing that was once farmland but now grew thick with waist-high grass and overgrown bushes. Ragged fences, with "no trespassing" signs, lined the left side protecting rag tag houses. Lakolo Johnson's mutts ran to the fence and barked as Max passed.

"It is me," Max said, softly.

Something is wrong today, he thought, and not just because of the fences Lakolo put up. The dogs feel it too.

Max crossed the clearing. Fruit trees, overgrown and crowded with ferns and vines, stood in rows, the lonely last vestige of a plantation. A slender mongoose picked among fallen fruit from a big lychee tree. It looked at Max with alert black eyes and froze. After sniffing the air it continued nibbling.

THE NIGHT MARCHERS   Daniel Braum

Behind the trees were rows of freshly tilled earth and irrigated ditches. Green tops of taro and carrots sprouted from the muddy mounds. Just beyond, a dozen young boys kicked around a soccer ball in a patch of dirt in front of a low, long house.

"Aloha," Max called.

The boys abandoned the game and surrounded Max in a noisy pack.

"Everything's done," a boy named Akani said. "We even already had dinner."

"Good, good," Max said, then he dashed for the ball.

The boys chased him. Akani looked strong and healthy and that made Max happy. He, like all of them, had been on the street at one point or another or in situations destined for no good. Here, living with him, they didn't have much, but had a chance to grow up with their heritage. There were others who helped, like the school principal Mrs. Makana. She added real Hawaiian history to the lessons and put the kids on the rolls with no problems and no questions. It was every Hawaiian's right under law to renounce United States citizenship, but they didn't. This help was their way. Until Hawaii was strong again, their help would have to do.

"Homework done?" Max asked, guarding the ball.

"It's Friday!"

"Right," Max said. He kicked the ball then ran up the steps to the porch.

He sat on an old plastic milk crate watching the boys play in the twilight. Behind him, the front door opened into a big kitchen that took up most of the house. Even though the dishes were not done he let them be. As the shadows of overgrown fruit trees merged with the growing darkness their game changed to a kind of tag that involved chasing fireflies.

THE NIGHT MARCHERS

When they began to tire Max called them to the porch. They gathered 'round jostling for positions on the steps and against the rail.

"Another story," said Kekipi. His name had been Paul once, but Max called him Kekipi because he always had something to say.

"Estaben Cruz, Bert Marin, and da rest of da kids at school are all seeing da new Batman movie this weekend."

"An den getting PlayStation games at da Plaza."

"If that's what you want," Max said. He lit an old kerosene lamp. "I figured you are all old enough to hear different stories now. The secret ones. The ones only for grown up Hawaiians. Do you think you are grown up enough?"

"Can't we hear the stories *and* get a PlayStation?"

Kekipi's buddies punched at his arm and told him to shut up.

"Alright, alright. Listen then," Max said. "I'm going to tell you about the Kahuakai Oka Po. The Ghost Marchers of the Night."

Trees and ferns rustled in the breeze, their overlapping shadows forming twisted shapes on the porch.

"Somewhere, down by the shore, where the beach meets the valley is the doorway to the Lua O Milu, the nether region. It is a place where spirits cross to and from our world."

Flashes of mischief and delight lit up in the boys' eyes.

"Don't bother looking," Max said. "You'll never find it. Only the spirits and keepers of Hawaii's secrets know where. And don't let me catch you trying, or then we'll never go to the movies—"

"Lua O Milu. That's like hell, right?" Akani asked.

Their minds are so full of haole ideas, Max thought.

"No. It's not like hell," he said. "It simply is a place. A place where the spirits go. At the end of each month, just before dawn, if you are lucky, their phantom forms can be seen on the beach and in the valley."

A round of excited murmurs rang out from the boys.

"Then how come I've never seen them?" Kekipi asked.

A lone dog howled, followed by a chorus of barks. The boys laughed nervously.

"I want to see them. Can we go?" Akani asked.

"There are many things about Hawaii that are dangerous. And this is one of them, "Max said.

"You can take us," Akani said.

"I cannot protect you from everything," Max said. "For now, I can tell you the story. Once a year all of the ghosts gather by the doorway. A great procession of the ghosts of kings and warriors marches through the valley and then back to the doorway to enter the underworld. Any in their path will die."

"The ghosts kill them?" Kekipi asked. "You're just saying this to make sure we don't sneak out at night and nick things from Lakolo Johnson's tool shed."

"There are some things you will never see, some places you should never go," Max said. "This does not make them less real. It does not make them less worthy of your respect. Your history is real, whether you believe in it or not."

Kekipi covered his shoulder to protect against another round of dead arms but all his buddies were listening raptly.

"They don't want to hurt us, do they?" Akani asked.

"Oh, no. Not if you are good Hawaiians," Max said. "If they want anything at all it is your belief. Which is why I am telling you this story tonight. Soon I will be asking more from you. For more help protecting the island. More responsibility. And in due time, if you are good, I intend to show you."

"Cool," several of the boys said in unison, then laughed.

"You guys are baboozes. He's telling us this because there's no cash to go into town and do stuff," Kekipi said.

THE NIGHT MARCHERS

"No," Max said. "I don't think you are stupid and in need of being tricked. The Ghost Marchers are as real as the flow of lava Pele sent across the highway last month."

Something white streaked across the edge of the trees. Kekipi's smug expression changed to fear.

"I think I see one," said Akani.

Max scanned the row of trees expecting to see nothing. By the big lychee stood a woman, her long blond hair shining white in light of the moon.

"Inside. Now," Max said to the boys.

He walked down the stairs and stood there, blocking passage, as the woman crossed the muddy taro patch.

"Easy, it's me," the woman said, holding her open palms outward.

"Nicola?" Max said in disbelief, recognizing the voice.

Her hair was longer and streaked with gray, her body leaner, and her face defined with fine lines at the corners of her eyes and lips, making it stronger, more beautiful than he remembered, but it was her.

"I wasn't sure if this was the right place," she said.

"How did you find me?" Max asked.

"Your boys by the bay. Don't worry, they're fine."

Some of the boys appeared at the window, watching intently.

"Just an old friend," Max said to them. "Nothing to be afraid of."

He wanted her away from the house. He hadn't seen her since the incident at Neveshir and his last days with the Department of Relics and Antiquities. He had always thought of the Department as protectors yet in the end he concluded that at best they were nothing more than a secret squadron of grave robbers posing as soldiers. After raiding the buried city like a band of common thieves Max resigned and returned to Hawaii. Nicola stayed at the Department. Max had feared for her, for the path she was taking. Mining the past for power and wealth without respect. Without context. Without responsibility. And his fears turned out to be true. Over the years he had heard she had left the department and gone mercenary. Rumors of her more notorious jobs, like the bargain for the Yeti's Hand and the hunt for the Tasmanian Tigers, had reached him, even here. He had hoped that the rumors would be all that would find him.

"Not going to invite me in?" she asked.

"We don't get many visitors. Come, we will go somewhere to talk."

The boys looked disappointed. Max led her deeper into the valley. They walked without speaking, the path noisy with chirping frogs and geckos. Max stopped at a large mound of earth. A huge rectangular stone poked out of its top corner. Smaller rectangular stones, like a ruined wall, framed the area.

"I can't believe I am standing here talking to you," Max said. "You scared the boys."

"You knew I'd be back."

"I suppose. I hadn't given it much thought lately."

Faces carved from wood and stone rested overturned in the shadows beneath the trees; the darkness beneath their angular brows and protruding noses, blacker than the surrounding night, gave the idols a sentient quality.

"I should say, welcome, then," Max said. "Forgive me that I have no lei of flowers or grass skirt."

He searched her face for a hint of the woman he once knew. He found only the result of years of obsession in her eyes and her ropy muscles. It only meant trouble that she had come.

"Hawaii is everything you said it was," she said. "Your connection to it is spoken of in certain circles."

He didn't like the sound of that.

"Ease my mind," he said. "Tell me you are only here for me, on some nostalgic whim."

"I wish I could," she said.

In the distance the dogs barked again.

"I serve the island now. No one else."

"Same old Max. Why do you torture yourself? We were soldiers. That wasn't our fault. You're still punishing yourself."

"We broke kapu," he said. "Therefore I must—"

"...suffer the punishment, I know," she said. "Kapu. Taboo. Same thing. Break no kapu or punishment will be swift, harsh, and clear. This Hawaii you long for never sounded like such a pretty place to me. Step on the shadow of a king and be put to death. Very enlightened."

"What else do you remember?"

"A lot."

It had been twenty years since he had told her that anecdote. He thought he saw a flash of the loyal, wide-eyed girl in her eyes. Then he noticed the bulge of a gun beneath her baggy khaki pants. She was not the girl he once knew, but a stranger. A dangerous stranger. He looked away.

"The only way to subvert the will of the Kings and escape punishment for breaking kapu is to find a priest or a city of refuge before a penalty is enforced," he said. "You stand in one such place. I have sought refuge and I serve my penalty. As a priest, a guardian of the *alli,* the Kings, I can offer you a new start."

"I was hoping for some help, not salvation."

Max pictured her the last time he had seen her, in Neveshir. They were packing up all the relics for Washington. The buried city was supposed to have been empty for centuries, the realm of no one. But it hadn't been empty. The realization he had stolen an entire heritage had been his spark for change, but it had only pushed Nicola deeper into obsession and ignited her spiraling fascination with the dark, forgotten corners of the world.

THE NIGHT MARCHERS   Daniel Braum

"It is said that the bones of your Kings possess the power to—"

"Stop," Max said. "Even you must know some things are still sacred."

He scanned her posture for sign of threat, uncomfortable at how easily his old soldiers' instincts came back to him.

"I don't want to hurt you," he said, surprised by the sincerity in his words.

"I haven't come to steal," she said.

Max wanted to believe her.

Bats swooped above them, devouring mosquitoes and bugs.

Someone was running up the trail. Nicola drew her pistol.

"Put that down," Max commanded just as Akani crashed through the brush into the clearing. Seeing Nicola, the boy threw his hands in the air.

"That's one of my boys," Max screamed.

Akani leaned forward, hands on his hips, out of breath. Nicola lowered the gun.

"You know never to come here," Max yelled.

"I'm sorry," Akani said, dropping a cell phone. "Kenjo called. Someone's in the caves."

Max grabbed him by the shoulders. "How many?"

"At least three," he said, through heavy breaths. "They were up top and rapelled in with ropes. He said he was going closer to get a better look."

"Caves?" Nicola asked.

She must not know, Max thought. Everything was happening too fast.

"You did good," he told the boy. "Catch your breath. Go back to the house. Tell the boys to stay inside."

Akani stole a glance at Nicola and slowly returned to the trail.

"My boat is at the shore. I can help," Nicola said.

THE NIGHT MARCHERS

If what the boy said was true, the Kings were in immediate danger. If it came to it, she was a capable fighter, from the looks of her more capable than he. And she could get him there fast.

"Come," he said, and as soon as he spoke the word, he knew that it would cost him.

Nicola's boat, a sleek black cigarette with a pair of oversized outboard engines, was tethered to a cluster of lava rock jutting from the shore, well hidden beneath a patch of palms. Nicola retrieved a small box from her pocket, clicked it, and an array of electronics beeped and whirred to life.

Max jumped in, then Nicola, perfectly counterbalancing the rocking boat.

Just like old times, Max thought.

Nicola pulled the cords and the engines roared. The boat sped into the waves and Max opened his arms and prayed. A cloud of spray engulfed him.

How had the unthinkable happened, he wondered as they bumped over the dark water. If the caves had been found by outsiders then our belief and the island's strength has truly faltered. He tried to figure how long a head start the intruders had. A half hour? Maybe more. Enough time to reach the Kings.

When they reached the cliffs Nicola slowed the engines. Heat lightning zig-zagged in the sky. The rocky silhouette showed no sign of intruders or of Iwani or Kenjo anywhere.

The boat rocked in the waves, drifting closer to the jagged rocks lining the shore.

"A little closer," Max said.

"A little closer and we're going to be smashed."

Max moved to the edge of the boat.

He took one last look at her, searching for some sign he could trust. Finding nothing, that lost and adrift feeling he'd often had as a soldier came back to him in an awful wave.

"Do not follow," he said, then dove.

The warm water embraced him and current pulled him close to the rocks. He kicked, tight short bursts. Still he felt himself being pushed by the swells. He kicked harder, dragging himself forward with his arms. The current spun him, and then he felt himself drawn into a small space as if guided. His back touched rock and he swam up, bursting from the water into more darkness, though a breathable darkness. He allowed himself a few greedy breaths then whispered a prayer, barely audible above the echo of dripping water. He wriggled out of the water onto slick, cool rock. He breathed deep and slowed his heart. From somewhere deep in the caves came rattling and faint voices. The intruders. The chamber they rapelled into was up ahead.

Max crept toward the sounds waiting for his eyes to adjust. The rock walls glowed with faint red phosphorescence as if they were angry. The air was thick with mist. It poured off the walls and moved despite the still air. Hidden in the crevices of the passages rested the bones of Hawaii's Kings. Some were so ancient he did not know their names.

He felt his way along the wall until he found an opening.

"Forgive me, great King," Max whispered, then reached in.

He groped cool stone then felt something dry, a bone, hardened with age and sediment. He ran his hand further up till he felt an edge, the stone head of an ancient spear, resting alongside the King. Max pulled it out and held the weapon in front of him as he continued on.

Light leaked into the passage from a large chamber ahead. Max approached silently and peered inside. Mist covered the floor to knee height. In the center of the room a patch of the mist glowed an artificial blue. Max crept over and felt along the floor. A cell phone. Kenjo's. Still juiced but no signal. The boy was supposed to just watch and call. Had he followed them in, in a fit of bravery or stupidity? Max pictured the boy sliding down the ropes, tailing the intruders into the caves.

He felt cold hands close over his and the spear shook. The mist circled him as if he were the eye of an ocean storm. A burst of sulfur and hot salt air wafted past. His mind's eye filled with the image of a great King. Perhaps Kahmehamea himself.

The King stood on a beach, the black volcanic rock and sand in stark contrast to his white robe and red-feathered hat. Lava oozed into the roaring waves, sending up clouds of hissing steam.

"My Kings, I am sorry," Max said. "Forgive the failures of your humble servant."

The chamber shook. The stones groaned like breaking thunder. The vision of the King disappeared and the mist was drifting out of the room into the passageways.

"Kill them," said a voice.

Max was almost certain it had not been spoken out loud.

"Yes, my Kings," Max said, unsure if the order included Kenjo.

The boy had violated kapu by coming into the caves. The Kings would not want him to kill one of their own, would they?

The report of a gunshot rang out from up ahead. Max ran, sliding as he navigated the twists and turns, until he reached another large chamber. A jagged hole had been blasted in the ceiling allowing moonlight in. Ropes dangled from the opening, their shadows twisting and changing shape on the curved cave walls, disappearing where they crossed the black tunnel mouths. A man clad in black, like a common thief, was frantically climbing, a canvas sack slung over his shoulder. At the foot of the ropes were piles of bones.

THE NIGHT MARCHERS   Daniel Braum

Mist poured into the chamber, rising in a circle to the hole in the ceiling.

The chamber rumbled and shook, then chunks of cave ceiling gave way. The man climbing the ropes fell along with fist-sized rocks. He landed with a solid thunk. Max ignored his moaning and unwrapped the canvas. It was as he feared, inside were the bones. He lifted the spear to plunge it into the man's chest.

The spear vibrated, or was it his hand shaking? He always knew he would kill for the Kings yet he had never had to. Before him was a man, here to rob what he held most sacred. Still, he was just a man, perhaps just as he himself might have once appeared to the guardians at Neveshir.

A face appeared at the hole up above. A woman, with bright yellow eyes, her face framed in white cloth. Max caught the glint of an ankh in the moonlight as she threw the ropes down, then disappeared. Max stood frozen, spear pointed at the man who had gone silent and still.

Footsteps clomped in the side passage. Max pivoted, ready to throw, but it was Nicola who emerged from the tunnel mouth. She was carrying Kenjo in her arms. Max lowered the weapon and ran to them. In the tunnel behind them another intruder lay on the floor, bleeding.

Max touched the boy's face. "You brave fool, you never listen."

"He's more shaken up than anything, but he'll live," Nicola said.

"I told *you* not to follow," Max said to her.

"And you violated kapu by coming here," he said to the boy. "There'll be a heavy price to pay."

A glimmer of understanding lit up in Kenjo's frightened eyes.

Nicola sat the boy down against a stone and wiped the grime from his face.

The last of the mist swirled at the ceiling and exited through the jagged hole.

THE NIGHT MARCHERS

"I want to help," Nicola said.

Max said nothing and sat next to them. In the moonlight Kenjo looked so scrawny and weak and the scattered bones so old and fragile. Nicola would be of service yet, he thought. Only watching her care for the boy, he wished there was another way.

They returned to the house as the sun was rising. Max sent Kenjo to the bedroom the boys shared, and insisted he stay there and rest, though his tone implied punishment. The other boys kept trying to sneak in so they could ask him about what he had seen. Nicola and Max retreated to the porch.

"Who is she? What does she want with the Kings?" Max asked.

"All that matters is that she will take them away."

For a few moments they sat in silence. Then Max said, "No. You will tell me."

Beneath the trees, the mongoose began its daily routine of picking through the lychees.

"When you left the Department you asked me to leave it all behind and come to Hawaii with you. Well, here I am. I finally came through, at least on that part. I stayed on at the Department for years, actually. Even you wouldn't believe what wonders are out there."

"Who is she?"

The boy's shouts from a game they were playing joined the din of morning birds.

"We met not long after you left. She helped me understand why you left the Department. At first we were partners. She was a lot like us. We were excavating a route on the Old Silk Road and one of the things we unearthed touched her."

Max imagined them lifting a linen wrapped figure from some desolate desert grave—pictured it jolting to life and reaching out a dusty hand.

"Touched her?"

"She was damaged. And was never the same."

From the way Nicola avoided specifics the reality of it was likely much worse than he could imagine.

"And you led her here. You want me to think you came to stop her but you came to beat her to the find."

"Does that matter now? I am here with you."

In the chaos Nicola could have absconded with bones if that was why she was here, Max thought. But her game was always deep cover, layers upon layers. The guardians of Neveshir had also thought she was there to help, at first.

Lakolo's dogs barked. A pair of young backpackers walked past the overgrown grove.

"Thing is, Max, last night would have caught her by surprise. She didn't expect a fight. I know her ways well. Even a lion would rather scavenge a meal than fight to make a kill. Now she knows she is up against you and me and some boys."

"Then she knows we will take the bones to a new resting place."

"She'll wait for when we are most vulnerable and come for the rest of them then."

"We shall have to count on this."

"I said I will help."

Evasion. Misdirection. It was how she achieved success in the old days. Was she doing the same here? No matter, Max thought. Perhaps she might really be here to help. If not—

"Alright. You can start by helping the boys bring the canoes to the shore. We have to make a run back to the caves then get everything in place."

THE NIGHT MARCHERS

The boys were eager and full of questions.

Were there grave robbers? Did you kill them? Will we see the ghost marchers tonight?

"No," Max answered. "Not tonight. You must watch the house and look after Kenjo. Make sure he stays in his room."

The mongoose stopped and sniffed the air, watching all the commotion with its black eyes, deciding if it was safe to resume its feast.

Max's wooden canoe bobbed in the surf. The moon, reflected in the water, caressed the boat with light. Max gently lifted one of the stone urns from the caves, out of the boat and onto the shore. The sticks he had placed inside clattered faintly.

I am sorry, my Kings, thought Max. You are alone in the caves and in the hands of outsiders while we set our bait.

"You sure they are watching?" Max asked.

"She's been watching since she set foot here."

Max counted the jars then looked at the moon. He hoped it would see killing tonight.

Nicola monitored a piece of equipment, some sort of tripod mounted scope she had retrieved from her boat.

The night was alive with the sound of frogs and sets of waves breaking on the shore.

"Movement," Nicola said, and pointed to the monolithic cliffs breaking up the glittering patterns of stars.

"Up top," she said.

He didn't take her binoculars. He recognized the silhouettes of his boys, Kenjo's scrawny frame and long hair among them.

"They never listen," Max said. "Stay here, I'm going to fix this."

"No," she said, and pointed to where the trees met the sand a few hundred yards away.

A group of black-clad men emerged from the tree line. They held their handguns straight as tin soldiers and moved in a perfectly uniform line. A tiny golden ankh hung from gold chains around each of their necks. He wanted to yell to the boys to run but he hoped they'd be smart enough to figure that themselves now. Nicola reached for her weapon. Max pushed it down with his open palm.

"This time you will listen," he said.

She wants to fight, Max thought. I understand. Queen Lilohani wanted to fight when Captain Cook came, but knew it would spill her people's blood fruitlessly.

Nicola raised her hands and they allowed the men to surround them.

Their eyes were far away and unfocused as they took Nicola's pistol and searched them both. A tall man with sickly purple veins visible beneath the pale white skin of his neck signaled to the tree line. A woman emerged from their shadows. She too was dressed in thieves' black. A white turban was wrapped around her face. She stopped in front of Max, barely standing as high as his neck. A fold of the turban covered her face below her nose. The rest of her features were delicate and her skin a healthy sun-touched gold. Her amber-yellow eyes were trained on them.

She stepped closer to Nicola and Max anticipated the words he knew were coming—a smug "we meet again," or an "I win."

Instead the woman flicked her wrist at Nicola without any fanfare, sending a cloud of dust into her face. Nicola let out a single cough and collapsed to the sand, the black-clad men not reacting to her or any of the action around them.

"Do not fret. It is not so bad," the woman said to Max. "Your Kings will be safe with me. I will believe in them"

THE NIGHT MARCHERS

A hint of cinnamon, lily, and something burnt and oily scented the air.

"You will not take them," Max said.

"Have you looked at your Island? Really looked at it?" she said. "Your Kings have grown so weak. No one believes in them. I will believe in them for you."

"I will not let you rape them."

She laughed. "I will sing to them. Nourish them the way they desire."

She opened one the stone jars. Finding only the sticks, she laughed again; her breath reeked like a homeless wretch on the streets of Hilo.

"Where are they?" she asked.

Max didn't answer. The woman stepped around Nicola laying in the sand and seemed to ponder Max's silence.

"Very well," she said. "Yesterday, at the docks, I watched you take the tourists' picture. I know you want to burn the hotels down. Return to the Hawaii that was lost when Captain Cook came. Yet you do not. Instead, you tell stories to children. Dig up tikis in the jungle. Your Kings still remember blood. They will not taste it here. This battle is lost. You are part of America. Fat and mighty America sitting on you with her suntanned bottom, and you are too weak to ever shake her off. There are places where your Kings will make a difference. I will take them there."

The waves went still as if the moon had decided to let go of its hold on the tide. The chorus of night sounds went silent.

In the back of his mind Max thought that he should be bothered by her words, only he was captivated by the layer of white mist floating just above the surface of the water. It thickened and rolled along the beach.

"You are haole," Max said. "Truly without breath. The Kings do not care for whatever your petty plans may be; they care for the wind and water. Fire and stone. For the Island they fought for and its sons and daughters."

The woman grabbed a pistol from the nearest man and cocked it, the click unnaturally resonant in the silence. "I wonder, do you really know your Kings at all?"

Max didn't flinch from the gun and the woman seemed confused. Then she saw the cloud of white surrounding them and jerked her gun to the side. Her men spun around, pointing their guns in all directions.

The mist coalesced into wispy bodies. Long lines of translucent ghosts were assembling along the shore. Grim, blank-eyed faces on the ones nearest. The procession of Kings appeared in the surf. Long robes trailed behind them. Max couldn't tell where the robes ended and the dark-green water began.

"Great Kings. Soon I will have all of your bones and—"

Max lunged for her. Then someone fired and the night erupted into wet pops like dud firecrackers followed by the metallic click-clicks of dozens of futile trigger pulls.

Max tackled the woman and they rolled in the sand, his hands finding their way around her neck. A pair of misty hands solidified around his. The mist formed an arm and then a body. Max thought he'd feel a sense of awe being so close to the Kings but all he felt was blood-lust, the need to wring the life from this intruder.

As he choked her he watched the other Kings reach for the men. The King's faces were stern, strong, and regal but blank, like an idealized picture and not the faces of real men. Bullets whizzed through their round, feathered hats.

I've been calling myself a peaceful priest when all along I was always just a killer, Max thought. Maybe the boys will grow up to have the luxury of hands that do not know death.

THE NIGHT MARCHERS

The men dropped their guns and fell to the sand, coughing and clutching their throats. Beneath Max, the woman gasped for breath. Her turban had slipped down. The bottom of her face was shriveled and wrinkled, like a shrunken head. Blackened teeth stuck out from turned out lips. Max could see how the scar almost formed a handprint, a slap immortalized in ruined flesh. She muttered in a foreign tongue with the last of her air.

Max squeezed the life out of her and a wave of nausea welled in his gut. It had been decades since he had killed. This felt different and horribly right. She was wrong to think she could take the Kings but she was right that they lusted for blood. He knew it now. With his hands around her neck he was in tune with them, an instrument of their desire.

The Kings turned to where Nicola lay on the sand among the dead.

Max moved in front of the great King. Max saw the veins in his feathered hat, the pores and scars on his solemn face, the tattooed bars and triangles on his arm as his hand reached out.

"No! This one defended you," Max said.

The surf bubbled and hissed as if lapping over molten lava.

"Intruder," said a voice, though neither the King's mouth nor opaque eyes moved.

"I am your priest. And I say spare her," Max said. "Without me there is no one."

The ghost raised its other hand and Max flinched. When he opened his eyes, the Kings were gone and the mist had rolled down the beach.

Nicola's eyes fluttered under shut lids. She moaned as Max pulled her away from the rising surf. His relief only lasted a heartbeat. The procession had moved toward the mountains, towards where the boys were still watching. Max ran, hoping to intervene again. The ghosts disappeared and reappeared on the mountain in the blink of an eye. Heat lightning flashed, and the sulfuric smell of lava, tinged with burnt flowers wafted past him. Max watched the boys scatter. He watched Kenjo's scrawny form in silhouette drop to his knees before the King.

"Run," Max said. He didn't have the breath to shout.

"He's just a boy. One of us."

Maybe they didn't hear. Maybe there was no place for mercy for one who should have known kapu.

Max sprinted but it was too late. Kenjo's body went slack. The procession of ghosts disappeared over the peak.

On the beach, the last tendrils of mist receded from the fallen intruders. The surf's murmur had returned and the chirp of geckos and peepers again filled the night. Up on the mountain, the boys were screaming.

The wind hissed through the palms shading Nicola as she slept. Monstrous orange birds of paradise and white orchids sprouted among the overturned tiki and remnants of an old stone wall.

Max stood in the shade, a lei of fresh flowers in his hands. He waited and watched as she opened her eyes.

"Good. You are awake," he said, his face rigid as one of the chiseled idols.

"I brought you to this city of refuge. I now offer you a chance to repent."

Nicola rubbed her eyes and brought her hand to her neck. "You're serious?"

"The Kings yearn for your blood. I hear their whispers in the shadows and the waves. This is your chance."

Nicola rose, slowly, sleepily and paced the borders, careful not to walk outside the line of stones.

THE NIGHT MARCHERS

"I'm leaving and will return later with your supper. Should you stay your first task is to begin to clean this place up. Clear the idols. Repair the wall. While you are working, think of your best stories for the boys. Only the true ones. They can be about me if you wish."

"I can just walk away?"

"Whenever you wish," he said. "The choice is yours. Leave without my absolution and I think they will find you."

Max knelt, carefully picked a white orchid, added it to the lei, and left her.

Max held the lei over Kenjo's grave.

"Will I see you draped in these next procession?" he said. "Someday, I will join you. But not yet, not yet."

Back at Kealakekua Bay Iwana and Kekipi were giving a tour. The real Hawaii, they called it. After what they had witnessed, they had been studying diligently. And talking a lot to the old timers.

Captain Cook's ship rested somewhere at the bottom of the bay. Someday all trace of the metal and wood would be gone, but the cliffs and caves would still remain.

Iwana and Kekipi didn't think that far ahead. They mourned the loss of their brother and friend and struggled to make sense of kapu and why it was he and not them.

He draped the flowers over the stone and walked away.

"It is a start, my Kings," Max said. "A start."

THE MOON AND THE MESA

Jamie and I have claimed a little bit of elbowroom. I can't hear her, or anyone very well, but that's okay. The bartender has his eye on her, as do most of the showboats drinking twenty-dollar cocktails at the bar. She's dressed down, for her, but even still, I'm very aware of her simple black top that doesn't even come close to hiding her curves.

We're silent. People-watching. Together. The wordless space between us is comfortable and familiar. The extension of a frankness and trust born of being drunk as sin together more times than I can count. My hands remember how they want to touch her but as always they stay at my side, obediently under dominion of my mind, my higher self, despite the alcohol.

Two guys at the bar are staring right at her. Both tall and blond. Their crisp shirts tightly tucked into well-tailored dark slacks. This bar is full of Euro-trash like them. It's why she brought me here. Midtown on a Saturday is always good for hunting.

Jamie's noticed their stares and encourages them with her smile. They come over. I didn't even have to say a word.

"You from here?" tall and blue eyes asks her.

"Why do you ask?" She tosses a ringlet of her long black hair.

They laugh and mutter something quickly in German.

"I'm Heinrich and this is Klaus. Klaus wants to know if this is your boyfriend?"

"My boyfriend? Oh no, no, no." She touches my arm. "Just my friend David. And he looks thirsty. Klaus, why don't you go get us a round?"

She plays with the silver chain disappearing beneath her shirt, like she always does when it begins. I used to think it was just a flirty habit, until the first time I saw the silver Star of David. Must be from her grandparents. Looks very old country. I never asked. I never needed to.

"So, are you New Yorkers?" Heinrich asks. He *so* wants to tell us he is traveling. He's dying to tell us all about what it's like for him to be in New York. I've seen it a hundred times before. For a second I almost feel bad but a childhood image of my grandmother prevents me.

A thin line of drool hangs from the corner of her mouth as she sits blankly on the couch in the house I grew up in. Often she'd spend the night during the High Holy days and when I'd get up in the night for water or to sneak a cookie I'd catch her unplugging appliances and asking the refrigerator questions about guard locations. Sometimes she'd just go on and on in Yiddish, her eyes all freakily far away.

"Where do *you* think *we're* from?" Jamie asks.

"Uh, here. New York, of course," he says.

"Nope."

Jamie and I laugh. He doesn't get it. He can't. There's nothing funny about it, except him and the way *she* said it. I've been worried about her lately and there's something different about the way she laughs tonight. Like the start of a twisted belly laugh she won't be able to stop.

After a second he laughs too, pretending to get it. His eyes dart to the line of skin showing between her shirt and her jeans.

THE MOON AND THE MESA

"Where do you think I'm from?"

Jamie starts to talk, but I interrupt. I'm more than worried about her taking it too far. Tonight I want to be the one.

"Wait, wait, wait," I say. "I know. I know, don't tell me. I have it between two places—"

"Just say," he says.

"Uh, I'm not sure. Say something. Say like, Florida Oranges. Say, the rain in Spain falls mainly on the plain."

He does. He's enjoying it. We're enjoying it more. Klaus is back with our drinks, trying to figure out what he missed.

"Fuck. I'm so close," I say. "It's right on the tip of my tongue. Okay. Whatever. New Jersey?"

His face is still smiling but the cheer has left.

"Where?" he asks.

"New Jersey. Around Hoboken. Right?"

Jamie's disappointed. I can tell she wanted to keep it going longer. As in all the way back to her apartment.

"I was thinking Jersey City," Jamie says, stirs her pink drink, tastes it, then licks her lips.

"No," he says, his smile now a forced grin.

"Damn, I should have gone with my second guess, Nashville, right? I should have heard that Tennessee accent right away."

"No. I'm from Hamburg. Klaus is from Vienna."

"Really?" Jamie says. "You look like Jersey boys."

They stare, not sure what to say.

I turn my back to them and make mindless small talk with Jamie. I make it a point to touch her shoulders, her arms, her back with every sentence. After a minute Klaus and Heinrich meld back into the crowd of showboaters. Jamie's pleased. Our stupid trick slams their type every time. But I know this wasn't why she came.

"That was great," she says and leans in for a kiss.

THE NIGHT MARCHERS   Daniel Braum

Her mouth barely touches mine. Her lips don't mean it. She doesn't mean it. It's just another song and dance, steps in a connect-the-dots that is supposed to form a picture of normalcy, but never does. Beneath I suspect she's nothing. Nothing but something very broken with no idea how to even begin to reassemble. I don't even want to think about what that makes me then.

"Fucking Nazis," she says in my ear. "It was too fast. Didn't you want to take them home?"

Her new Glock is at home. She keeps it on her pillow, its angles and blackness obscene among the plush get up, like a sex toy among teddy bears. She tells me about it when we talk on the phone and I sense her staring at it when she's supposed to be listening. Someday soon, she's gonna use it. She's right, it was over too fast. We've done much, much better, and I thought that someday soon might have been tonight.

We push our way through the hot maze of cologned bodies and emerge into the relative quiet of the street. She fishes in her purse. Instead of taking out a pack of cigarettes she pulls out the little black gun. She holds it up admiring it in the streetlight.

"Didn't you want to take them home? Didn't you want to—"

"Aw fuck. What the hell are you doing with that? Don't take it out here!"

I snatch the gun and stuff it back into her purse.

"Hey. Easy there," she says. "Don't you dare tell me you're not going to. You said."

She's much too calm. It's that calmness that scares me.

"I know I said and I'm going to," I say.

"When then? Tomorrow?"

"I already called Larry. He's in. Not tomorrow, but soon. Real soon. For real. I promise."

214

THE MOON AND THE MESA

"Take it, then."

She kisses me. This time for real. And she deftly slides the gun into the waist of my slacks. It feels horrible against my skin, but I let it stay, savoring the floral shampoo smell of her hair and her hot alcohol breath on my ear before she pulls away.

───────────

Larry flips through my stack of pictures stopping at a black and white landscape of a lonely mesa.

"That's a good one," Larry says.

"Is it?" I ask.

"Yeah. Fuck, yeah."

This is where *he* tends bar. I brought Larry because he is strong. A black-belt now. And smart, but just dumb enough to listen to me. We're both in from the City for Rosh Hashanah family obligations.

"What the hell were you doing out there?" Larry asks.

"Dworkin was looking for the place on the map farthest away from everything. The place the farthest away from any city—the place with the least sky glow so we could see the stars. He wanted to fulfill a dream to lay on his back in the middle of the night in the desert and play the guitar as loud as he could. I wanted to take pictures, so I was in."

That's what I say but really I was doing everything I could to avoid coming here. Now that I'm back, Jamie's having no more excuses.

───────────

Dworkin found the place on the map, a secluded campground near the Reservations on the Arizona-Utah border. He said to meet him in the airport in Flagstaff. He'd take care of the rest. He rented a little Honda four-by-four and packed it full of his instruments, camping gear, and a gas generator.

The place on the map turned out to be a crowded trailer park. So much for the power of Triple-A. I mean we were so freakin' tired we just drove on in, pulled into our spot and went to sleep. We woke up in the morning and realized we were surrounded by RV's. What a nightmare.

("That must have sucked," Larry says.

"It did.")

So we just rolled on, figuring we'd hit the scenic drive through Monument Valley, cruised the Rez, and found a new spot.

Highway 166 turned into County Road 75 and took us into the heart of the Rez. Signs admonished that we were leaving the U. S. of A. and entering Navajo-land, to stay on the road unless given permission.

The road snaked into the deep, wide chasm that is Monument Valley, a white line weaving into hundreds of ancient red-rock formations. Two Native American dudes waited at a roadblock, a two-by-four laid across the road, collecting a toll. We paid and followed the road and pulled off at the most awesome little vista as it began to wind its way down.

Two mini-buses took up all the spaces in the small parking area. A few dozen wheelchair-bound people were jostling into position for a group photo. Two aides were helping them line up. One of them, a blond, in denim shorts and a white cut-off shirt, was walking backwards, looking into a camera instead of where she was going.

Dworkin hit the brakes yet she walked right into us.

"Move," she said to Dworkin along with something in German that I took to be curse words.

THE MOON AND THE MESA

("Dworkin Spreken-ze Duetsch?" Larry asks.

"No. But you know Dworkin. He doesn't like to be told what to do.")

So I told him just to chill, get his guitar, and to trust me. I jumped out of the car and asked the woman if she'd like to get in the photo. The wheelchair crowd was watching the exchange like a television program.

She handed the camera over to me. Since I couldn't fit them all in the frame, I climbed on top of the Honda, noisily going right over the hood and onto the roof. They all cheered. And it was a hell of a photo. The blond. All the wheelchairy people. And in the background one crazy-ass bird's eye view of Monument Valley and its majestic mesas and winding roads snaking into the corners of Navajo Country. It's the kind of sight that makes you believe in God.

So Dworkin lightened up and is posing for pictures with everyone, hamming it up doing Elvis impersonations and windmills on his guitar, just getting them to be silly and shit.

The German chick is having a smoke behind the bus. She's staring at this mesa. Fucking beautiful. The mesa. Like Devil's Tower from Close Encounters. A flat top. Sloping sides. All red rock, the shadows constantly shifting and the tones changing as the clouds crossed the sky.

"That was good," she says. Her German accent is thick and she speaks slowly.

She's enjoying her cigarette like it's her last. She looks me up and down and wasn't shy about it. Really casual and unashamed, like Europeans are. I could sense her sizing me up, deciding what to think. I wished I wasn't covered in sweat and all the red dust that was everywhere.

"That was very good, for them," she says. "They loved it."

"How long's this show been on the road?" I ask.

"Two months," she says. "We're heading to Disneyland and are flying back to Germany out of L.A. Just came from the Grand Canyon."

"Fuck. Two months," I say. "I've only got two weeks."

"Fuck is right. You Americans need to learn to take more time."

"It's been good?"

"I get to see the states, for free. But not a lot of people to talk to, eye to eye. Where you staying?"

"Not sure. Somewhere around here, we hope. My friend brought his guitar to play out here in the middle of nowhere. I'm gonna take pictures."

"Cute," she says. The fine white hairs on her stomach are coated with red dust. She has a faded scar running along the left of it. I wonder if it was a C-section.

"We're up at the lodge in the little tourist trap up the road," she says. "Just for tonight. I'm sharing a room with the other two so you can't meet me there."

"I'd invite you for a drink or something but well, you know. Can I buy you a water?"

"Just meet me at the mesa. Tonight. After midnight."

"I'd hang with you guys more often if I knew you rolled like this," Larry says.

"Okay. So why don't you?"

"I dunno. Work. And I've been the one stuck taking Grandpa to fucking chemo."

Larry's grandfather escaped from Dachau. And then went back. Became part of the underground railroad smuggling escapees into

Italy. I remember when Spielberg's people came to the city to interview him and other survivors.

"He's become so small," he says.

The bartender looks over. It's him. No doubts at all. I can feel the blows in my gut. See his face as a boy, standing over me. It wasn't easy for Larry and I being the only Jews in our grade. And there never was any other reason needed to chase us after school. Sometimes they'd catch me.

"That's him, right?" Larry says.

"Yeah."

"You sure?"

"Yup. We gonna do this?"

"Uh, yeah."

"All right. A couple more beers then. We wait till it empties out."

"Okay."

I think of Jamie out hunting in the city without her new gun and the unlucky fucker who thinks he's found a hot date.

Larry's putting 'em away to mask his nervousness. I keep the beer flowing and the story going to prevent any second thoughts.

———————

So we leave the overlook and cruise on into the Valley. We spend the day looking at stuff and taking photos. Dworkin's getting antsy and has his guitar on his lap in the front seat.

There really isn't any place to camp. And we're not supposed to just pull off on the side of the road but come late afternoon we pull over anyway. Dworkin has to piss and runs off behind a big rock. I walk a ways up the road with my camera. There's a fence and a little stable. A white horse absently flicks its tail at flies in its shade.

I raise my camera to take a shot and notice there is a man in a ten-gallon white hat standing in the shadows. The hat and his clothes are stained red from sand.

"Didn't see you there. Sorry," I say. "Can I take a photo?"

He emerges from the shed without answering. He's a white guy or maybe he once was. His old skin's wrinkled, leathery and tan, and marked with spots of age. His shirt is stretched thin to its fibers.

"I dunno," he says. His mouth is almost toothless. "I shouldn't let you but it's been a dry one. The horse needs hay and all."

I think about this for a second.

"I don't have any hay, but how about a couple of bucks?"

"That'd be fine, fella."

I hand him a couple of bills and snap the picture of the horse. Dworkin has come out from behind the rock.

"What you boys doing here?" the man asks.

"Looking for a place to stay. He wants to play his guitar as loud as can be in the middle of the desert. I'm gonna take pictures."

"'lectric guitars? You boys got power?"

"Yup. A generator. He thought of everything."

"Hmmmn. All this land is in the care of my boss, Mr. Yiskil. I suppose maybe if you had some gas money or what not it'd be okay for you to stay. You don't look like trouble. I could ask him."

"Sounds good."

"'K then. Be right back."

He disappears behind the shed and a few seconds later pulls out in the ricketiest pick-up truck you can imagine.

It arcs across the desert throwing up clouds of red sand behind it. It's just a far away speck when it stops. I can make out a little trailer in the distance.

Three vultures are high overhead sweeping around the mesa in long lazy circles. Small holes are everywhere at the bases of all the cacti. Snake holes. Spider holes. Homes for the world of things that come alive at night.

Fifteen minutes later the pick-up returns. Our host steps out and leaves the door open. The most beautiful long feather hangs from the rear view mirror. It's white and flecked with a dozen shades of brown, like from an owl. An eagle, maybe.

"My boss don't think you're here for the music, but that's okay. You can play as loud as you like. You won't bother nobody. He hopes you find what you are looking for in the desert. You can't sleep under the moon and the mesa and not be changed. Pitch your tent anywhere you like."

In the distance I see a man standing motionless by an old trailer. Mr. Yiskil, maybe. I sense I am in the presence of something very, very old and primal. Not just the ancient stone. I feel it watching. For a second I envision Jamie and me returning here, holding hands, smiling in a normal way.

"If anyone gives you any trouble just say you have the permission of Mr. Yiskil and you are under his protection. You know, sometimes guys get drunk and might pull that white man can't be here shit on you. Remember to say that."

I pull out a fifty from my wallet. Dworkin takes out a twenty.

"That's a lot of gas money. Mr. Yiskil will be pretty happy."

I hand the bills to him.

My father places a few dollar bills in my hand for my brother and me, crisp ones, good for the vending machines in the basement.

We spend every other Sunday at the home where grandma is. I hate it there. Even the ocean right across the boardwalk, the tons of bleach and antiseptic can't mask the smell of old sick bodies.

THE NIGHT MARCHERS   DANIEL BRAUM

I have to kiss grandma hello and stay for a few minutes, then I'm free to go.

Grandma usually sits blankly, drooling, her old clothes smelling of mothballs. Her scraggy white hair barely combed. Sometimes we play gin rummy. She's good at gin rummy. She calls out "Rummy" in a thick Russian accent.

Today she is waiting for us at the door, her coat on, her bag packed.

"How can you bring the kids here? To such a place like this" she says to my father.

She grabs my wrist and runs. The strength of her grip surprises me.

"Let her go. Don't scare her," an orderly says.

She turns the corner and tries to hide us in the janitorial closet. She's muttering the S'hma prayer. Does she think we're going to die?

I see the green tattoo of numbers on the inside of her arm just above her wrist. I don't want them to touch my skin.

My arm is red and mottled with little bumps from so much sweating. The heat of the day has gone with the sun—vanished with the warm wind sweeping from the mountains into the valley—a wake-up call to the sleeping creatures of the night. The air is alive with bats. Coyotes prowl on distant mesa tops. I don't see them but I sense them waiting for the rising moon and I want to hear one howl like in the movies.

"No glove, no love," Dworkin taunts as I leave to hike to the mesa. Then he gets serious. "I need this time. Thanks. But come back later, I'd love a photo or two."

The moon rises over the mesa, drenching the night in a white glow. The cacti. The scrub. A steer skull with broken horns. A shell of a pick-up truck half buried in red sand. They all take on a new starkness and poignancy. Being here I feel I am like them. A survivor. Even if I've done nothing else to earn it besides being born.

This close the mesa is huge, a monolithic fist rising from the earth. It dwarfs me and the sea of cactus and all the creatures who run the course of their lives at its feet.

With the oppressive heat gone, the desert is alive with life. Things can flourish in the night. Movement is everywhere. Kangaroo rats scurry to and from their holes. Coyote disappear among the cactus and I hear them yipping and snarling somewhere else nearby. Things rustle in the scrub. Lizards and snakes. I try to watch where I step. A shiny black scorpion crosses my path with a lizard twice its size impaled on its stinger tail.

Without the noise of the city, without my ringing phone and the bombardment of ideas from billboards and TV I notice that the world is a quiet place. I sense their absence. The open road has opened someplace in my mind.

Dworkin's chords echo off the mesa. I wonder if I could ever convince Jamie to come here with me. I wonder what my grandmother would have looked like had she lived till a ripe old age. Would my family still be in Europe if it weren't for the war? If so, what would have become of me?

Someone is sitting on a big rock at the foot of the mesa. I close the distance and realize it is a thick cactus—its spiky arms emulating a rag-doll human shape in the shadows and moon-glow.

Then I see her. The German Girl. She's on a plateau just up the slope. She's wearing the same white shirt and shorts. Not a speck of red dust anywhere. Her legs are crossed and she's leaning back on her arms. She's as motionless as the cactus.

I feel myself get excited. Then I stumble. My vision wavers and threatens to go black. I should have brought more water.

THE NIGHT MARCHERS DANIEL BRAUM

I climb the slope and park myself next to her on the rock. With the change of vantage I can see the maze of cactus and rock. The nighttime city.

The moon-glow has smoothed over her scar. The tiny lines around her eyes are gone. I want to hear her talk. Hear her accent.

"What are you thinking," I say, to get her talking.

She shakes her head no and places her finger over her lips. The movement is meticulous and as fluid as an ant cleaning its mandibles. Her breasts are fuller than I remembered this afternoon. Her legs longer. Smoother. There's not a drop of sand on her.

That sense of proximity to primal-oldness fills me and like that I realize she's not the German girl. I try to scoot away but I am frozen. It looks just like her, whatever the fuck it is. It's pretty blond-haired head slowly turns, fluidly, not a drop of movement from the rest of her.

Am I talking to myself? Am I like my grandmother? Mad and talking to things no one else can see?

Green numbers appear on her moon-white skin. The arm becomes Jamie's and now it is Jamie sitting next to me. She's caressing her gun as if it were a lover's hand.

"No, you're not crazy," the Jamie-thing says. "What's crazy about wanting to make them suffer? Don't you want to kill them all?"

Dworkin's chords erupt into an obscene grinding riff. The moon is just above the mesa top. A perfect round companion to its unyielding square-topped form.

Now I see my grandmother. The smell of her is too real. Mothballs and bleach and stale fish and sweat and drool.

"I'm tired of this," I say. "I want to stop fighting."

"So stop," it says. It doesn't sound like my grandmother at all. It sounds like some bird from the zoo that has learned how to talk.

THE MOON AND THE MESA

Her mouth is black and inside something glows like a far away star. Thorny spines poke from her flesh.

Her skin shines like a scorpion's in the moonlight. She takes my hand. Her grip is stronger than I expect. She pulls me to her kiss and tastes bitter, like fried cactus. My heart races and I think I am going to be swallowed and die, my bones left to be covered by the sand. But I can't stop kissing it and as I do I'm filled with the oddest notion that a scorpion isn't evil. It just is. It stings and kills because it is its nature. I wonder if what Jamie does is *her* nature. And if what she wants me to do, and why I have come here tonight is mine. No it's just a justification. It's all wrong. Nothing changes that. Then I remember Mr. Yiskil and I break away.

"I'm here with Mr. Yiskil," I say. "I have his permission."

It smiles. Then I am sitting alone. Just the thorny rag-doll cactus next to me.

I look away and see a woman climbing the slope. The German girl. She's in cut-off jeans and a purple Mexican poncho.

"Here with who?" the German girl says, climbing up the rocks. Yiskil knew it would boil down to her and me. This is why I am here. Alone, I feel like I am the scorpion now. But I get the sense I'm still being watched by the cactus-thing, the looming mass of the mesa its eyes.

"Guess you've been waiting long? You look like you need a fuck even more than me."

I start to ramble. She tells me to shut up. She takes my hand. Hers is solid but surprisingly tender, her skin slightly damp with sweat, welcomingly cool on my burnt skin.

Somehow I know whatever it is that is watching cares about nothing that has or will happen here. The drama of my life meaningless as another lizard succumbing to a poison sting.

I sing along with Dworkin's chords in the distance.

"Your friend sucks," she says. A mechanical crackle disrupts the riff and one final guitar chord rings out and fades into the canopy of sound that is the desert night.

An owl lifts silently from its perch on a cactus at the foot of the mesa, a squirming mouse in its talons.

This is where Jamie would turn it around. This is where Jamie would take her down. This is where we kiss.

I roll on top of her, press her shoulders into the ground. Her hands dig into my back. We shed our clothes, two more creatures of the desert naked in the sand. Our sounds drown in the crackles of Dworkin unplugging his guitars.

Last call went out and the last of the patrons slipped out the exit. It's just Larry and me and *him*. Larry's good and drunk. So am I.

"So you fucked her right and let her go? Right?"

The bartender looks over at us and walks over cradling three beers.

I shoot Larry a look that says get ready.

"David. Larry. Thought it was you two. We're closed but I can stay open for one more, that is if I can join you."

Larry's face is red but not from the alcohol. He's remembering. School. His grandfather. The fucked up world. Me a part of it. The biggest part of right now. He'd rather be anywhere but here. I know. Yet here we are.

A text pops up on my phone. It's from Jamie. "Did you do it yet? Tell me. xoxo—J."

"How long has it been?" he asks. "Heard you went off to college and the city."

He swigs a beer.

THE MOON AND THE MESA

Jamie's gun feels horrible against my skin. I want that feeling to go away. I'm tired of it.

"I'm sorry, you know. I'm really sorry," he says, ingenuously. "I was such a stupid kid."

I believe him.

"I'm sorry too," I say. And he's saying something. Talking with Larry but I'm back at the mesa, looking into the blackness of that thing's mouth, watching the German girl trudge away from the mesa back towards her lodge. I remember how I stifled one last urge to follow, one last urge to surrender to the scorpion's nature, but then let her disappear into the alien, moon-lit landscape of the desert night.

THE SPHINX OF CROPSEY AVENUE

Nathan is about to hit Exit 13 on the Belt Parkway when the Sphinx of Cropsey Avenue lumbers onto the westbound lanes. She's at least as tall as the house in Canarsie he grew up in. That would put her three stories high at her shoulder. A story equals a floor, right? He can never keep that straight. He's heading to the house now. He doesn't want you to know the address. His mom still lives there and he thinks his line of work can be dangerous.

The Sphinx's lion body is twice as long as she is high. Her golden hair, straight and even, hangs just past her round, feminine shoulders. Her back is bare. Patches of dirty snow and ice that accumulated from sitting motionless on Cropsey Avenue for the last few weeks still remain on it. She's walking diagonally across the lanes heading for the swampy beach on the other side of the Belt so he can't see her face.

Nathan hits the brakes to avoid the stopped cars. With his right hand he instinctively reaches for Kirk. Kirk is Yael's six-year-old son. The reason Kirk is even in the car at all, is because Yael didn't come home last night. Again. Nathan's late to meet the broker at his mom's house. He couldn't leave Kirk so he took him along. Nathan and Yael are lovers. For now.

"You okay?" Nathan says.

"Yeah, of course," Kirk says.

Nathan looks over to make sure.

"She's so big. I've never seen one up close."

"Me neither," Nathan says.

"What are they?" Kirk asks.

"No one knows," Nathan says.

"A mystery?" Kirk asks.

"Yeah, very good," Nathan says. "A mystery. Something like that."

"If you ask it a question it's supposed to tell you the truth, right?"

"Where'd you hear that?"

"TV," Kirk says.

"I think it's supposed to be if you answer a Sphinx's riddle it's supposed to tell you the truth," Nathan says.

But he knows the way it goes is that if you correctly answer the riddle you are allowed to pass, and live.

"Is it true?" Kirk asks. "Can they talk?"

"No," Nathan says.

He meant to say no one knows. Because no one does.

What in the world are you, he wonders. And why the hell are you here?

For a second he thinks the Sphinx of Cropsey Avenue has stopped in response to his musing. But no. It is only that her left front paw is caught on a car, her first step into the eastbound lanes. Her hair does not move in the breeze as she crosses. Stopped cars in her path are crushed underfoot. She lumbers onto the shoulder, then onto the marsh and stops on the sand at the water's edge facing east. She settles down on her rear legs and tucks her front legs in front of her. Like a cat. In that sphinx pose. Her face is beautiful. Chiseled cheek bones. Small eyes. Thin brows. Symmetrical thin lips with only a hint of pinkish red. Her eyes, all the parts of her eyes, are different shades of white. Her breasts are smooth half globes without nipples, centered in her chest. All her human parts are perfectly white. Perfect alabaster white only covered with the grimy patina of Canarsie. Sandy brown lion fur covers her to her mid-navel.

Scars and matted patches mar her fur. In the fall, he and Yael took Kirk to the zoo. The big lion's fur wasn't perfectly uniform like a cartoon and Kirk had asked what's wrong with him. Nathan didn't know how to explain that the cuts and skin irritations and scars, like our skin, bore the telltale signs of the lion's daily struggles. "It's real," was all that he could think to say.

Only when he's watching the Sphinx later on the news, with his mom, will she seem unreal to Nathan. Right now she seems the most natural thing in the world to him, just sitting there in sphinx pose on the shore on the side of the Belt Parkway. The gray and black patches of dirty snow on her back and on the sides of the road contrast with the cleaner white snow of the beach.

A news helicopter circles overhead. Sirens in the distance grow louder. One lane of eastbound traffic is crawling forward. Nathan hopes Kirk doesn't ask if the people in the crushed cars are okay. He sees that some have gotten out unscathed but he's not sure about all of them. His heart slows in relief that Kirk is unharmed.

Later, after Nathan's mom's pain subsides and they are just talking, she will say "I don't understand how it moves," in the same perplexed tone she uses when she says she doesn't understand how a fax sends a piece of paper from one telephone to another. Nathan does not understand the sphinx but somehow it feels right sitting on the side of the parkway he has traveled countless times before.

THE NIGHT MARCHERS   DANIEL BRAUM

Kirk rolls down the window and barks at the Sphinx. The air smells of ocean salt and car fumes. It is the first non-freezing day since the big January storm and all the ice has begun to melt. Spring is two weeks away. Nathan hopes when it comes things will feel lighter. His mom has finally agreed to move but he won't believe it till it's done. Kirk likes to pretend he is a puppy more and more these days and that worries Nathan even more.

———————

Nathan parks behind the house where he grew up, in the alley between East Eighty Fifth Street and East Eighty Fourth Street. The "alley" is wide enough for two lanes of traffic and to park cars, the long way, on each side. So it's more like a road. An unnamed, unnumbered road. He always thought that was cool. And that the house number was lucky. He trusts you a little more now, enough to know the streets but not the house number. Nathan's boss confirmed the number was lucky when he ran checks on him when he first started work. Numerology. Astrology. Past lives. Susceptibility to suggestion. Those sorts of things.

Nathan opens the car trunk to get the video cassette he has brought for his mom. She still uses a VCR and has trouble programming it. Nathan grabs the tape labeled "Ruthie's shows".

"Cool, what's that?" Kirk says and reaches for the black rectangular case among the small cardboard packages in the trunk.

Nathan gently moves Kirk's hand away. He wants to say don't touch that. Don't touch any of it, it's dangerous. But he knows that will only pique Kirk's interest.

"It's just junk," Nathan says. "Boring."

In the case is a rifle. His boss gave it to him. So far it has never been used but his boss wants it there just in case. The packages are

232

from his boss too. He thinks the packages are even more dangerous than the gun. Two of the packages have been in his trunk for weeks without instruction where to drop them. One of them vibrates and rattles of its own volition from time to time even though he knows nothing can be alive in there. The other one makes him feel cold when he touches it and once he thought he heard the most unearthly whisper coming from it. He hopes these packages aren't just in case also.

Nathan closes the trunk and he and Kirk walk through the alley to wide concrete stairs filling the space between the house he grew up in and the neighboring houses. All are three stories high and attached. This is the only break. Besides the driveways on either side, this is the spot where you get out of the alley. A pack of teens are tromping down the stairs. They stop and fan out, blocking the way.

"Hey mister. Can I get a few bucks?" the tallest one says.

"Sorry. No," Nathan says.

"I don't think you heard me," the teen says. "Gimme what you got."

Nathan is infuriated. The neighborhood wasn't like this when he was growing up. He feels his temper rising and that makes him angrier. He steps in front of Kirk to protect him.

"Get out of my way," Nathan says. "Don't make me hurt you."

Nathan's father taught him how to punch. You have to punch back or you'll always be scared, he had said. Now Nathan is scared of hurting them. And of Kirk seeing him lose control.

The teen pushes him. Nathan pushes back. The teen falls. His tailbone connects with the concrete step so hard Nathan can feel the hurt. Another one lunges. Nathan grabs his arm and pulls, sending him careening forward and down. The teen knocks his head as he tumbles down the ten steps to the bottom. The rest of the pack scatters.

"You okay?" Nathan says to Kirk.

Kirk nods his head. But Nathan sees he is trying not to cry.

"I don't want to go to Morocco," Kirks says with a sob.

"Don't worry, no one's going to Morocco," Nathan says. "Here. I want to show you something. See that tree?"

Nathan points to the mimosa tree in the small yard and they walk up to it.

"In a few weeks those buds are going to open and become pink flowers. Sort of like dandelions. But weirder. And pink."

Kirk looks up at the two forked boughs.

"Yeah. It's a good tree for climbing," Nathan says.

The branches rise a little past the second story into the space above the stairs between the terrace and the neighboring terrace. Nathan's mom is on her terrace. She'd been watching. Her home health care lady wheels her inside to greet them. He hopes she didn't hear what just happened. Part of him hopes she did.

Nathan holds Kirk's hand as they climb the steps to the front door. Kirk has stopped sobbing and wants to hear all about climbing the tree. Nathan lifts him so he can ring the top button. A harsh buzz replies, letting them in. A tarnished Mezuzah hangs on the doorframe. The hallway needs to be cleaned. It is dim and smells like Indian food from the first floor tenant's cooking. The door to the first floor apartment is down the hall to the right. Next to it is the door to the basement that leads to the alley. The basement is where Nathan used to catch his dad smoking. In his dreams of the house this is where he usually runs into his dad. In the dreams his dad tries to convince Nathan that he is not dead and that Nathan doesn't have to wake up. The dreams have become more and more frequent.

On the wall at the tiny landing at the top of the stairs hangs the wooden "Home Sweet Home" sign Nathan made in grade school.

THE SPHINX OF CROPSEY AVENUE

Nathan's mom is on the phone in the kitchen when they walk in so he can't see her.

"This is Ruthie Umanski at East Eighty Fifth Street. I'd like to order a pizza. My son is here visiting me."

The living room to the left has snow white carpet and a sky blue plush couch with pillows worn almost white in places. The portraits on the wall are of Nathan's mom and dad on their wedding day. The photographs are painted over in oils. Framed photos of Nathan at his bar mitzvah and of his sister Veronica and her two sons hang around them.

"He likes it very cheesy. And well done. Who are you sending? Why not Jerry? Can you send Jerry? I like him."

Nathan walks into the kitchen and nods in greeting to the home health care person. They come late. They leave early. Sometimes they don't show at all. In general they give his mom a hard time. Last month one of them gave her a double dose of arthritis pills and no heart medication and she ended up in the hospital.

"Nate, my boy. How are you, darling?"

Nathan and his mom kiss each other on the cheek.

"You look tired," she says. "You're not using your mask, are you?"

"No, Ma. You know I hate that thing."

"You need to."

"Not now, Ma."

"I think the mask is cool," Kirk says.

"How are you, Kirk darling," Nathan's mom says. "You want some pizza?"

Kirk barks.

"I hope you've been a good puppy," she says. "What's new in puppy land?"

"A lot," he says. "My pack of puppies just met a new pack. They all don't have moms or dads or are puppies whose moms couldn't care for them so they all live together on the street."

"A pack of wild dogs, that sounds terrible," she says. "You're not scared?"

"Why would I be?" he says. "One of them might turn out to be my puppy wife or puppy husband."

"Puppy husband," Nathan's mom's health care lady says. "Where'd you learn that, child?"

"Shush," Nathan's mom says. "I'm talking with my son and his...Kirk."

She winces and rubs her swollen fingers.

"Did I take my afternoon pills?"

The health care lady goes into the living room to get pills. The living room has been made into a makeshift bedroom for Nathan's mom. The real bedrooms are on the third floor. In Nathan's dreams he is in the attic looking down into his parents' bedroom and his dad's tiny office room next to it and his sister's bedroom down the hall. The dreams are so real he can recall the feel of his hand on his dad's big wooden armoire. He spends what feels like hours in the dreams going through the drawers and the boxes of his and his sister's drawings and handmade cards. The house does not have an attic. He wakes up from these dreams choking.

"How's Snakey?" Nathan's mom asks.

"Snakey's good," Nathan says. "I'm working a lot. I gave her to Josh to take care of."

"Oh good. But I'm not living in a house with a snake."

"Veronica already told you we'd get rid of her."

"It's big enough to eat Josh alive."

"No she isn't," Kirk says. "She's only three feet long. Nate, can I have her?"

"Ma you can't walk steps. And it isn't safe here."

"Nathan. Shush. It's perfectly fine here."

"What did the broker say?"

THE SPHINX OF CROPSEY AVENUE

"She didn't come. Traffic. 'Cause of the Sphinx."

Nathan's mom takes her pills and turns on the TV on the wheeled cart in the kitchen. It makes Nathan sad to think this is how she spends her time. The news shows a traffic copter view of the Sphinx of Cropsey Avenue. The sound is turned down.

"I don't understand how it moves like that," Nathan's mom says.

"It's a Mystery," Nathan says.

He and Kirk share a smile.

The image changes to a split screen of the Sphinx of New Delhi. And the one in Chicago.

"I don't like that it sits on the Sears Tower like that," Nathan's mom says. "It's going to fall and hurt someone."

"Maybe it can fly," Kirk says.

The words "Breaking News" scroll across the bottom of the screen. A celebrity Nathan knows but whose name he can't remember is walking towards the Sphinx of New Delhi. The celebrity's mouth is moving and his hands are in the air. The Sphinx's paw lashes out, lightning quick and flattens him.

"Cool," Kirk says.

Nathan's mom gasps and changes the channel. A commercial for Saturday night's showing of a Yanni concert is on PBS.

"He's such a handsome man," Nathan's mom says. "Such nice music."

"He's coming to the Garden this summer," Nathan says. "I'll get tickets."

"No. I don't want to."

Nathan knows that means No, I'm not able to.

"When's the broker coming back?"

"She's not. I don't think I can move, Nathan."

She rolls to the window.

"I remember when there was nothing there across the street. Just fields. You could see all the way to the bay. This is my house. This is where I live."

This is the way it always ends. With Nathan showing her the code for the burglar alarm she never uses. He wishes he could convince her that living with Veronica would be better.

"I gotta get Kirk back," Nathan says.

Nathan's mom has stopped hiding the disappointment on her face when he leaves. He's learned not to look.

———

Nathan is in Yael's tiny apartment wondering if she will return. Kirk is in the one bedroom, the room he shares with his mom where he is supposed to be asleep. Nathan knows he is awake looking at the pictures in his mom's astrology books and playing with Nathan's sleep mask.

They had more pizza for dinner. The box is on the black folding card table with Yael's things. Maps of Morocco. Paperback books on Tarot. Bottles of Nyquil. Insulin vials. Yael has drawn a Hamsa in chalk on the wall. Nathan sits on the floor facing it with a pillow behind his back, against the opposite wall. There is no other furniture. His phone vibrates. It's his boss.

"I've got a pickup for you. My table at the Sexton."

"I'm still watching the kid," Nathan says.

"Fine. As soon as you can, then. Let me know when you're on your way."

"Soon as the kid's mom comes back I will."

———

THE SPHINX OF CROPSEY AVENUE

The Sexton is the Manhattan bar where Nathan met Yael last year, on Purim. It is not like most other bars. Or most other places. Someone has to tell you how to find it. And how to find your way in.

Nathan had just handed off a drop at his table when he noticed a woman dressed as a cat going from table to table offering to read fortunes. Yael. The first thing everyone notices about Yael is her long, dark hair. That night in the dim light of the bar it seemed to disappear down her back and merge with her slender cat-suit-clad form. The next thing people notice about her is her smooth, brown skin. And her green eyes, which are so green people think they must be lenses but they are real. He wasn't sure if soliciting like that was against the Sexton's rules but it violated people's expectations of quiet anonymity despite the closely packed tables. He wondered how long she could stay on her feet in those leopard-spotted, high, high heels like that. It *was* Purim and he had a full schedule so he didn't give it a second thought until later. After his drops and pickups he left through the staff's back exit that led into an interior courtyard. Yael was there. His surprise that she had known about the staff-only egress was overshadowed by his anger. Two men, well-dressed like most of the Sexton's patrons, were pushing her back and forth between them as she unsteadily tried to get away.

Nathan didn't know what it was all about. He told himself he wasn't going to get involved, that he was just going to ask if everyone was all right but found himself throwing punches before anyone said a word. The two guys were soon on the ground. Yael steadied herself with a hand on Nathan's shoulder and placed a strange machine in his hand. It was white plastic and not much larger than a small tablet but thicker and had a Velcro strap.

"Feed me. Sugar," she said.

She looked very, very out of it. Drunk or something else. She slumped onto him then woke up, startled.

"Sugar," she said and passed out, again.

Nathan carried her through the courtyard and into one of the surrounding buildings, out its lobby, and onto the street around the corner. He hailed a cab. While riding he figured out the machine was an insulin pump. An inch of thin white tubing protruded from the back of the machine. Nathan gently lifted the bottom of Yael's sheer black shirt exposing her concave belly. He found a thin scar and a hole among the soft almost transparent fuzz to the right of her belly button. He guided the tubing into the hole. The machine beeped and the display came to life. He held the machine in place so it wouldn't detach.

Yael woke ten minutes later.

"Who the fuck are you?" she said.

"It's alright. I got you out of there. I was going to take you home until I could figure this out."

Yael ordered the cabbie to head to a new destination. Her apartment.

"You're really here to help?"

She opened the machine's Velcro strap and wrapped it around her waist.

"I am," Nathan said.

"Okay. Good. Then we need to go to Morocco to find my grandfather."

The cabbie laughed. "Not in my cab."

"How about let's get you home," Nathan said.

The sun was coming up. She allowed him to help her into her apartment. Kirk was sitting at the folding table eating cereal from a bowl without milk. He silently watched them enter. Nathan got the sense this was a child who had seen a lot of things and was used to taking care of himself.

"Kirk, I want to tell you who this man is," Yael said.

THE SPHINX OF CROPSEY AVENUE

"You don't have to, Mom. I know."

Yael looked surprised. "Tell me, honey."

Kirk became shy. He motioned to his mother and whispered in her ear but Nathan could hear.

"He's my father. You've finally brought him here. In case you go away and never come back."

"No, honey. This man is not your father. Your father is a bad man who wants to hurt us. This is the man who is going to help us find your grandfather."

"I think I'm the man who's going to go to the store and get some groceries for this place," Nathan said. "After that, we'll see."

<hr />

Nathan falls asleep looking at Yael's chalk Hamsa.

He dreams he is in the attic of his Mom's house that does not exist. The attic leads to spaces behind the walls and closets. Impossible spaces with too much room that also do not exist.

"Wake up."

Yael is shaking him.

"I was at my house," Nathan says. "Having another vision."

"No. You were dying. Your body was telling you to start breathing again and wake up. You need to use your mask."

She stumbles to the bedroom and peeks in on Kirk.

"I'm glad you're still up," she says to Nathan. "I read the fortune of a woman tonight. Get this. She has family in Morocco and knows all about Fez…"

"Still up? I'm still here. It's been two days!"

"I knew you'd be here for him."

With some effort she lifts her shirt over her head and takes it off. Her insulin pump is Velcroed to the side of her body. She detaches it and places it on the table. Nathan knows what this means. She comes to him and kisses his neck. He does not respond.

"What?" she says.

"You've been staying away longer and longer. One day you're not going to come back. I know what you're doing."

"I come from a family of fortune tellers. I'm meant to tell fortunes."

"True, but—"

"You believe in me," she says. "Don't take that back."

"You're his mother, too. You're also meant to be his mother."

"Yeah, well he has you," she says.

"Does he? I'm not his father. He has a father."

Yael makes a spitting sound. "No. Don't you say that. That deadbeat savage is not a father."

"You haven't said anything about the court case in a while."

"His *father*, deadbeat-dad-sperm-donor, doesn't get to see him until he's all paid up and the court says it's safe. What else is there to say? His *father* wants him to grow up and be a doctor. Or lawyer. Or an astronaut. Or a baseball player. Or whatever it is little American boys are supposed to grow up and be. No. He's going to grow up like my grandfather, in Morocco."

Yael loses her balance and bumps into the table. She steadies herself and slams her fist down.

"A lot of help you've been with that."

"I never said I was going to get you two to Morocco."

"If you really loved me you would."

"I'm not stopping you. I never have. Go."

"Just like that? Go? Go you say?"

"Yeah. If that's what you want," Nathan says.

"I do want. But what about Kirk's father? It's not that easy."

"So, take care of it," Nathan says.

"No, why don't you take care of it? You could," Yael says.

"Me take care of it? Do you even know what you're asking?"

"Kill him for all I care. There I'm saying it. Kill him. Kill him. Kill him. He deserves it. Do it. For me."

"I can't."

"You won't."

"I just spent the last two days…I'm sorry. I'm not doing this. I'm leaving."

Nathan gathers his things into his overnight bag. He stops at the door to the bedroom not wanting to wake Kirk by retrieving his sleep mask.

"Please. Don't," Yael says and slides her arms around him from behind.

He doesn't want to but he finds himself kissing her. Kissing her is the last thing that still feels right. It would be easier if it did not. Time disappears for a few minutes then she slumps forward onto him like she did that first night in the courtyard. She shouldn't have her meter off for so long, Nathan thinks. He carries her to the bedroom and tucks her in next to Kirk.

What kills Nathan is that she doesn't understand that the reason he isn't taking care of things for her is because he does love her.

———

Nathan arrives at the Sexton early and is waiting at his boss' table to make the pickup.

A man wearing an expensive suit pulls out the chair across from him. Nathan knows something is wrong. Clients are never early. Everyone else knows their place. The man has a well-groomed, short beard in the style that is popular among young Middle Eastern men.

"I'm told you know my wife?" the man says.

"You must be mistaken," Nathan says.

The man sits down.

"If you don't want any trouble you'll get up and leave."

"I'm not mistaken. You're right I don't want any trouble. I just want my son."

Yael's husband, Nathan thinks. He glances to one of the back exits, contemplates a quick escape, and then decides to stay.

"You can see your son," he says. "As soon as the court says you can."

"The court?" Yael's husband looks around. Nathan notices he is slim and fit. The suit hangs on him well.

"Oh. I see," Yael's husband says. "Look at this place. Only in America. It makes sense why she'd come to a place like this. A fool is born every day."

"I have nothing to do with your son," Nathan says.

"You don't understand," Yael's husband says, calmly. "There is no court case. There never was. There never will be. I don't want any trouble for her. Money is not the problem. Is that what she told you?"

"Maybe you don't realize that I'm working right now," Nathan says. "My boss isn't going to be happy you're in that seat."

Yael's husband takes a thick envelope out of his jacket pocket.

"Your boss told me you'd be here early. I have this for you."

The man slides the envelope to Nathan. It dawns on him what is happening.

"Go ahead," Yael's husband says. "It's bad for the both of us if you don't."

"No."

"Energy flows back and forth between everything," Yael's husband says. "Everything in the universe. Including you and I. When we don't do what we're supposed to do it breaks that flow. And that's an imbalance. You know this. When we don't do what we need to do the universe comes knocking. And knocking. Most people spend their lives surrounded by the universe knocking. And they don't hear a thing. Or won't. I don't know why. But I know you are the kind of man who knows what happens when one doesn't answer the knock."

"The universe knocks louder," Nathan says.

"Yes. Then tries the window. Or breaks down the door."

"Or sends something we can't ignore," Nathan says.

"Very good. You are with my wife. You must know this concept well. She and I, we're from the same place but we walk in different worlds; you know what I mean. That's okay. That's how it goes. Things change. Things end. Things serve their purpose. You're here to bring me to my son. And to take this."

Nathan does not touch the envelope.

"You can't buy your son back," he says.

"Your boss told me this was what I have to do. So I'm doing it. I wish Yael only happiness and good fortune. That which wasn't meant to be with me."

"Oh, really?"

"Yes."

"You didn't hurt her?"

"Did I hurt her? Is that what she told you?"

Yael's husband stands. He takes off his jacket and unbuttons his white, collarless shirt. His shoulder is a knot of scars.

"This is where she stabbed me when she tried to kill me. I'm lucky she's better at telling fortunes than she is at killing people. There's no court case. And no police. Don't believe me. Check. The money is yours because it is bad for you to perform a service without compensation and bad for me to accept one without paying fair value. What you do with it is up to you."

"You don't get to decide what to do with him."

"I know. I'm his father. It's supposed to be something Yael and I decide together."

"I don't want any part of this."

"I mean you no harm. I mean her no harm—"

"Go straighten it out yourself. That's what I told her too."

"I want to. But I need your help. I'm here with my hat in hand asking for your help. You know she may not know many things but she knows how to run. I take one step. She knows I'm coming and she's ten steps away. I've been trying for years and my son is getting older. Until I procured the services of your employer I had little hope left. Help me, please. You look like a good man. Inquisitive. Cautious. I can tell you've been looking after my son well."

"We're finished here. Go."

"Take my card. Check on me. Do what you have to do. I'm not here to get between you two."

"She's nothing to me," Nathan says. "Just someone I know."

"Then doing your job shouldn't be hard."

———

The morning home health care person doesn't show and Nathan has to come and get his mom out of bed, to the bathroom, and make breakfast.

"Veronica found Snakey a new home," Nathan says. "A nice man out in Suffolk who rescues turtles from the side of the road and breeds reptiles."

"Oh good. She'll have herself a nice Snakey-husband."

Nathan's mom is in bed. In the room that used to be the family room. Nathan and his sister's bronzed pairs of first shoes sit atop the big old Zenith console television. Two decorative swords hang on the wall. Nathan remembers when he was Kirk's age he used to think that they were real and that he could use them for protection if he had to. Nathan opens the closet. He knows there is no room or space behind it but he is compelled to check.

"We don't have an attic, right Ma?"

"No, of course not. Nathan. Sit down. Promise me you're not going to run off and go to that Sphinx like that man on TV."

"Ma, of course not."

"Promise me. Swear. You have that crazy look in your eye. You're my son. I know you."

"I promise, Ma."

"I worry about you. I don't want you to end up like that man. Celebrities think they can fix the world."

"I promise."

On the TV an image of the Sphinx of Cropsey Avenue cordoned off with police tape is displayed behind a news panel. A white-bearded Rabbi is saying he thinks the Sphinxes are the Pharaohs' revenge and that we must find the answer to their riddle. A man who has written conspiracy theory books says he thinks that the Sphinxes themselves are the riddle. A woman who has helped the police track down serial killers with her psychic insights says that our governments will fail us and that we must trust people who deal in the unexplained for a living.

"Who are these people?" the news host asks.

"They live and work among us. They have a whole society. Rules and laws and codes. Like the mafia, most of us don't even know we're living next door to them."

"And what if we don't answer the riddle?" the news host asks.

"Then we don't pass. So to speak. Which means we, all of us, do not survive."

"Turn that rubbish off," Nathan's mom says.

Nathan turns the sound down.

"Nate, my boy. I'm meant to be here," she says. "I can't be what I'm not. Nothing good will come of it otherwise. I don't have much time. I'm meant to pass here. In my home."

"Ma, don't talk like that."

Nathan's mom takes her son's hand. "Feel me. Sometimes I really think I'm dying. It hurts so bad. I can't handle getting out of bed. How am I going to handle moving?"

The afternoon health care person walks in. Seeing them holding hands and in tears she quietly walks back the way she came.

"You're not going to die, Ma."

"And I'm not selling this house. You might need it."

"I don't need it."

"Maybe you'll have a family someday."

"Maybe, Ma. Maybe someday."

"For you. And Yael and Kirk."

"Yael is a long way away from that. She's getting her act together. Perpetually."

"People don't change, Nate. Unless they really, really want to. Either you love them for who they are. Now. Or you don't."

"I know, Ma."

The news image zeros in on the piece of shredded car caught in the paw of the Sphinx of Cropsey Avenue. In the background cars on the Belt Parkway crawl by as drivers slow down to look.

———

Nathan hands the envelope full of money to Yael.

"You saw him? Where?" Yael says.

"At work. I know there's no court case."

Yael utters a string of profanities in several languages.

"What did you tell him?"

"Nothing," Nathan says.

"Is he coming here?"

"No. He paid the money for me to tell him where you are. But I didn't tell him anything. And I won't. I don't want to be involved. Now you can go to Morocco or wherever you want."

Yael flips through the money. Kirk is sitting with headphones on barking along with 101 Dalmatians on Yael's tablet.

"I still think you should just take care of this head on," Nathan says. "But it's your life. Do it when you're ready, I guess. If you ever are. I'll throw him off your trail. You'll have a big head start."

"You're not coming with us?"

"I can't."

"You can. But you won't. Why? When I said I loved you it meant I'd do anything for you. Why isn't that the same for you?"

"I'll go say goodbye to Kirk."

"No," she says. "Just go."

Kirk sees that his mom and Nathan are looking at him and he waves and smiles. Puppies run and frolic in the movie on the tablet's screen. Kirk barks.

The Sphinx of Cropsey Avenue rises from her place in the sand on the side of the Belt Parkway. She walks along the road to where it changes to the Southern State. The piece of shredded car in her paw scratches on the asphalt. She walks along the Southern State to the Wantagh Parkway where she turns south and heads for Jones Beach. The Sphinx lumbers through the lot and over the dunes and tall grass of the beach called West End Two.

Yael and Kirk are in an old Jeep Yael bought with some of the money. All of their possessions are in it. They pull into the West End Two parking lot at Jones Beach. It is almost spring but despite the sun it is still terribly cold. The beach is empty except for a small group of wet-suit-clad surfers. The two surfers in the water pay the Sphinx no mind.

"What are you doing?" one of the surfers asks Yael. "Get out of here. That thing's dangerous."

"I'm looking for someone before I go," Yael says. "I was sure I'd find him here."

The Sphinx lumbers in their direction. The surfers on the sand move out of its way.

"You said we could say goodbye," Kirk says.

He lets go of his mom's hand and runs for the Sphinx.

The Sphinx does not slow down. Kirk is in its path.

"I know the riddle," Kirk says. "I know the answer."

He barks. The Sphinx keeps coming until it is right before him. It raises its paw. The two surfers from the water have left their boards and are running for Kirk. Yael is running too. They will not get there before the great paw lowers.

Kirk drops to all fours and barks louder.

The Sphinx lowers her paw back into the huge indentation of sand she lifted it from. Her head lowers as if regarding Kirk, then she turns her body ninety degrees towards the water.

Yael reaches Kirk. She wraps her arms around him and pulls him to her.

"You're okay," she says, and kisses him.

"Where do you think it's going?" a surfer says.

"Not sure. Fire Island, maybe," the other surfer answers.

Kirk squirms away from his mother's kisses.

"What did you say? What did you say to it?" Yael asks.

THE SPHINX OF CROPSEY AVENUE

"I said it in puppy language," Kirk says. "If you don't understand I can't tell you."

"I think I get it," the first surfer says. "I think they're here for us. All of us. Here to ask us why we're all being so stupid."

"Like why Auntie Ruthie won't move from Canarsie," Kirk says. "And why Nathan doesn't use his mask."

To Yael and the surfers it appears that the Sphinx of Cropsey Avenue is going to lumber into the water and disappear like a Saturday afternoon movie monster. She stops at the water's edge. Diaphanous wings unfold from her back. The wings are so thin one can barely see them. In the sun they take on the sandy color of West End Two and the steel blue gray water. The Sphinx takes a step into the water then lifts into the air.

"I didn't know they had those," Yael said.

"You didn't?" Kirk says.

"You did?" Yael says.

"Of course," Kirk says. "You just have to know to look."

Yael lifts him into the air and holds him up to the surfers.

"My son," she says. "Six years old and already seeing the unseen." The surfers let out a mock cheer.

"Alright. Whatever," one of the surfers says. "Glad he's alright."

"You're a mystic like your grandfather, Kirk," she says, and kisses him. "And a gypsy just like me."

"Does this mean we don't need to go to Morocco?" Kirk asks.

"Maybe," Yael says. "Maybe we are meant to go to Mexico. Or Miami? What do you think of Miami?"

"Will you tell Nathan? In case he wants to come and see us?"

"Why not," she says.

Yael carries her son to their car. The Sphinx of Cropsey Avenue flaps her wings. Her lion paws hang beneath her clawing the empty air as she flies over the cold Atlantic Ocean.

Nathan drives to his mom's house. 9109 East Eighty Fifth Street. He trusts you enough now to know the numbers. He hopes his mom will live forever but he knows she will not. Someday you might go looking. But she will not be there.

Nathan checks on the night health care person. He checks on his mom. Yael and Kirk called earlier to say they are heading to Mexico. There are plenty of places to tell fortunes there. The money will go a long way. If they stay, Kirk will grow up a free spirit like Yael desires. Maybe someday he will see them again. He doubts it.

He makes two phone calls. First he calls his boss and quits. Then he calls Yael's husband.

"Morocco?" Yael's husband says. "I should have known. She's still stuck on finding her crazy grandfather."

"She doesn't have much of a head start. Maybe you'll catch up with them in Fez. I've heard it's a nice place. Everyone living side by side in peace."

Nathan goes upstairs. He lays down on the floor of his old bedroom. He wants to explore the spaces behind the walls he has seen in his dreams. He hasn't brought his mask. When he closes his eyes the Sphinx won't leave his mind. The scarred fur of the Sphinx of Cropsey Avenue and her expressionless alabaster face, melting snow streaking through Canarsie's grime. He lays there trying to fall asleep. He hopes the dreams will come soon and that his dad will be there.

STORY NOTES

NOVEMBER 2022

There is part of me that wants to tell my real-life stories and inspirations behind the stories in this book. One time when I did that I was told the real story was much more interesting than the one on the page so, for now, I shall refrain.

However, what I offer here, bits of where I was and what I was thinking when I wrote these, serves as a chronicle of my journey into understanding and finding my place in horror and in that way is a part of my story.

When I first started writing if you asked me if I wrote horror my answer would have been "no". I would have never believed it if you told me that someday I would be a horror writer.

After "Across the Darien Gap" was purchased by Cemetery Dance Magazine I began thinking about how to classify my stories. My interests and creative process remained the same but for the first time I began to consider that my writing might actually be considered horror. Certainly others thought so. Now, that old headspace seems far away and maybe even hard to believe but with the exceptions of Stephen King and Clive Barker I had not (yet) been exposed or introduced to much horror and so I had never considered my work through that lens.

Richard Chizmar went on to purchase "Jellyfish Moon" and "The Green Man of Punta Cabre". After that Norman Prentiss approached me to acquire a collection of my work, (this book!), for the eBook division. Richard, and Norman and the stories of Cemetery Dance were my gateway. I was delighted to learn of the multi-faceted, wide-reaching breadth of the genre. Eventually I came to realize where I fit in. It was a journey and a process, but there was one specific moment, one epiphany, one turning point (that I credit to the late, great Peter Straub) that did it for me. I will tell you about this later in these pages.

It is mid-November 2022 as I write this. A long and late Indian Summer has left us and just like that it is cold again here in New York. The sounds of the last of the peeper-frog hold outs in the trees are gone from the nights and I've been looking back on at each of these stories in the order I remember writing them. So, here we go back to the year 2002 as I was the drafting of the first of the stories included in this bunch.

HURRICANE SANDRINE

"Hurricane Sandrine" I believe is the oldest one in this collection. The first draft was written in 2002 though the idea, (the idea of a ghost of a storm), goes back to one I remember having very early in the 1990s. In 2002, my drafting process was very slow. It involved getting feedback from my colleagues, teachers, and peers on multiple drafts over a period of months or even years. An early bit of feedback on the story from my teacher, Terry Bisson, stays with me because it was an early bit of validation of my instincts and decisions on that early draft and what were seeds of my style and process of storytelling. This was important to me because most of the voices offering feedback were saying things like you can't write like this and this is wrong.

Today I have come to write with more awareness and experience; I have more "tools" at my disposal and feel I have control whereas then I was going more by instinct and trial and error. My process now, in the year 2022 often involves consciously making decisions to "push" things in a story one way or another, with the intent to move the story or elements within closer to or farther away from certainty or intentional ambiguity.

I have fond memories of discussing a draft of this story with my colleagues at the World Fantasy Convention in 2003 in Washington D.C. I have a vivid memory choosing to include of an image of the storm over the island. The memory and image reminds me of the decision making aspect of my drafting process. A large part is deciding what to show on the page and this is an early memory of doing so.

Also at that same convention, another of our instructors, the generous and kind Karen Joy Fowler briefly introduced our group of fledging writers to Kelly Link. Kelly Link's stories and teachings went on to become very important to me which is why I chose to recount this here even though it is not a story note. Also not a story note is one of my favorite stories to tell, a fond memory of Neil Gaiman who was in front of us on the very long line for brunch in a narrow and long alleyway that same day. I usually say "this is an anecdote that illustrates why Neil Gaiman is the coolest person ever" when telling it but there's no room here so I shall save it for another time.

THE GHOST DANCE

The first draft of "The Ghost Dance" was also written in 2002.

At the time I had very little understanding of genre other than very broad strokes, and as such I thought very little about genre when drafting.

THE NIGHT MARCHERS   Daniel Braum

The seeds of inspiration for it go back to the early and mid-1990s when the subject of persecution and subjugation of Native Americans was frequently on my mind. The story itself was born of my desire to embody a notion from a line in a Robbie Robertson song. If you revisit the story you might be able to guess the song and the line.

While I didn't know about genre terms or the names for things back then I knew that the kind of stories I liked to read were stories that I referred to as "stories that were open", as in open to interpretation as to what is really going on. It doesn't surprise me that I was trying to write stories like this though I have no clear memory of trying to do so intentionally. Later on this notion of "an open story" dovetailed with an element of strange tales (as I perceive them) that I call "intentional ambiguity". This understanding, other notions I have of weird fiction and strange tales, and writing with awareness and control came much later on for me.

Like "Hurricane Sandrine", "The Ghost Dance" is a ghost story. Technically. Definitionaly. Because both do have ghosts in them. I say technically because they don't feel like what we might think of as classic ghost stories. Back then I for sure was not setting out to write a ghost story. Now I'm really interested in everything about ghost stories and I'm really glad that I wrote some. I talk endlessly about ghost stories on my You Tube channel called DanielBraum so you are very welcome to join me there for more about this.

For those curious for more about the subject of the story I recommend the book "In the Spirit of Crazy Horse" by Peter Matthiessen and the album "For the Native Americans" by Robbie Robertson.

The story found a home in Electric Velocipede which was a 'zine known for publishing slipstream. The editor told me that it was the imagery that won him over when he accepted it.

STORY NOTES

ACROSS THE DARIEN GAP

From checking e mails of back up documents of initial notes and rough sketches of scenes I deduced that the early drafts of "Across the Darien Gap" were done in 2004.

I was not thinking about notions of horror at the time, I was thinking a lot about "magic" and how to depict it in fiction. While I see some of these attempts to portray "magic" are present in the story- looking back I also see some of what I call "hallmarks-of-a-horror-story" present too, such as ghosts and demons. Like I said before, I'm happy to have written a ghost story but when drafting I wasn't thinking about the story that way at all.

My earliest memory of an inspiration for it is the image of the characters standing in the shallow ocean with the bioluminescence, watching the heat lightning. It is a moment where some of the characters are in the presence of profound beauty yet are unaware of their proximity to terrible danger. The main character is full of a sense of duty and tension and is struggling to protect them. Once upon a time I was in a place and situation like that. In early passes and sketches of the story I was trying to capture that feeling and that place. Often the first thing that comes to me is that I know that I want write about a place or something very specific about a place. I've spoken at length about setting and this part of my process in several interviews so despite the temptation to dive in I'm going to move on.

The main character of "Across the Darien Gap" is full of unrealized dreams, shattered dreams, and failures. He is outgunned and outmatched and on the run and in a strange place with no help coming. What I had not learned yet when I was drafting the story was that Horror as a genre, or as a category can be said to be or thought of to be about emotion. In retrospect, through the lens of horror-as-emotion "Across the Darien Gap" is a story that portrays strong emotions and as such I came to see why people thought it fit in as horror.

This is a good place to say while I knew very little about structure at the time I knew that I liked reading stories that didn't have happy endings and ones that did not feel all neatly wrapped up in the end. It makes sense to me that I would be trying to do this back then, though I have no memory of aiming for such an ending with this one. Story structure and how it might affect genre and perception is something I've thought a lot about over the years since this one was published. I've observed that certain structures and endings are often used in horror stories and have come to be associated with them. Without going into my perceptions of horror structures here I want to say that the notion that it is okay to have stories that end in a place where it feels like the story is still going on and having stories that are not "wrapped up in a bow," are teachings I first learned from and that I associate with Kelly Link. While endings and structure were not things I was consciously processing back then I think a hell of a lot about them now.

The story was purchased by Cemetery Dance in 2005 and appeared in the Magazine in 2006. I first began thinking about and reading horror around this time.

MYSTIC TRYST

"Mystic Tryst" is another ghost story. I realize this is now the fourth ghost story in a row in these notes. And that I'm repeating myself in saying that I did not plan this when writing them. Then again, I also was not judging or censoring my ideas. Setting and imagery is often what comes first for me. For this one, the image of the spectral lionfish floating in a dark corner is what I remember coming first. I remember figuring out a scene and then the story to hold the image.

Before I had landed on who the characters would be I knew that "Mystic Tryst" would be a story about letting go. And that there would be tropical blue imagery. For a while my working title was "Blue Heaven". I never was in love with the title "Mystic Tryst" but I went with it because as the name of the record I felt it shifted focus toward the main character. While writing the draft I had a good sense of where the story was going to end up and where the characters would "be" at the end.

I could not wait to show people that I'd wrote about ghost fish, which I was sure no one had ever seen before. I was so surprised when almost all the of the initial feedback I received on drafts and submissions was that they'd been seeing a lot of stories about ghost fish. And then I learned of the great Karen Russell and her story "Haunting Olivia".

A memory that is not a story note is that I got Karen Russell's autograph at KBG Bar's celebration of the Best of Lady Churchill's Rosebud Wristlet! A memory that is a story note is that I figure the first drafts of this one were done in 2004 or early 2005. I surmise that some of the imagery must have been inspired by a 1995 trip to Mexico.

The story was published in Farrago's Wainscot which was an online journal of interstitial works. When accepting it the editor told me something along the lines of that he thought the ghosts as metaphor for the relationship between the characters was well done. I never let on, until now, that I had not contemplated that at all. I like it when things like that happen. When I put what feels right on the page, authentic feelings even if not literal ones, I am perfectly fine when people see things in it different than what I saw or intended.

THE NIGHT MARCHERS Daniel Braum

THE GREEN MAN OF PUNTA CABRE

I remember writing early drafts of "The Green Man of Punta Cabre" in Belize in what must have been 2004. I had mummies on my mind because at the time I was putting together "Spirits Unwrapped" a chapbook of mummy stories which was published in 2005. (The chapbook has the same name and subject matter as the 2019 anthology I edited for Lethe Press.) In many ways this story belongs with the four stories in that chapbook but I made the decision as an editor not to include my own story in a project I was helming.

I had a desire to write about the problem of how genetically modified corn is driving heirloom corn to extinction. Also the phenomenon of seeing the faces of religious icons in ordinary things was on my mind and the first idea for the story was that it was going to be a story about seeing a face in a stalk of corn. While set in Mexico the place is a fictionalized. I think the green man of the story was what I was thinking of as the mummy at first and the "imposter" and the "saint" figures came later on.

I remember reading and making notes on a print out of a draft at an open air bar over dinner alone and receiving comments of commiseration from other patrons that I was doing work while on "vacation". My replies were smiles and quick small talk so I could get back to writing. However, one curious person sat down next to me and was genuinely interested in what I was writing. Over the course of our conversation I was told a travel tale about a place and that inspired the saint figures in the story. Since I did not yet have an ending and was writing without a direction in mind I remember feeling fortunate that "the ending" simply walked over and sat down next to me.

STORY NOTES

JELLYFISH MOON

I have a pleasant memory of talking about my ideas for "Jellyfish Moon", "The Green Man of Punta Cabre" and I think some other story ideas (that may not have ever been drafted) with my friend the author Brendan Day, in Madison Wisconsin in 2003. We were at an outdoor area near water and we were taking a break from the WisCon convention. One of the things I like to do is talk through a story with someone before putting words to the page, if I can.

The setting of "Jellyfish Moon" is also fictional. I remember the process of envisioning the physical locations so I could write about them. There are some places that feel to me like they are at a crossroads or turning point of change and growth. I wanted to depict that and related notions in a story without writing about actual persons or places. Once I had "that part" decided I went about creating characters and their stories and conflicts in which these ideas could be embodied and played out. When creating characters, I often ask myself, what do they want? What is in the way of their getting what they want? I often think of what the internal stakes for them are in addition to the external.

SPARK

I was still looking at my stories as being about magic and speculative ideas when I drafted this one in what I am pretty sure (but not certain) was in 2006. (I know the story was sold in late 2006 and published in Spring 2007.) I was developing an idea I remember thinking of as "contagious" fire.

The supernatural element in "Spark" is intended as literal and I don't think of the story as a "strange tale" as I like to define it. I remember being happy with how the story turned out. I still like it today even though I suspect that if I drafted the story today I would likely take the idea in a different direction which would likely be pushing it in the direction of being a strange tale. I did the final edits on the proof for the publisher sent in a hotel room in Sydney in early 2007 during the last days of my stay in Australia.

While in that Sydney hotel I had ideas for Australia-set stories on my mind. One of them went on to be written and appears in the book Underworld Dreams. Several those Australia-set ideas remain (at the moment) in the idea and sketch phases.

I began my Australia trip in late 2006 writing a story and ended the trip editing one. "Spark" I believe was the last story I drafted before the trip. It might be the last of its kind as far as my process and intent goes. Starting with the next story in the notes that follow I think there was some sort of shift.

MUSIC OF THE SPHERES

During the winter of 2006 in the weeks before departing for my trip to Australia, I remember feeling on the verge of some sort of change. I didn't quite know from what to what but I felt like I was at a threshold of… something. I remember missing old friends. I remember feeling like I was standing still and that the world was changing and was going to change around me. I remember feeling nostalgic about and a longing for days past.

I wrote the first draft of "Music of the Spheres" in a hotel room at LAX in last days of 2006 waiting for my flight to Brisbane which departed on New Year's Eve. I can see the tiny desk and dim light. I remember listening to Jeff Bridges narrate an audiobook of The Sun Also Rises when I showered. The drafting process was different. I don't remember doing any pre-writing or outlining. A first draft just came out and was written from beginning to end in a short period

STORY NOTES

of time. I think I had reached a point where I had internalized a lot of the lessons years past and was ready to write more stories. I felt pretty good about the draft and it was set to be my first story to be workshopped in Australia.

The first instructor to discuss the story told me things along the lines that you can't write like this and this is not how it is done. I knew they meant well. I remained open minded to learning. I was fortunate enough to have a thick skin and confidence in my instincts. I'd been told before that there would come times when we might receive "good" advice but that advice would not necessarily be advice that was "good" for a particular story. Keeping this in mind helped me be confident about the story and the direction my writing was going with the story. I also had support and enthusiasm from my friend and colleague, Peter Ball and then from Kelly Link. Kelly Link acquired the story for Lady Churchill's Rosebud Wristlet, a publication that had once published Karen Russell's first story. The opportunity to discuss the story with Kelly and receive editorial guidance from her was a milestone experience. Her notes and guidance, some of them as specific and finely-tuned as word choices and punctuation, strengthened the subtlety and intentional ambiguity of the story. Reading Kelly Link's work and listening to her talk about story formally and informally has been the source of countless lessons for me.

MOON AND THE MESA

I wrote the "Moon and the Mesa" in early 2007 in Brisbane.

While writing these notes it strikes me that I might have wrote a setting forward story because setting is comforting and natural territory for me and I was veering into a difficult subject matter. The flip side of that hypothesis is that I always write setting forward stories and the desert is a location I am always eager to write about.

THE NIGHT MARCHERS   DANIEL BRAUM

With jumps back and forth in time the structure is unorthodox yet the result is one I remain happy with because I feel like I wrote a successful strange tale and work of weird fiction at a time when I knew nothing about such terms. There is controlled ambiguity at play. There are strange elements that may or may not be supernatural. And the heart of the story is with the characters and the weight of their struggles.

The story was selected for Midnight Echo the magazine of the Australian Horror Writer's Association a publication which had never published work by an American author.

TOMMY'S SHADOW

"Tommy's Shadow" is the true ghost story of this bunch because it is not here in the book at all! It was originally intended to be part of the collection but eventually found its way into my third collection, Underworld Dreams. I debated whether to include the how and why it left one book and joined another but have opted to only mention the occurrence and thus have it connected to The Night Marchers at least in this way. I will say the bright side of the happening chronicles the kindness, generosity, support, and professionalism of Richard Chizmar, Norman Prentiss, Sarah Langan, and Steve Berman, a group people I look up to and who remain important to me.

THE NIGHT MARCHERS

While the "Night Marchers" is the title story it is one of the few that is not a "strange tale" at least in the way I have come to use the term. The elements of the story are not ambiguous and are not intended to be. I'm happy the way it operates as a ghost story. The ghosts are real and are meant to be so. The main character is haunted by his past.

266

STORY NOTES

And the weight of history looms large as does a palpable concern for the future.

I wrote the story in 2008. I'm happy with it as a potential introduction to or representative story of my work however it secured the spot as the title story because it simply sounded like the title of a horror book to my ear and I wanted to deliver that to Cemetery Dance.

THE SPHINX OF CROPSEY AVENUE

The image of a Sphinx walking along the Belt Parkway was an image I had been carrying around in my head for a while. It remained in my list of ideas of stories to write "file" for a long time before I wrote it in early 2015. By this time, I was free of the notion that all things in my stories had to be explained.

When writing a story like "The Sphinx of Cropsey Avenue" with a lot of different things in play, I know I run the risk of the pieces not coming together or that it just won't work for any given reader. For me, part of the process is being aware and okay with this. If I've done what I've set out to do, I know it will reach and resonate the right audience.

While everything may not be explained, the story is not nonsense, there still a logic to it- a "night time logic" meaning it has a weight and aspect that is not consciously being processed.

A GIRLS GUIDE TO APPLYING SUPERIOR CAT MAKE UP AND AVOIDING COMMONLY FOUND SUBURBAN DEMONS

I read this story at the book launch party at the Museum of Morbid Anatomy in Brooklyn in May of 2016. My nephew was there and sitting in the front row when I read so I was squirming when I hit the curse words. My brother tended our makeshift bar of mojitos. My friends were in attendance. It is a wonderful memory.

This is the story that found its way into the book after "Tommy's Shadow" departed. This edition marks the first time the story is being published by Cemetery Dance and I'm really happy it is back in print and at home with Cemetery Dance.

I knew Halloween was a time of year associated with horror when writing it, but I was interested in the supernatural or perception of the supernatural as a catalyst for the human stories and conflicts and not for the atmosphere or scares often connected with Halloween. A strange experience is depicted but it is ambiguous if the occurrence is supernatural or something else, something human perhaps? For purposes of the story the answer does not matter. The choices we make in life matter and I believe characters making choices often makes for good fiction. By the time I drafted this one I had learned what a "strange tale" was and was intentionally drafting them, this is one of those strange tales.

This is the end of the story notes.

While there is a part of me that wants to be like Robert Aickman, who spoke very little about his creative process or the meanings and inspirations for his stories, I've spoken way too much about my work and enjoy doing so far too much for this ever to have been a realistic consideration for me. Speaking of Robert Aickman, onward to my essay and that epiphany I promised I would return to.

AFTERWORD:
"STRANGE TALES, A SWORD, AND A PAINTING."

The following is the text of a guest blog post that went live in June 2016 around the time of the original launch of The Night Marchers and Other Strange Tales eBook. I cleaned it up by removing a few links, artifacts of the format, and the actual text of the Aickman and Link stories so we could print it here. I call the resulting essay: "Strange Tales, A Sword, and A Painting."

Let's begin with a question.

What explanation could there be for a person who could survive multiple stabbings from a sword unscathed?

Think about it. And hold your answers in the back of your mind as you read this post.

Here's a second question.

What is a strange tale?

My answers to both of the questions are I don't know. And I'm not sure.

THE NIGHT MARCHERS   DANIEL BRAUM

Hold these thoughts for a bit. It is a beautiful New York summer morning (in June of 2016) as I write this. I'm in a bit of shade from the nice sun. The bird chirps are masking my worries. The sprinkler is going. I have a novel in progress I'm anxious to work on today and a wonderful pile of dark fiction stories to review. I've got this post to write yet I am distracted by my yearning for pancakes. I can handle this. Yet my attempts to summon them, using only my mind have been failing. I'm told of some strange alchemy one of my author pals calls a "recipe" but these are the days of science and reason and such tales of spinning culinary gold out of grocery store staples is just too farfetched for even me to believe.

It has been a great year for short fiction. I'm very excited to be a small part of it with my first collection of short stories The Night Marchers and Other Strange Tales. I'm proud of my stories and I've always believed in them but I never quite knew just where they fit in. I've been writing with the intent to publish for a decade and a half. It has only been recently that I feel I have found a context for some of my work, the stories and kinds of stories that appear in the Night Marchers. You've asked me to talk about horror and short fiction in this guest post. My caveat is I'm far from an expert. All I have to offer is some insight into my writing journey. I'm grateful to share a glimpses into my exploration, my questions and my perceptions on genre. I'm one guy. One reader. One writer. One who is grateful to be a small part of an exciting time in fiction. With that said, let's go!

A beginning point is to mention that as a reader and writer I'm not terribly concerned with genre labels or labels at all. Well maybe just two. Fiction and non-fiction. As a kid I went for the fiction in my local library. Why? Because in fiction anything could happen. That was the only "rule". The only distinction. Be it rocket ships, magic, or ghosts or adventures with none of these things, fiction was stories that were not bound by truth. Or the rules, or so called rules, of this

AFTERWORD: "STRANGE TALES, A SWORD, AND A PAINTING."

world. Why I think I've found my way to horror is that I've found that horror, or at least horror today as I know it, seems to run by this same anything can happen spirit. Yes, I know there are divisions and subdivisions and labels and genres and subgenres all with their expectations and stereotypes, I'll leave explorations of these categories for people much smarter and more well-read than myself. What excites me about horror today is that editors, publishers, and readers seem to be very willing to go anywhere in a story. At its widest and most expansive definition horror in my opinion can be "anything" so long as it is dark, or remotely dark. If this darkness is in space or with robots or time travel, (gross oversimplifications of science fiction as a genre or category), horror will still "take it" and accept it as horror. If this darkness appears in a story with magic, swords and sorcery, urban or historical witchcraft (again my gross oversimplifications of the fantasy genre), horror will take it too. I've found that horror embraces all the hard to classify, cross-genre, genre-bending, interstitial work out there. All the weird fiction and strange tales. Horror accepts these stories as its own too. This is very exciting to me. This is as close to that no rules, just a party of imagination, I experienced as a kid set loose in my library as I've come. Thus horror feels like home. Horror and the wide net it encompasses is the fiction I'm excited to read. As I sit here and write this I'll try to zero in on the stuff I'm excited about and have been excited about. I'll try to close in on why I might call these stories, or kinds of stories, strange tales.

I think this is the place in this post where I have to proclaim Spoiler Warnings. There is a good chance I'm going to spoil elements of the short stories The Swords by Robert Aickman. Some Zombie Contingency Plans by Kelly Link. And the movies The Neon Demon and It Follows.

Let's start with Robert Aickman. There is so much to say about Robert Aickman and the term 'strange tales' he coined for his stories.

THE NIGHT MARCHERS DANIEL BRAUM

I'd like to focus on one story in particular; The Swords. I mention the Swords because it was my gateway to Robert Aickman and to weird fiction. I was lucky enough to attend a panel at World Fantasy Convention in 2014 where Peter Straub, and Chleasea Quinn Yarbo and others were discussing Aickman and his work. I had never read Aickman before and the conversation had me so intrigued. Peter Straub mentioned many reasons why he loved Aickman's work. He also cited those same reasons as to why one his notable friends and collaborators disliked Aickman. If you have not yet read any Aickman his stories are about people's encounters with the supernatural. But Aickman's supernatural elements are not ghosts or goblins. In fact they rarely are anything explained.

On the panel Peter set forth a theory or formula as to how an Aickman story works. I'm going by memory here so apologies to Peter or anyone if I miss a nuance or get this wrong or mis-quote him in anyway. But as I remember it Peter said he usually find three elements in play in an Aickman story:

1.   A story grounded in prose a sense of place and voice. Aickman's narrators were usually disaffected, longing British Men.

2.   Then we have some sort of what Straub calls a coincidence. Some sort of action or occurrence that if handled by a lesser author, or in less grounded prose you would just throw your hands up and say, no way. Not real.

3.   Then we have a supernatural element. A supernatural encounter. And they are rarely, if ever explained.

If you can, seek out and read a copy of the Swords now. In any event let's talk about it.

As to Straub's point one:

The narrator in the Swords is a young British man. The point of view, the voice, the setting are all incredibly well grounded and well presented. Reading this story the reader believes the character and where he is both in place and in history. The narrator in the swords comes across something that is part side show, part sex show. In a carnival tent, a young woman (wearing green powder) is pierced by with swords by men watching in the audience. In the beginning of the story the narrator experiences this then leaves the scene of this event.

As to point two: The coincidence.

The narrator returns to the carnival place to find the woman and her carnival barker like handler, (who he calls the seaman or showman), gone. Then this happens:

"...and all the while mulling over and around what had happened to me, until the time came for dinner. I had planned to eat in the café where I had eaten the night before, but I found myself in a different part of the city, which, of course I didn't know at all, and, feeling rather faint and queer fell instead into the first place there was.

And there, in the middle of the floor, believe it or not, sitting at a Formica-topped table, was my girl with the green powder, and, beside her, the Seaman or showman, looking like a run-down boxer."

So the coincidence is that he runs into these two people again. This coincidence and coincidences like it are what the panel pointed out could be both hallmarks of Aickman stories and elements handled in the hands of lesser writers or any writer other than Aickman that would cause a story to fail, that would cause a reader to stop suspension of disbelief.

But then we have point three. The supernatural element. The coincidence is not the supernatural element. In The Swords the green-powder woman not only survives the swords side show, something else very unusual happens to her. Our narrator has a private date, a "session" with the woman. In the course of this session the woman loses her arm. Then she reattaches it and flees. No explanation as to what has occurred is given. Aickman only gives us this, as he follows her and runs into the Seaman. And pays the man for his session with the woman.

(I've omitted the part of the original blog post containing the excerpt from the ending of "The Swords")

So let's revisit the question I began with. How can a woman survive being stabbed by a sword? How can a woman lose and arm and reattach it? You all are very smart and creative. You could come up with dozens of creative and plausible things. So not only do I say I don't know. I submit to you that it doesn't matter.

It is this lack of knowing. This intentional lack of an answer that Aickman was after. And a large part of what give his stories their punch.

What he delivers this way is a sense that emotion and consequence for our narrator. And hopefully us the reader.

Had Aickman presented the woman as a robot the story could veer toward science fiction. Had he presented the woman as using magic the story could come across as fantasy. Had he presented the woman as a vampire or other creature perhaps the story reads as horror. But he does none of these things. The story comes across as supernatural. Something akin to science fiction, fantasy, and or horror. But something different.

Is this a strange tale?

It is certainly a Robert Aickman strange tale.

What did Robert Aickman do?

After reading the swords I thought a lot about the story. And how it was operating. And why it appealed to me so much.

The answer, for me, is Night Time Logic.

Night Time Logic is a term coined by author Howard Waldrop.

There is a great article out there on the Wall Street Journal where author Kelly Link speaks about this. It appears to now be behind a pay wall.

Even if we do come up with the link I'd like to talk a bit about Night Time Logic. It is never optimal to define something by explaining what it is not but I'm doing so anyway.

Daytime logic. Daytime logic is the kind of logic that operates with your conscious mind. The rules of the supernatural elements in a story are known. And clearly defined. For example day time logic is Vampires. Vampires operate in known way. Anything with clear and known rules are operating with "daytime" logic.

Night Time Logic is about what is felt. It is about the unconscious mind. I'm tempted to say Night Time Logic is about "no rules" but this is not the case. Night Time Logic is about supernatural things operating by rules that are not given. That are not known or fully known. What is happening is not explicit. You don't "get" the rules in your brain or your conscious thoughts.

You feel thing.

In your gut.

In your heart.

In Aickman's the swords something is happening. We get the sense the Seaman knows what is going on. But we aren't privy to it. We are privy to the emotion. To the sense that something is happening.

Author Tim Powers has spoken about something akin to this. I don't believe he is speaking directly about Night Time Logic but he sums it up quite well. Back in 2004 he gave a Key Note or Guest of Honor speech at I think what was the ARISIA convention or perhaps it was Boskone. I once thought it could be found online but I can't seem to find the link.

As I recall, he was talking about chickens who had been raised for generations indoors. Generation after generation of these chickens were raised without ever seeing the sun. Without ever seeing a predator. One day some researchers did an experiment. They ran some sort of a zip line along the ceiling of the giant chicken coop warehouse and attached the shape of a Chicken Hawk onto it. They moved the fake chicken hawk along the ceiling and watched as the chickens who had never seen a predator react in fear. The point was not about genetic memory. The point was that an author's job is to operate as that "fake chicken hawk" does. To elicit real emotions and responses from readers with the so called cardboard cut outs of our words.

This is Night Time Logic to me.

If done right the emotion is delivered. The emotion is felt.

Readers will react and respond to something in their guts. Not in their brains.

Can they tell you why? Maybe. Perhaps. What is key is not knowing about the lady with the swords. It is feeling it. Being affected by it.

(I've omitted a link from the original blog post to an audio version of "The Moon and the Mesa".)

The supernatural element in the story, if it is a supernatural element at all, I believe works on Night Time Logic. Was it effective for you? Why? Several stories in the Night Marchers and Other Strange Tales operate this way. I hope you will give them a read.

If you spend any time around me talking about fiction. Night Time Logic and Kelly Link are topics that are sure to come up. I recently tried explaining Kelly Link's fiction to a pal who had not yet read Kelly's stories. And without thinking much about it I told him that some of Kelly's stories operate like Aickman's stories work on Night Time Logic. This may or may not be true. This may or may not be intentional. But the story I had in mind is one of my favorite Kelly Link stories. It is called is "Some Zombie Contingency Plans". Despite the name. It is not really about Zombies.

AFTERWORD: "STRANGE TALES, A SWORD, AND A PAINTING."

(I've omitted a link from the original blog post to an audio version of "Some Zombie Contingency Plans.")

Kelly Link begins the story by directly addressing the reader, telling us what the story is about:

"This is a story about being lost in the woods."

On the surface the story is a story, about a con just released from prison with a very young girl and her even younger brother at a house party. There is a lot of natural tension and conflict built into the scenario. Link does her job in presenting a setting and situation that feels so real you or I or any of us could have attended. But, like she said in the first line the story is ultimately about is being lost in the woods. What does that mean? What does being lost in the woods mean?

Soap was in prison for stealing a painting from a Museum heist. Only the painting was never at the Museum in the first place. So sneaking up on us this is a story about.... A man who is mad? Or maybe a magic painting? Or maybe something else entirely. As the story nears its end we realize that despite the story not seeming like it is a supernatural story at all that something magical, something supernatural might be at play here. Like in Aickman's work, what exactly this is, is not explained. But certainly it is felt and the story delivers great emotion and perhaps even something akin to the sense of life being lost in the woods using Night Time Logic.

Aickman and Link write stories that are hard to classify. Stories that transcend the categories they sometimes find themselves in.

These stories and these kinds of stories are what excite me. There are so many wonderful examples of this. From my vantage the state of horror today looks very exciting.

Thanks to a demand by readers and a willingness by publishers to give us fresh voices and exciting perspectives it is a very exciting time. Movies like "It Follows" and "The Neon Demon" are bringing and popularizing this kind of fiction on the Silver Screen.

With that, I'll wrap it up. I could go on all day.

I ended the original post with well wishes and some banter about pancakes that reads as a non-sequitur now, very fitting and very "me". And with that this afterward and revisiting of this essay is now done.

ACKNOWLEDGMENTS

First and foremost, thank you to Kevin Lucia, editor of Cemetery Dance eBooks and Trade Paperbacks for acquiring the book to be re-issued in this edition.

Thank you to Norman Prentiss who acquired and edited the book for Cemetery Dance eBooks in 2015. Thank you for your friendship, advice, generosity, professionalism, years of support, and for making working on the book such a great experience for me.

Thank you and much gratitude to Richard Chizmar and the entire Cemetery Dance team, now and through the years.

Thank you to Nicholas Kaufmann for writing the heartfelt and generous introduction to the 2016 edition. Thank you for years of friendship, encouragement, and support. For reading so many of my stories in rough draft. I learned so much about horror and writing by reading your stories and notes.

I want to thank everyone who has supported me and shown support for these stories along the way. Thank you to my friends, my colleagues, my workshop partners, my teachers, and the editors who acquired these stories for first publication:

Lee Thomas, Ben Francisco, David Wellington, Sarah Langan, Stefan Petrucha, Rhodi Hawk, KZ Perry, Victor La Valle, Peter

THE NIGHT MARCHERS　　　DANIEL BRAUM

Ball, J.J. Irwin, Chris Lynch, Kelly Link, Trent Walters, Rudi Dornemann, Sharon Woods, Catherine Dybeic Holm, Brendan Day, Jack Dann, John Foster, Matthew Cheney, Anya Martin, Dan Studer, Chad Stroup, Rich Duncan, Tonya Hurley, Laetitia Barbier, Ellen Datlow, Marc Laidlaw, Peter Straub, Dallas Myer. KGB Bar, Pseudopod, Clarion Writers Workshop and Clarion South, Museum of Morbid Anatomy, Green Hand Book Shop, Jim Freund, Fred Coppersmith, Gardner Dozios, and Michele Souliere. Tim Powers. Karen Joy Fowler. Simon Brown. Alice Turner. Leslie What. Terry Bisson. Lee Battersby, Mark Rudolph, Darin Bradley, John Klima, Bailey Hunter, Robert Morrish, Gavin J. Grant.

Thank you for purchasing and reading the book.

And thank you to my family, especially my mother, father, and brother for everything. Without them, their support, and love this book and nothing at all would not be possible. As I said in the original dedication to the book without them I would be one of the lost.

FIRST PUBLICATION
HISTORY AND
HONORABLE MENTIONS

"Music of the Spheres"
First published in Lady Churchill's Rosebud Wristlet #25
Small Beer Press, April 2010

"Hurricane Sandrine"
First published in Full Unit Hook Up #5,
Conical Hats Press, Spring 2004

"Mystic Tryst"
First published in Farrago's Wainscot #8,
Resurrection House, October 2008

"A Girl's Guide to Applying Superior Cat Make Up
and Dispelling Commonly Found Suburban Demons."
Original to this collection. May 2016

"Across the Darien Gap"
First Published in Cemetery Dance Magazine #55
Cemetery Dance Publications, June 2006

Honorable Mention in the The Year's Best Fantasy and Horror,
Volume 20, edited by Ellen Datlow, Gavin Grant, and Kelly Link

"Spark"
First Published in Dark Recesses Press April 2007
Dark Recesses Press, April 2007

"The Ghost Dance"
First Published in Electric Velocipede # 8,
Spilt Milk Press, Spring 2005

Honorable Mention in the The Year's Best Fantasy and Horror,
Volume 19, edited by Ellen Datlow, Gavin Grant, and Kelly
Link

"The Green Man of Punta Cabre"
First Published in Cemetery Dance Magazine #71
Cemetery Dance Publications, Summer 2014

Honorable Mention from Writers of the Future 2nd Quarter
of 2007

"Jellyfish Moon"
First Published in Cemetery Dance Magazine #67
Cemetery Dance Publications, August 2012

"The Night Marchers"
Original to this collection, May 2016
Honorable Mention in the Best Horror of the Year, Volume 9,
edited by Ellen Datlow

"The Moon and the Mesa"
First Published in Midnight Echo #4
Australian Horror Writer's Association, Fall 2010

FIRST PUBLICATION HISTORY
AND HONORABLE MENTIONS

Honorable Mention in the Best Horror of the Year, Volume 3, edited by Ellen Datlow

"The Sphinx of Cropsey Avenue"
Original to this collection, May 2016

ABOUT THE AUTHOR

Daniel Braum's unique brand of storytelling effortlessly blends genres and defies conventional categorization. His multidimensional characters encounter the unexplainable in places at the edges of civilization as they navigate the heartbreak, loss, wonder, and horror of the human condition.

Primarily a writer of short stories, Braum loves to read and write tales that explore the tension between the psychological and supernatural. He often calls his work "strange tales" in the tradition of author Robert Aickman. His work operates in the borderlands of the horror genre sharing territory with some his favorite authors such as Aickman, Kelly Link, Lucius Shepard and Tanith Lee.

The Night Marchers and Other Strange Tales, his first collection, was released from Cemetery Dance eBooks in 2016. Reissued in trade paperback by Cemetery Dance Publications in 2023, the book contains stories ranging from his appearances in Cemetery Dance Magazine to Lady Churchill's Rosebud Wristlet.

Later in 2016, Braum released the Dim Shores Chapbook Yeti. Tiger. Dragon and in 2017 the Twilight Zone-esqe collection The Wish Mechanics: Stories of the Strange and Fantastic which Jack Ketchum called "a skilled collection that turns old tropes on its head."

His third collection Underworld Dreams released in 2020 from Lethe Press and contains the story "How to Stay Afloat When Drowning" which also appears in the Best Horror of the Year Volume 12 edited by Ellen Datlow. His first novel is forthcoming from Lethe Press.

Braum also works as an editor of books and publications of short stories and is the host of the Night Time Logic series and the annual New York Ghost Story Festival.

He is grateful for his long association with Cemetery Dance; in addition to his three appearances in the magazine, he appears in the Shivers 8 anthology, his column runs on Cemetery Dance online, and his novella The Serpent's Shadow is being reissued in Sept 2023 as a trade paperback.

You can find him on his You Tube channel Daniel Braum, on social media, and at https://bloodandstardust.wordpress.com

CPSIA information can be obtained
at www.ICGtesting.com
Printed in the USA
BVHW042324190523
664485BV00007B/618